Dedication

For Kristin Morris
God is a refuge and our strength, an ever-present help in
times of trouble. ~ Psalms 46

I0671614

A Thousand
Little Blessings

Claire Sanders

This is a work of fiction. Names, characters, places, and incidents either are the product of the author's imagination or are used fictitiously, and any resemblance to actual persons living or dead, business establishments, events, or locales, is entirely coincidental.

A Thousand Little Blessings

COPYRIGHT 2014 by Claire Sanders

All rights reserved. No part of this book may be used or reproduced in any manner whatsoever without written permission of the author or Pelican Ventures, LLC except in the case of brief quotations embodied in critical articles or reviews.

eBook editions are licensed for your personal enjoyment only. eBooks may not be re-sold, copied or given to other people. If you would like to share an eBook edition, please purchase an additional copy for each person you share it with.

Contact Information: titleadmin@pelicanbookgroup.com

Scripture quotations, unless otherwise indicated are taken from the King James translation, public domain.

Cover Art by Nicola Martinez

White Rose Publishing, a division of Pelican Ventures, LLC
www.pelicanbookgroup.com PO Box 1738 *Aztec, NM * 87410

White Rose Publishing Circle and Rosebud logo is a trademark of Pelican Ventures, LLC

Publishing History
First White Rose Edition, 2014
Paperback Edition ISBN 978-1-61116-409-1
Electronic Edition ISBN 978-1-61116-408-4
Published in the United States of America

1

Burnet, Texas - March 1919

Henrietta Davis clenched her jaw and forced herself to look at the casket. The spray of yellow roses covering her mother's final resting place was oddly cheerful for such a somber occasion. Not even her mother's favorite flower could lessen the shock that quaked through Etta's soul. Her mother's life had been whisked away like a fragile blossom before a bitter winter wind, leaving Etta grasping for the cherished flower and finding nothing but cold air.

Reverend Martin stood in the Davis family cemetery and read from his dog-eared Bible in the same deep voice Etta heard every Sunday morning. The reassuring words stilled her trembling hands. Her mother was with her Lord, surrounded by love and reunited with her parents and grandparents. But the words did little to relieve the cold stone of grief lodged beneath Etta's heart.

Next to her, Etta's father shifted in the rickety folding chair the funeral home had supplied. Henry Davis had donned his most stoic face that morning, giving no hint of the keening grief she'd heard coming from his bedroom a few nights ago.

It was early spring, a time when birds sang with renewed vigor and dormant trees budded in promise.

But her father and she weren't thinking about new

life. They were burying the person who'd given them love, comfort, and joy.

Etta's nose tingled, a sure sign tears were imminent. She took a deep breath and steeled herself. She wouldn't embarrass her father by crying. He'd schooled her to portray their family as upright members of the community, always in control, never fodder for the town gossips. She raised her lace handkerchief and sniffed.

Her mother's best friend, Sara Benson, leaned against Etta's right shoulder. "It's almost over. Almost."

Etta nodded slightly and lifted her gaze. Through the black netting attached to her broad-brimmed hat, the cloud-dotted sky shone. How many times had her mother encouraged her to daydream on early spring days such as this? "What about that cloud?" she'd ask, her face as animated as a child's. "It looks like an elephant."

"No," Etta would disagree. "It's a poodle with a leash."

"It's an elepoodle," her mother would pronounce, as though her word was the last to be uttered on the subject. "What? You've never heard of an elepoodle? They're native to Finland." Then she'd dissolve into girlish giggles and dare Etta to find another imaginary animal.

Etta's father cleared his throat and stood. Was the service already over? He shook Rev. Martin's hand and then crooked his elbow toward his daughter. Etta slipped her arm through his and walked down the gently sloping hill. Decorum surrounded her father like heavily-starched linen as they made their way toward the house.

Fellow mourners trailed after them.

Etta would be expected to fill her mother's role as hostess, a job for which she felt woefully unprepared. How could she smile and chit-chat when all she wanted to do was crawl under the covers? Her queasy stomach clutched as she pasted a false smile on her face and stepped through the door.

Two middle-aged ladies dressed in black pushed themselves up from generously upholstered chairs in the parlor. The two matrons formed the church bereavement committee, a detail Etta had forgotten amidst the confusion of the week.

Mrs. Henrichson approached with open arms. "You poor thing. Come and sit down. We've got everything under control."

Mrs. Stoutman nodded vigorously, causing the black feathers on her hat to quiver. "Don't worry about a thing, Henrietta. We found your mother's china and set out refreshments."

Etta allowed Mrs. Henrichson to lead her to the dining room table. Her grandmother's antique gold-rimmed plates held slices of cake and finger sandwiches. A silver coffeepot and a crystal pitcher of lemonade sat nearby.

"Mother never used these dishes," Etta began and then censored herself. Her mother had cherished each dish as a memento of her own mother and kept them stored away, never to be endangered by careless hands. But it seemed trivial to make a fuss over dishes when the ladies had come to help. "Oh, it's all right. Thank you for taking care of everything."

A crescendo of noise swept into the dining room as friends and family made their way to the refreshments.

Her father shouldered his way through the crowd, shaking hands and nodding before exiting through the casement doors that led to the side courtyard.

Another tug of sympathy wrenched Etta's heart.

Her father must want to get away from the crowd as much as she did. Her guests were quite content visiting with each other. Perhaps she could shirk her hostess duties for a few minutes. She forced herself to walk slowly up the polished oak stairs, but once out of sight, she ran into the quiet stillness of her bedroom.

After closing the door, she placed a hand on her roiling stomach and blew out a breath. How long would the guests stay? An hour? Two? She removed her hat and gloves, laid them on her dresser, and then, crossed to the windows that overlooked the courtyard.

Through the massive limbs of the live oak, Etta watched her father. He slumped in the wicker chair, slowly rubbing his left temple. She'd bring him some pills to relieve the pain as soon as she got downstairs. A soft knock sounded on her door. "Come in, Rosa."

"It's not Rosa. It's me." Sara entered the room carrying a cup and saucer. "Rosa's in the kitchen. Do you need her?"

"No. I'll be down in a few minutes. I just wanted to..uh...to take off my hat and gloves."

Sara patted Etta's arm. "I know, honey. Stay up here as long as you need. I brought you some coffee. Two sugars, no cream, just the way you like it."

"Thank you. You know me so well."

"'Course I do. I was there on the day you were born."

Sara was unlike her mother in so many ways, yet the two women had been best friends for years. Etta's mother had been fair-haired and petite, but Sara was as tall as most men and her hair was as black as the jet beads she wore around her neck.

Etta sipped the hot coffee and returned her gaze to the courtyard. Several men had joined her father. "I'm worried about Papa."

Sara leaned against the window frame. "Me, too. I wish he'd take some time off, but knowing him, he'll be at the bank tomorrow."

Several automobiles drove up and more people piled out.

"I can't believe how many people are here. Seems as though the whole town is parked in our front yard."

"Lots of people want to pay their respects. Catherine will be missed." Sara pursed her lips in a sign of disapproval. "I see your Uncle Carl decided to show up. You'd think he'd make it to the services for his only sister. But then, he's always been more interested in fun than in paying his respects. That man thrives on being the main attraction of whatever social circus he can find."

Etta choked on the coffee.

Sara's description of Uncle Carl was almost identical to her father's. More than once Papa had referred to her uncle as "the family clown."

Sara patted Etta's back. "You OK, honey?"

Etta nodded and cleared her throat. "I'd best go downstairs."

Sara brushed her fingertips through Etta's hair. "You're so pale. Why don't you lie down for a while? I'll bring you something to eat."

Etta leaned her head toward the older woman's shoulder, willing to surrender her constraint for a moment of maternal affection, but the unmistakable crash of dropped dishes jerked her to full attention. "I should go," Etta said as she brushed her hands down her black serge skirt. "I'm sure Rosa needs help."

Sara reached for her, but Etta couldn't give in to her desire for comfort. One kind touch and her false bravado would collapse.

The family's housekeeper stood at the sink, elbow deep in suds while Mrs. Stoutman and Mrs. Henrichson threw away broken pieces of china. Rosa's dark brows were drawn into a fierce scowl, an ominous portent of the scolding brewing in her mind.

Although she didn't think it was possible, Etta's heart fell even further as she looked at the ruined dishes. "Thank you so much, Mrs. Stoutman. I'll finish this." Etta set her cup and saucer on the counter and took the broom and dustpan from the large-bosomed woman. "You, too, Mrs. Henrichson. It's so kind of you to help at a time like this."

Mrs. Stoutman pulled Etta's head down to her shoulder. "Oh, Henrietta, I know you're going to miss your momma. Sometimes I still pine for my momma, and she's been gone for nearly thirty years."

Etta's nose itched dangerously from Mrs. Stoutman's honeysuckle-scented talc. She sniffed in an effort to stifle the sneeze, and Mrs. Henrichson threw her arms around Etta, sandwiching her between the two matrons. "Go ahead and cry all you want," Mrs. Henrichson said. "Nobody would fault you for crying on a day like this."

"I'm all right." Etta's voice was muffled between the women's soft bodies. "Just let me get these broken dishes cleaned up." She struggled to escape, but the two ladies crowded closer.

"You're so lucky you still have your mother," Mrs. Stoutman said to Mrs. Henrichson. "There's nothing worse than burying your mother."

"I know that's true," Mrs. Henrichson replied. "I remember your mother's funeral as if it was yesterday. So many flowers."

As the two ladies talked on, Etta slid slowly toward the floor until she was free of their suffocating condolences. Breathing deeply, she backed away from the pair and picked up the largest pieces of broken china.

Mrs. Stoutman retrieved a tray of finger sandwiches. "How many pies do we have left?"

"Only three." Mrs. Henrichson slid an apple pie onto a silver platter. "Maybe I should cut thinner slices."

Mrs. Stoutman backed through the kitchen's swinging door. "Good idea."

Etta's shoulders slumped in relief once the ladies left the kitchen. She wanted her normal life back. She wanted her mother.

Rosa touched Etta's arm. "Are you all right, *mija*?"

As Etta looked into Rosa's kind, dark eyes, gratitude welled in her soul. *Mija.* Rosa had used that endearment since she'd first come to work for her family fifteen years ago. Did Rosa really think of Etta as her daughter? "I'll be all right. Don't worry." Etta emptied the dust pan. "Let me help you with the dishes."

Rosa made a clucking noise with her tongue. "No, no. Why don't you check on your Papa? Bring him some coffee."

Etta tied a white linen hostess apron around her waist, slipped a small tin of pain reliever into the pocket, and prepared a tray.

Her father and four other men sat in wicker chairs

beneath the live oaks that shaded the house. As she approached, all of the men stood.

"Keep your seats, gentlemen. I've brought fresh coffee. Who would like a refill?"

Judge Thompson raised his cup and saucer. "Right here, Henrietta. I was just telling your father what a lovely service your mother had."

Etta set the tray on the wicker table and turned to fill his cup. "Thank you, Judge." She turned to the man on his right. "What about you, Mr. Mayor?"

Edgar Robinson rubbed his balding head. "I probably shouldn't but...oh, go ahead, fill 'er up."

Etta complied and moved on to James Moore, owner of the largest store in town.

Mr. Moore put his hand over his cup. "None for me, Henrietta. If I drink any more I'll be awake until three in the morning."

She moved to her father's side and offered him the pills. He shook his head, declining the medication, but held up his cup for more coffee.

The youngest of the men stood. "Why don't you take my chair, Miss Davis?"

Etta smiled at William Clark, the county prosecutor. He had a reputation as a tenacious lawyer with a notable record of convictions, but his round baby face and blond hair gave him the appearance of a young boy, rather than a determined officer of the law. "Thank you, Mr. Clark." She returned the coffeepot to the tray and settled into the chair.

The men were curiously quiet. Perhaps her presence put a damper on their conversation, but she'd sat in on many of their meetings before. The four men formed the bank's Board of Directors.

Etta studied her father. His graying hair was

combed as meticulously as usual, and his starched collar showed no sign of wilting, but his face bore witness to his grief. The lines on his forehead had deepened and his usual quick smile had abandoned him. He rubbed a palm along the crease in his trousers and broke the silence. "I plan to stay home tomorrow. I have quite a bit of correspondence to catch up on. I'll be in the office the next day."

Judge Thompson's bushy white eyebrows drew together. "Don't rush it, Henry. The bank's not going anywhere."

"The judge is right," Mayor Robinson said. "The bank will run as smoothly as ever until you come back."

"I need to keep busy," Papa said. "Otherwise..."

"Perhaps you'd like some time to work with your horses," William Clark suggested. "My mother says you're sure to win top prize at the Travis County show this summer."

Etta sent silent thanks to William. Her father's only interest outside the bank was his Arabians, and William had hit just the right note to lift his mood.

"I hope you're right about that," Papa answered. "My wife used to say my horses were as beautiful as a well-kept secret. My stallion--"

"Here you all are!" Everyone turned to see who had hailed them in such a jolly manner. Uncle Carl lifted a hand in greeting. "I see you're enjoying this beautiful spring weather."

The men sighed unanimously as they turned their attention away from Carl.

Oblivious to their unenthusiastic response, Uncle Carl pulled a small side table into the circle and sat on it. He looked like a parrot in a group of crows. All the men had dressed in black, but Carl sported a beige suit with a bright blue vest. His sharp-pointed shoes were polished so brightly they reflected the sunlight. "What were you all talking about?"

Mayor Robinson answered first. "We were just advising Henry to take a few days off."

"I hope you do," Carl said to Henry as he straightened the blue bow tie that matched his vest. "I'm simply bereft at having lost my dear sister. I can hardly imagine going back to work right away. You take your time, Henry. I'll take care of any business that can't wait until you return."

The members of the board exchanged gazes.

"Carl," her father said, "would you please carry that tray to the kitchen for Etta?"

"Of course." Carl smoothed his sandy-blond hair and lifted the tray. "You coming, Etta?"

Her father's request was as transparent as a liar's promise, but Carl didn't see through his ploy to get him to leave.

Etta trailed Carl into the kitchen.

Most of the visitors had left, and the women of the Bereavement Committee were packing up.

"Thank you, ladies," she said. "My father and I appreciate your help."

Carl placed a hand over his heart. "Losing someone is never easy, but the kindness of neighbors eases the pain."

Mayor Robinson's wife slipped her arm around the crook of Carl's elbow. "I know you'll miss your only sister. We'll all miss Catherine."

The other ladies made noises of assent.

Sara Benson held out her arms the way a hen uses its wings to gather chicks. "Time for us to leave, ladies.

Etta and Henry need their rest now."

"Allow me to carry those boxes," Carl said to Mrs. Stoutman. "I'll be leaving as well, Etta," he said over his shoulder. "But I'll call tomorrow to see how you and Henry are doing."

Etta accompanied them to the front door, thanked them again, and watched them drive away. When the last automobile had disappeared, she slumped against the door frame and allowed the quiet to seep into her bones. Things would never be the same without her mother, but at least she and her father could relax now that everyone had left.

Sara walked through the front parlor and hurried to Etta's side. "Oh, Etta. Are you all right?"

Etta straightened her spine and faced the other woman. "I'm fine."

Sara wrapped her arms around Etta's shoulders and held her close. "I know I'm not your mother, but I hope you'll call when you need something. I'm only a few minutes away."

Etta returned Sara's embrace, glad to have her mother's best friend looking out for her. Sara had been part of her mother's life as long as Etta could remember. She'd often traveled to Pennsylvania with her mother to visit Etta at school, and her mother's letters always contained news about what she and Sara were working on. They co-chaired church committees, worked on numerous fund-raising campaigns for the town library, and hosted one social after another. If Etta could step away from her own sorrow, she'd surely see how sorely Sara grieved the loss of her best friend. "Thank you for all your help, Sara. I couldn't have handled everything without you."

"I don't believe that for a second, but it's the least I

could do. Would you like to walk over to my house? We could have a cup of tea and a long talk, or simply sit and do nothing."

Sara's house was only five minutes away, but even that short walk seemed overwhelming. "Maybe later. I want to make sure Papa gets some rest."

"That's good advice for you, too." Sara kissed Etta's forehead and stepped through the front door. "I'll check on you both tomorrow."

After watching Sara make her way to the footbridge connecting the Benson property to the Davis land, Etta closed the front door and walked quietly to the wall of windows in the dining room. Her father sat by himself in the courtyard, his head resting in his hand. "Help my Papa, Lord," she whispered. "Only You know the depth of his grief. Only You can alleviate his pain."

Etta's footsteps echoed on the stairs as she made her way to her bedroom. She'd wanted the visitors to leave, but now that the house was silent, the hollow feeling at the pit of her stomach intensified. Her mother's gentle presence was gone from the house but not from her heart. She'd see her mother again someday, but Etta dreaded the years of sorrow that lay ahead of her.

At the top of the staircase, Etta came face-to-face with the closed door of her mother's sewing room. A shaft of afternoon sunlight blinded her as she swung the door open, and her mother's scent, a blend of lavender and vanilla, wafted around her. A man's unfinished dressing gown lay on a table, probably a gift for her father, and piles of folded fabric were stacked on a ladder-back chair. How her mother had loved to sew. Etta knew little more than how to hem a skirt or mend a torn seam, but her mother had loved to design everything from evening gowns to curtains.

Etta sat at the machine and ran her fingers over a stack of blue and white quilt squares. Her mother hadn't made many quilts, but she did occasionally join Sara's quilting bees when the ladies of the church gathered to make one as a way to raise funds.

Etta caressed her cheek with one quilt square. Just last week, her mother had been her usual busy self, softly singing a hymn as she arranged yellow roses in a crystal vase. This week, she was gone, one of the many victims snatched away by Spanish influenza.

How long would it take until grief loosened its jagged talons? If Etta could open a doorway to heaven, she'd step right in, pay a visit, and then return to her normal life. She yearned for her mother's loving touch, but she wouldn't feel it again for many, many years.

ৡ৽৻ৡ

Lantana shrubs brushed the hem of Etta's brown cotton work skirt as she stepped into her mother's flower garden the next morning. So much needed to be done. She retrieved hand pruners from her basket of tools and began to deadhead the yellow roses.

From the nearby stable, horses sounded their morning greetings as her father led them from their stalls and turned them out to pasture. He allowed no one to care for his prize-winning Arabians except himself, a task which included mucking their stalls. Her father, who was seldom seen wearing anything other than a three-piece suit, donned work pants and a chambray shirt to work in the stable.

Etta pulled on her mother's gardening gloves and

dropped to her knees. Nettles grew beneath the bright green foliage of Mexican heather, and she'd learned the hard way that pulling them with bare hands would lead to painful stinging. Growing flowers was yet another skill she'd neglected to learn. But then, she'd never had to work for her mother's affection and approval. Her mother's esteem had been given as freely as the air she breathed.

If only her father's approval could be so easy to attain. It was no secret he'd wanted a son to carry on his name and his business. But complications from Etta's birth had sealed her mother's womb. She was his only heir, and, although he'd provided for her care and education, it had been her mother who'd lavished love and affection.

Etta rested on her heels and watched the antics of the half-feral cats that made the stable their home. As a child, Etta had begged for a kitten as a pet, but her father hadn't allowed that indulgence. "No animals in the house," he'd pronounced in his strictest voice.

"Except for little monkeys," her mother had said with a wink and a hug, soothing away the hurt of her father's denial.

A painful yearning rose from Etta's heart to her throat, and she wiped away tears with the back of her gloved hand. "Am I still your little monkey, Momma?" she whispered.

No answer came, but the horses neighed loudly as they cavorted around the large field. The bay stallion, Antares, made his way to the lead mare, Mira. He nuzzled her neck and huffed a loud breath. Mira shook her head and turned away from him, but the stallion was undaunted. He repeated the action with the three other mares.

How easy it was for the horses, Etta mused as she moved to another part of the garden where chickweed had invaded. The Arabians knew their places in the world and managed the give-and-take of equine society. But as a dutiful daughter who worked alongside her father six days a week, Etta was on her way to spinsterhood.

Things could be worse, she reminded herself. The world of finance intrigued her, and maintaining a healthy balance between fiscal risk and security was challenging. If she kept at it, perhaps her father would reward her with more responsibility.

Etta pushed a strand of hair away from her face and watched her father stroke the stallion's neck. She loved the horses almost as much as her father did and often ended the day grooming them by his side. In June, they would travel to the state capital for the annual horse show. It had always been her mother's favorite trip, although Etta suspected her mother went for the many social gatherings rather than anything related to equine husbandry.

Etta repositioned herself near the green shoots of the daffodils. How her mother had loved their cheerful announcements of spring. But as Etta worked in the dirt, a chorus of horse calls pulled her attention back to the pasture.

Antares's head pointed to the sky as he trumpeted one squeal after another and the mares formed a circle. Perhaps they smelled a predator, or one of the horses was hurt.

Etta rose to her feet and scanned the field.

The mares snorted in agitation and moved restlessly in their defensive circle.

Etta dropped the gloves into her basket of tools

and walked down the hill toward the stable. The stallion galloped to the wooden fence and neighed loudly as she approached.

"Papa?" she called as she entered the stable. The opened stall doors and the empty wheelbarrow meant her father was half-finished with his morning chores. "Papa?"

The horses answered, but there was no response from her father.

Etta passed through the stable, opened the gate that lead to the pasture, and closed it behind her.

What was her father doing?

Then Etta recognized a dark shape within the mares' protective circle. "Papa!" The frigid hand of fear grasped her heart as she picked up her skirt and ran.

The mares parted, allowing Etta access to her father. Panic gripped her throat as she dropped to the ground and turned him over.

A deep moan came from his twisted face and his left arm swung wildly.

"What's happened, Papa? Did you fall?"

Her father answered her question with an unintelligible grunt.

"Can you stand, Papa? Or sit up?"

His eyes were dazed and his body rocked from side to side.

Etta slipped her arm beneath his back to help him to a sitting position, but he pushed her away with a wordless groan. She gasped for air as she fought her rising panic. She couldn't leave him alone, but he needed help. The house was too far away for Rosa to hear her shouts. Etta removed a handkerchief from her father's shirt pocket and wiped his face. "I'm going for help, Papa. I'll be back as soon as I can."

Against everything in her heart, she left him in the pasture, the morning sun beating down on him, and ran to the house. "Rosa!" she screamed. "Rosa! Call Dr. Russell!" Etta's dry throat ached from exertion and panic. "Rosa!"

The housekeeper opened the back door and shielded her eyes against the sun. "What's wrong?"

Etta bent at the waist, her hands on her knees, and struggled to catch her breath. "Papa...call Dr. Russell...Papa's had some kind of accident."

Rosa's dark eyes grew wide with alarm. She hustled into the kitchen, leaving Etta panting outside.

Knowing she could count on Rosa to get in touch with the doctor, Etta ran back to where her father lay moaning on the dusty ground. With each step, she sent a desperate prayer heavenward. She couldn't lose her father as well as her mother. No one could expect her to survive such a loss.

The mares had reformed their protective circle, but upon hearing Etta's approach they nickered and disbanded. Etta knelt at her father's side and raised his head until it rested in her lap. His eyes were closed and his breathing labored.

Rosa carried a crockery pitcher and a glass into the pasture and bent over him. "Oh my, Miss Etta. He looks bad. His face is all crooked."

Impatience flared in Etta's chest. The last thing she needed was Rosa's dire prognosis. "Give me some water."

Rosa followed the order, and Etta held the glass to her father's lips. "Papa, here's some water for you. Dr. Russell is on his way. Here, Papa. Drink some water." She tipped the glass into his mouth, but the water ran down his chin. She reached for the handkerchief she'd used earlier, soaked it with cool water, and placed it in his mouth.

Her father groaned and bit at the wet cloth.

If only she could get him into the house. But if he'd broken a bone or suffered internal injuries, moving him might prove worse. "Stand over there," she directed Rosa, "and block the sun." How long would her father have to lie in the dirt before help arrived?

Rosa moved to the location.

The horses nickered nervously as Etta wiped her father's face with the wet cloth and prayed. *Not my father, too. No, Lord. Please.*

❧❦

An hour later, Etta stood as still as an alarmed rabbit outside her father's bedroom.

Dr. Russell had finally arrived, given her father a cursory examination, and then returned to his car for a litter. It had taken all three of them to carry her father into his room, and, once there, the doctor had ordered her out.

If only her mother were here. Her mother always knew what to do.

Etta resumed her prayer. "Help Papa, Lord," she muttered in the darkened hallway. "Please help him recover. Show me what needs to be done." Her words were disturbingly similar to the prayers she'd made when her mother fell ill.

The door to her father's room eased open, and Dr. Russell stepped out. "Your father's sleeping," he said, slipping his arms through his gray suit jacket. "He's had a stroke. At this moment, I can't know the severity of his condition, but he's paralyzed on his right side, and he's lost the ability to speak. However, he is able to follow commands and to give a simple yes-no response."

Etta's hands flew to her mouth to stifle the tumult of emotions that threatened to escape.

Her father was only in his fifties, much too young to suffer something so debilitating.

"I've called a nurse to stay with Henry tonight, but he'll need much more than that in the weeks and months to come." Dr. Russell smoothed his salt-and-pepper hair, picked up his bag, and walked down the stairs. "I gave your father something to help him sleep through the night, and I'll be back tomorrow morning to check on him." The doctor put on his hat and turned to Etta. "If he makes it through the next few days without having another stroke, I'll look into admitting him to a convalescent home in Dallas where he can receive the care he needs."

Etta felt as though her feet had been cast in iron.

Dr. Russell strode to his car, threw his medical bag through the open back window, and drove away without one word from her.

Etta heard a floorboard creak and turned to see Rosa standing in the dining room.

"Your Papa, he's all right?"

Etta's tears would no longer be denied. Her face crumpled in hopeless sobs as her knees buckled.

Rosa ran to Etta's side. "No, no, mija. This is not the time for tears. Come on, now. Be strong for your Papa."

Etta hid her wet face in Rosa's worn calico apron. How could Rosa tell her to be strong? Her mother was the strong one.

Rosa caressed Etta's hair. "I called Señora Benson. She'll know what to do. Now come into the kitchen, and I'll make you some lunch." Rosa slid one arm behind Etta's back and led her toward the kitchen.

∂∘∾

"I'm not sending my father to a convalescent home."

Sara reached across the round kitchen table and patted Etta's hand. "I agree. Henry would wither away in a place like that. But he wouldn't approve of you taking care of him. Your father is a proud man, Etta. The last thing he needs is his daughter feeding him or, worse yet, bathing him."

Etta winced at the thought of having to care for her father's physical needs. He would be humiliated if she tried. "If a convalescent home is out of the question and caring for him by myself is inadvisable, there's only one option left."

"Right."

"But where in the world will I find 'round-the-clock nurses?"

"You could start with the convalescent home. They may have names of people looking for a job. Dr. Russell could probably give you several contacts, or you could run an advertisement in the newspaper. Lots of people need employment, Etta."

Etta breathed her first hopeful breath of the day.

No wonder Sara had been her mother's best friend. She had a no-nonsense way about her that blew away confusion and disorder.

"I suppose I could find someone to care for Papa's horses, as well. You know how particular he is about them."

A sparkle lit in Sara's eyes. "I know exactly the right person for that job. Gabriel's coming home in a few days!"

"Gabriel? Your son?"

"One and the same."

"I didn't realize…I mean, I'm sure Mom said something about him, but…"

"Catherine didn't know. We got a telegram just last night. Oh, Etta, I can hardly wait to see my boy."

Since she'd spent most of her girlhood away at school, Etta knew little of Gabriel Benson. He was older, tall, and lean with black hair and dark eyes. He'd gone to Camp Bowie with almost every other young man in the county when America had entered the Great War, and from the snatches of conversation she'd overheard between her mother and Sara, he'd seen action in France. "Is he all right?"

"In his last letter he wrote that he was fine, but I won't believe it until I see him with my own eyes. I hope life in the Army has cured him of his wanderlust. After he got that engineering degree in college, he told us about job prospects in Chicago. As if that wasn't far enough from home, he joined the Army and went to France."

"Do you think he'd be willing to care for Papa's horses?"

"Of course. Horses were the only thing on our farm Gabriel didn't object to. Besides, Etta, you need to get back to the bank and make sure nothing happens in your father's absence. In one way or another, everyone in town depends on the well-being of that bank. You find someone to help your father. I'll send Gabriel over to take care of the horses, and then you march right back to that bank and do what needs to be done."

Etta's breath caught in her throat. "Go back to the bank without Papa? I'm merely his assistant. There is no way I can take over his responsibilities. What if I...?"

Sara's eyebrows raised in question. "What if you fail?"

Etta's chest tightened. Failure was a very real possibility. She'd been her father's unpaid assistant for two years, and she understood the day-to-day operations required to keep the bank solvent, but she'd never imagined herself filling his shoes.

Sara touched Etta's wrist. "What if you don't fail? You're a young woman at the dawn of a new age. We'll have the vote soon, and women are making their way in the world like never before. Why shouldn't you be one of them? Show the people of this town what Henrietta Davis can do."

Despite her anxiety, Etta smiled.

Sara's words sounded so much like something her mother would have said. Catherine Davis wouldn't have sat in a corner, wringing her hands with worry. Etta's mother would have done whatever she could to solve the problem.

Etta stood, a renewed sense of determination filling her. "I'll drive to Dallas and talk to the doctors at the convalescent home. Would you like to go?"

"Not today. That's an overnight trip, and I wouldn't want to be away when my boy gets home. Besides, I've got a powerful urge to bake his favorite cake."

2

Gabriel Benson stepped off the mail train two days later.

"Here you go, Lieutenant." The brakeman was holding his duffel bag and jacket. "How's it feel to be home again?"

Gabriel set the bag on the wooden platform and put on the olive drab jacket that completed his Army uniform. "It feels like I've landed on another planet. Sure this is Earth?"

The brakeman's shaggy moustache quirked at the ends. "Felt about the same when I came home from fighting in the Philippines. But it gets better. Just takes time, that's all."

Time. That was about the only thing Gabriel had plenty of. "Thanks again for the ride."

"Couldn't let a fine soldier like you spend the night in a rail yard." The brakeman scanned the empty platform. "Nobody's meeting you?"

"My family's not expecting me tonight."

"The railroad put a telephone in the station house last month. Want to give your family a call?"

It was almost ten o'clock. If his parents kept the same routine they'd followed before he left, they'd already be in bed. "Don't worry about me. A long walk will do me good after being cooped up in that mail sorting room for the last three hours."

The train whistle blew, signaling its imminent

departure. The brakeman offered his hand. "Good luck to you, Lieutenant. Maybe I'll see you again sometime."

Gabriel shook the brakeman's hand and ignored the infuriating doubt swimming through his veins. It would be easy to jump back on that train and keep riding all the way to San Antonio. He could go anywhere he wanted, find enough work to keep him from going hungry, and keep moving until his soul found rest. But he'd never been the kind of man who ran away. As tempting as the open road may have been, his family expected him.

The train groaned to a labored start, and the brakeman pulled his hand free of Gabriel's grip. He yelled something, but Gabriel couldn't hear him over the clamor of the steam engine. He lifted his hand in farewell and watched his chance to escape disappear down the dark tracks.

As the noise receded, the otherworldly quiet of small town darkness bore down. The back of Gabriel's neck prickled. He turned slowly, his gaze straining to see the sniper rifle trained on his back. But there was no one.

Only the ghosts who relentlessly whispered memories into his ear.

Gabriel picked up his bag and blew out a breath. He'd come home to visit his parents and to get his bearings. Standing on the platform wouldn't accomplish either. The station door was locked, but the baggage room was open. He'd lugged forty pounds of equipment all over France, but no more. He'd come back for his duffel bag tomorrow or the next day.

It really didn't matter. Not much did anymore.

The smell of early spring awakened memories as

Gabriel walked north along the dusty road. March meant planting time and worming the cattle, two jobs he truly hated. He'd enjoyed working with the horses, but every time he raised a calf only to see it shipped to market, he swore he'd never be a farmer.

But what would he do now that his military service was over? Would time help him settle into his skin and quiet his mind? Perhaps he'd be able to sleep more than a few hours once he adjusted to civilian life. It would be a relief to worry about mundane things instead of artillery bombardments.

A cloudless sky stretched over flat land on either side of the road. Even with the bright moon, Gabriel easily picked out the constellations he'd known as a boy—the same ones he'd taught his fellow soldiers in France. How immense the universe must be for Orion and Cassiopeia to be in almost the same positions when viewed from different continents. There'd been so many quiet nights with nothing to do except exchange stories. Monotony and tedium were the soldier's lot, interspersed with terror and panic.

He knew one thing for sure—he'd never return to the Army. He'd live on the streets and become a beggar before he commanded men to follow him into harm's way again. Captain Brooks had written to the parents and wives and sweethearts of the fallen, had tried to console their loss with sincere praise for the men he'd commanded, but nothing could ever exonerate Gabriel.

No wonder those men haunted him. Living with ghosts was a fitting penance for someone who'd led them to their deaths.

Gabriel stopped at the bridge that crossed Hamilton Creek and veered off the road. Thanks to the full moon, he could follow the creek to his family's farm. The sound of water rushing over limestone rocks was just as he'd remembered, but he couldn't see the cold, clear water where he'd often played as a boy. Did children still catch tadpoles and hunt for arrowheads? How easy life had been before the war.

Lights from a nearby house caught his eye. That place was new, although the three-story structure was more mansion than house. He'd seen similar buildings in England, manor houses that served as part home and part agricultural center. But who would build such a place in Burnet?

He smiled sardonically as the answer came to him. The richest family in Burnet, of course. Henry Davis probably owned half the land in the county, not to mention, the only bank.

Gabriel picked up a rock and tossed it in his hand. While he'd been in France, fighting for the common man's right to live without being invaded, Henry Davis had been building a mansion next to his family's farm. His parents could probably see that house from every inch of their place.

He threw the rock into the creek and continued his walk. Didn't make any difference to him how the banker spent his money. As long as it didn't hurt Gabriel's family, Henry Davis could build a mansion on every acre of his property.

The wind picked up, blowing Gabriel's hair into his eyes. He'd have to get a trim soon, a job his mother would probably undertake as soon as she saw him. He'd never admit it to anyone, but he'd missed his parents. While in France, he'd sometimes fallen asleep to memories of his mother's gentle touch or his father's proud smile, but just like carefree days, he'd taken his parents' love for granted.

The familiar sound of a horned owl sounded from his right, almost like a welcome home greeting. Another owl answered from his left, and a small part of Gabriel's battered soul rejoiced to know the birds had found each other in the darkness. Night sounds didn't alarm him, unless they were the booms of approaching artillery or the unexpected slide of a bolt as an infantryman loaded his rifle. But he was in Burnet, where nothing more than owls monitored his trek home.

Gabriel walked on. A hundred yards farther, he would reach the footbridge that marked the beginning of his family's property. Perhaps he'd spend the night in the barn and surprise his mother at breakfast.

Another gentle breeze wafted around him, carrying a soft, feminine voice. Gabriel held steady, straining to hear. Why would a woman be out at this time of night? He crept forward, scanning the banks of the stream. A few yards later, he saw a young woman sitting on a large flat-topped rock on the opposite bank, the moon illuminating her white blouse. Gabriel ducked behind a large cottonwood.

The woman looked up into the starry sky. "Fear not for I am with you. Be not dismayed, for I am your God."

She was reading the Bible, Gabriel realized, but then amended his conclusion. There was no book in her lap, only a piece of blue and white cloth she sewed by lantern light. She must have been reciting the verses from memory.

"I will strengthen you, I will help you, I will uphold you with my righteous right hand," she continued.

Who was this young woman? She was on Davis land. Was she one of the family? There'd been a daughter, Gabriel remembered, but she was still a child.

"I'm going to need Your strength to get me through this trial, Lord," the woman said. "Please lead me to the right people to help Papa."

She was praying. She'd come out into the quiet night to talk with God. He had no right to eavesdrop, but if he moved now he might startle her.

Peace settled into Gabriel's soul. Something about the woman's quiet prayer and rhythmic sewing had eased the tension that gnawed at him. He didn't know her, but neither could he leave her. Some force drew him to her, as though she had something he needed. The quiet night closed around him, cloaking him in its protective mantle, and still Gabriel watched. He'd stay there till dawn if necessary.

Just as his eyes grew heavy, lulled by the peaceful night, the woman stood and brushed off her skirt. She was of average height with a trim waist and slender shoulders. A dark braid hung down her back, but there was no other way to identify her. "If I'm being tested, Lord, help me to remember You're with me every step of the way." She picked up the lantern and walked toward the big house.

Gabriel watched until the lantern light disappeared, then left his hiding place and walked toward the footbridge, feeling part interloper and part blessed. He'd seen plenty of people pray, especially in the trenches, but something about this woman's earnest plea had touched a dormant part of his heart. What trial was she facing? Why did he want to help her even though he didn't know who she was?

Gabriel turned at the footbridge and put the Davis land at his back. He'd keep an eye out for that young woman. In a town as small as Burnet, he'd be sure to run into her somewhere.

᙮᙮

Gabriel rubbed his bristled cheek and squinted into the morning sun as he walked out of the barn. The smell of frying bacon meant his mother was up and about, and since there was no way to warn her of his early arrival, he simply walked up the back steps and knocked at the kitchen door.

"Sara!" his father's voice bellowed. "Who's at the door?"

Gabriel's heartbeat quickened at the sound of his father's voice.

Ethan Benson could be a gruff father, but he'd always been a fair man. When Gabriel had gone to college, and then joined the Army, his father hadn't voiced any disapproval.

But Gabriel hadn't wanted any part of the farm or his father's life. He'd wanted adventure. Little had he known the heavy price such adventure would cost. Excitement mixed with happiness as he opened the door and walked into the kitchen.

"Oh!" His mother dropped the bowl she'd cradled in the crook of her arm. It shattered on the stone tile, sending rivulets of white batter onto the floor. Her hands flew to her face.

Gabriel blinked away tears. His mother. His beautiful, kind mother. The one who'd scolded him when he'd needed it and loved him when he didn't deserve it. He stepped toward her, arms open.

"Sara!" his father shouted again. "Who is it?"

Tears ran down his mother's cheeks as she threw herself into his arms, wrapping her hands around Gabriel's neck. "My boy. Oh, Gabriel. At last." She pulled his head down to her shoulder and clung tightly. "Thank You, Lord," she whispered again and again.

Gabriel embraced the only woman he'd ever loved. She smelled of Christmas mornings and Sunday dinners, and her warm embrace soothed him just as it had when she'd treated his boyhood cuts and scrapes. If only she could ease the kind of pain he carried with him now.

His mother stepped back but kept her hands on his arms. "How did you...when did you...?" She rose to kiss him on the cheek. "I'm so glad you're home, son."

"Sara, what in the world is...?" His father's voice died as he stepped into the kitchen and saw his son.

Although his mother looked the same as she had when he'd left for the Army, his father had aged beyond his years. Wisps of white hair now covered a nearly bald head and a pronounced stoop bowed his once strong back.

His father's eyes grew wide with surprise followed quickly by a wide smile. "Welcome home, son."

Gabriel stepped away from his mother to shake the hand his father offered but drew his father into an embrace instead.

"There, there," his father said, patting Gabriel's back. "It's all right now. You're home at last." His father pulled a handkerchief from his pocket and wiped his eyes.

In the trenches, men had given up trying to hide their emotions. Fear, anxiety, defeat, and humor had been put on view for all to judge. But now that he was home, he'd have to remember that men like his father didn't express tender feelings.

"Can you still eat four pancakes and ask for more?" His mother dabbed her eyes with the hem of her apron. "Let me clean up this mess and make some fresh batter." She brushed straw from his hair. "Where'd you spend the night? In one of the stalls?"

Gabriel kissed his mother's cheek. "I haven't had any good food since I left your kitchen. I promise to eat every bite."

His mother embraced him again. "There's nothing I enjoy more than cooking for my son."

His father blew his nose and gestured toward the kitchen table. "Sit down and tell us what you've been up to."

Gabriel took in the scene. His mother busied herself at the counter while his father removed three white cups from the sideboard. It was a tableau frozen in his memory, unchanged since he'd left.

His father looked up through white eyebrows. "Go ahead and have a seat, son."

Gabriel touched the back of the wooden chair, outlining the flecks of red paint that had worn away over the years. He must have sat in that chair a thousand times to eat, to study, or to work on one of his many building models.

"Is something wrong?" His mother touched his shoulder with a gentleness that only mothers possess. Her hair was pinned into a bun at the nape of her neck and her kind eyes shone.

He'd never be able to explain why a plain kitchen

chair had suddenly become a precious artifact. He shook his head and sat in his usual spot.

"Now then," his father said as he passed a cup, "tell me about life in the Army."

"There's not much to tell. Hey, I noticed you've got a new automobile."

His father pulled out the chair at the head of the table and sat down. "Not exactly new. I bought it from a guy down in Marble Falls. They call it a pickup truck 'cause you can drive it where you want and pick up what you need. Funny word, don't you think?"

"Must come in handy around the farm."

"Sure. I've been using it to make deliveries for Adler's Hardware. Remember that store?"

His mother poured hot, black coffee from a speckled tin pot. "Do you still take cream and sugar in your coffee?"

Niceties such as sugar and cream could be scarce commodities on the front line, so Gabriel had learned to drink his coffee plain. He stared at the sugar bowl and cream pitcher as though they could lure him into a sense of false security. "Black's fine for me, Mom. Thanks."

"In fact," his father continued, "Victor Adler's expecting me at the store at eight o'clock. I hate to run off so soon after you've come home, but after breakfast, I'll need to get going."

Gabriel dipped a spoon into the sugar bowl and watched the tiny grains cascade from the spoon. "It's OK, Dad. I'll be here when you get back."

Ethan clapped a hand on his son's forearm. "I hope you'll stay for a long time, son. Your mother's missed you."

Gabriel grinned at his father's unspoken

sentiment. It was all right for his mother to have missed him, but his father was above such emotions.

His mother joined them at the table and chatted amiably during the meal, telling him about neighbors he'd forgotten and distant family members he seldom saw. But even in the safe comfort of his mother's kitchen, memories menaced him. The sugar glared at him from its crockery dish, daring him to give in to its sweet temptation, and the pancakes reminded him of Corporal Hutchins. Sam Hutchins had been so skinny he could lie down in the shade of a clothesline, but that hadn't stopped him from eating more pancakes than any other man in the platoon. What right did Gabriel have to enjoy breakfast when Hutchins and the others would never eat again?

His mother removed his plate and frowned. "Are you sure you're finished? You didn't eat very much. Can I fix you something else?" She scraped the uneaten portion into the trash bin and slipped the plate into the sink. "How 'bout some eggs and toast?"

Not even his mother's cooking would sit well in his guilt-ridden stomach. "No, thanks, Mom."

"I'd best be going," his father said, clapping a weathered hand on Gabriel's shoulder. "Feel like going into town today? Lots of folks been asking 'bout you."

His mother answered for him. "Not today, Ethan. I've just got my boy back. Let him rest for a bit."

"All right, all right," his father grumbled as he put on his hat and walked through the back door.

Through the kitchen window, Gabriel watched his father shuffle slowly toward his truck. "Dad doesn't look well. What happened to him?"

His mother turned from the sink and dried her hands. "One day he came in from the fields and said he was finished being a farmer."

"Just like that?"

"Just like that." Sara poured a cup of coffee for herself and joined her son at the table. "When I met your father, his head was full of dreams. He wanted to go to college and become a history professor, but your grandfather expected him to take over this farm. When your grandfather died, your father gave up his dream in order to take care of his mother and sisters."

"I thought Dad liked being a farmer."

"He came to accept it, but he never really liked it. When it became clear you'd never take over, he began to question why he was still working from sunup to sundown. About three months after you joined the Army, he told me he'd had enough."

Uncertainty pricked Gabriel's gut. Had his rejection of farm life hurt his father or freed him from toiling at a job he hadn't liked? "How are you making a living?"

"We lease our land. That brings in money every year. Plus, I still sell eggs, and your father gets a salary from the hardware store."

Something was missing from his mother's explanation. "How could working less age him so?"

"Worry. His only child was far away, fighting in a war no one here really understood. Every time we'd get a letter from you, I'd see him relax for a few days. But then dread would creep up his spine and settle on his face, troubling him until the next letter arrived."

He should have written more often. But there'd been little to write home about until he saw combat, and then there'd been too much to tell his parents.

"Now that you're home," his mother continued, "I expect he'll recover a bit of his old self."

Gabriel carried his empty cup to the sink and dropped it into the soapy water. He'd assumed he'd spend his days helping his father with farm work. Now that there was no farm to tend, how would he keep busy? "I need to go into town sometime today and pick up my duffel bag. I left it at the train station."

"Dad will take you to town when he comes home for lunch. I still can't believe you walked all the way home in the dark instead of calling us. You know we would've come for you, no matter the hour."

"The walk did me good." Gabriel leaned against the window frame and gazed at the Davis's house. Now that it was day, he could see the house was built of native white limestone with black shutters and black trim. "I see Henry Davis built himself a mansion while I was gone."

Sara joined him. "I've got some bad news about our neighbors. Catherine Davis died last week."

Gabriel studied his mother's face. There was sorrow there, but not defeat. "Sorry to hear that. She was a good friend to all of us."

A sparkle lit his mother's eyes. "Catherine and I met in first grade. I always thought we'd grow old together. She used to tease me about which one of us would become a grandmother first."

"How did she die?"

"The Spanish influenza hit several church members. We went to help the Marsh family. All three of the children had it and one died. I suppose that's where Catherine picked it up."

Such a cruel irony. Just when the killing on the battlefield had ended, an invisible enemy had struck the home front. "What about you, Mom? Did you get sick?"

"Not even a sniffle. But that's not the end of the bad news. The day after Catherine's funeral, Henry had a stroke."

Two tragedies in one week. The Davis family had been hit hard. "Is he all right?"

"Henry survived the stroke, but his full recovery is doubtful. Poor Henrietta has her hands full."

It took a few seconds for the name to register in Gabriel's memory. Henry Davis had named his only child after himself. "Is someone coming to take care of his little girl?"

Catherine shook her head. "Henrietta Davis is twenty-five years old, Gabriel. She's no child."

"She can't be that old. She was away at school when I left."

"She was away at college. She graduated and came back to work in her father's bank."

An image of the woman by the creek formed in Gabriel's mind. "How tall is she?"

"About my height. Why do you ask?"

"I may have seen her last night. I took the shortcut, and I saw a young woman on the Davis side of Hamilton Creek."

Anxiety crept into his mother's voice. "What time was this? Was she all right?"

"It was late, but she was all right."

"Thank goodness. I'm so worried about Etta. She's got so much on her shoulders."

No wonder Henrietta had been praying by the stream. Dealing with her father's illness on top of her mother's death was no small burden. "Who's in charge of the bank now that Mr. Davis can't work?"

"Etta, of course. She's been working at the bank ever since she returned from college."

"She works? A rich girl like her?"

"Etta's no society girl. Catherine wanted her daughter to have opportunities she never had, so she sent Etta to an aunt who lives in Philadelphia. Etta attended a girls' academy and then went on to college. Miss Henrietta Davis is an intelligent girl with a loving heart and a head for business." Gabriel's mother walked to the kitchen counter and removed the lid of a cake tin. "How about a slice of lemon cake?"

Gabriel's eyebrows lifted. "Since when do you offer cake for breakfast?"

A mischievous lilt entered his mother's voice. "I'm trying to soften you up."

"What are you up to, Mom?"

"Do you remember Henry Davis's horses?"

"The Arabians? He's won every trophy and blue ribbon in the state with those horses."

"Well...Etta needs someone to take care of them until her father recovers."

"Don't tell me the banker doesn't have a trainer and at least a dozen stable boys."

"Not a one. Henry's always insisted on doing everything for those horses."

"I bet he doesn't muck stalls."

"You'd lose that bet. But I'm sure Etta would hire someone to do it now. I volunteered you to make sure the horses are being taken care of properly."

He hadn't been around a non-working horse in years. The Army took good care of its animals, but they were expected to do their duty as well as any other solider. "I don't know much about training show horses."

"That's not Etta's main concern. She just needs someone to feed them and clean the stalls until Henry's up to the task. Plus, you could ride all you want. You still like to ride, don't you?"

The feel of a fast horse, the sound of its heaving breath as it raced through unfenced land, the smell of sweat and leather. Gabriel smiled as the memories floated through his mind. The Arabians would be a welcome diversion from the awkwardness of returning home.

"Tell you what, Mom. Let me get a bath, a shave, and some clean civilian clothes, and I'll pay a visit to Mr. Davis's Arabians later today."

Gabriel's mother patted his shoulder. "I knew you'd be willing. I'll call Etta and tell her to expect you. And when you finish your bath, I'll trim your hair."

❧◦❧

Irritation nipped at Gabriel's heels as he left his parents' house and headed to Henry Davis's stables. He'd been glad to see his parents, but after a few hours, his mother's soft humming had pricked his nerves. By the time his father came home for lunch, Gabriel had jumped at the chance to ride into town. But he'd fisted his hands on his knees and ground his teeth as his father crept along potholed dirt roads. He longed to drive fast, to feel the wind in his hair, and to outrun his ghosts.

Gabriel crossed the footbridge connecting his family's farm to the Davis's acreage. Ahead of his steps, startled meadowlarks rushed into the cloudless sky, their disapproving calls warning him of nearby nests. Maybe tonight, in a land where nothing threatened him except birds, he'd be able to overcome the persistent irritability that plagued him. If he could sleep, if he could get just one night of deep, uninterrupted sleep, he might be able to ease his nerves.

Gabriel bypassed the house and went directly to the stables. The wood siding was painted white with black trim around the windows and doors. A copper cupola capped the slightly peaked roof and a horse-shaped wind vane topped it all. Five horses browsed contentedly in the spacious pasture behind the stables. The stallion was a dark bay and the mares ranged in color from roan to dun.

Gabriel pushed one of the wide doors. A hidden wheel slid sideways along a track, making the heavy door easy to move. The windows were open, and a cool breeze passed from one side of the stable to the other. Each stall bore the name of a star--Antares, Mira, Vega, Chara, Gemma. A tack room, a feed room, and a small office were at the other end. Gabriel walked slowly through the stable, noting the saddle trunks at each stall. In the office, a glass-fronted case displayed numerous trophies and ribbons.

The door to the feed room was closed. Although the knob turned freely, the door stuck in its frame. Gabriel leaned his shoulder against the door and shoved. As he stumbled into the room, a loud screech pierced his ears and a black blur sped across his boots. He crouched into a defensive posture, his breath reduced to frantic pants, and reached for his absent pistol. How had he been caught unaware, after vowing to never allow himself to be so vulnerable? His body tensed in anticipation of an attack as his gaze darted around the small room.

The screech sounded again from outside the feed room. Two tabby cats chased each other out of the adjoining office and through the open stable door.

Gabriel mumbled under his breath. He was in Burnet, Texas, not France. He'd been ready to attack, to take on the enemy with his bare hands. But there was no enemy here. He was home, where no one wanted to kill him or his comrades. He wiped a line of sweat from his upper lip. Would he never be able to put the war behind him? His skin still prickled at every unexpected noise and his normally even temper had dissolved into a morass of irritability.

He took another deep breath and pushed away from the wall. He'd come here to do a job. Might as well get on with it. He filled a bucket with feed and moved to the first stall. Someone had already cleaned it and put in fresh straw and water. All he had to do was distribute the food and lead the horses in. Hopefully, the animals would show him which stall was theirs. He had no way of knowing their names.

Once the feed was allocated, Gabriel picked out a lead rope and headed to the pasture. A dun colored mare was closest and she walked slowly toward him. Gabriel held out his hand, and she placed her forehead against his palm.

"Hey there, beautiful," Gabriel said in a gentle voice. "Ready to turn in for the night?"

The horse nickered, flicked her ears forward, and took half a step toward him. "I've got your dinner all ready for you." He hooked the lead rope to her halter and turned toward the stable. The mare followed compliantly, her head bobbing in time to her easy pace. When Gabriel turned to close the gate, he realized the other horses knew the routine well. They were already gathering for their turns.

He led the mare into the stable and watched her

enter the stall labeled Mira. That was easy enough. He unhooked the lead rope and slid the stall door closed. He stepped outside to retrieve the next horse.

A woman leaned against the fence, her gaze fixed on the animals. She reached out her hand and the stallion walked toward her. "How are you?" she asked the horse. "Did you have a good day?" The horse sniffed her hand and then moved toward the fence. She stroked his shoulder. "Is Benito doing a good job?" The horse took one step back and the woman petted his jaw. "Where's Mira? Is she investigating the far side of the pasture?"

It was the same woman who'd been at the creek. Her hair was pinned up, and she wore a blue skirt and matching jacket, but the voice was the same.

Gabriel moved out of the stable. "I've already put Mira into her stall."

The woman whirled in obvious surprise. "Oh! Sorry, I didn't see you there." She placed her palm on her chest, blew out a breath, and walked slowly toward Gabriel. "I'm Henrietta Davis."

Gabriel shook the small hand she offered and gazed into her eyes. They were the color of the Atlantic at sunset, blue with a hint of gray. This was definitely the woman he'd seen praying by the stream, but he would've never recognized the Davis's grown-up daughter. "I'm Gabriel Benson."

She smoothed her hair and stepped into the stable. "Thank you so much for coming, Gabriel. I haven't seen you since I went away to college. That's been at least six years. Welcome home."

How had he missed knowing this lovely young woman? Despite being neighbors, he'd rarely seen her through the years. An occasional glimpse of her at church or while their mothers visited was all he could remember. She'd simply been Catherine Davis's little girl. Until now.

"Sorry to hear about your parents," Gabriel said.

Etta rubbed her hands on her skirt. "Thank you. Did you find everything you needed in the stable? Our housekeeper's nephew comes in the mornings to clean the stalls and put the horses out for the day, but they need more than that." Her features were as delicate as a sparrow's wing, and her fair complexion a contrast to her dark hair.

"I'll enjoy giving your horses some exercise. Has Mr. Davis entered them in any events?"

"We always participate in the Austin show, but I don't see how my father can participate this summer. I'll need to cancel our entry."

"That's probably a good idea. I'm not familiar with the special training they need for participating in show events. But don't worry, I'll make sure his Arabians get a good workout."

A wide smile lit her pretty face, and her shoulders dropped. "That's such a relief. I can't thank you enough." Etta stepped into the stable, retrieved a lead rope from a nearby peg, and walked outside. "I'll get Antares."

Gabriel nodded and followed her through the gate. She turned to make sure he'd closed it and then walked to the stallion.

"Why are the horses named after stars?" Gabriel asked.

She hooked the lead rope to the stallion. "You know the stars?"

"A bit."

"My father loves astronomy. When I was little girl,

he taught me all the constellations and showed me how they move through the northern hemisphere."

Gabriel retrieved a nearby mare and walked beside Etta toward the stable. "Do you still stargaze?"

"Almost never. Not lately, anyway." Etta opened the gate, waited for Gabriel to pass through, and closed it.

Once inside the stable, Gabriel unhooked the mare and watched her enter the stall labeled Gemma. Then he returned to where Etta had fastened the stallion to a grooming post. She held a currycomb in her hand.

A tight band of irritation encircled Gabriel's chest. What was Henrietta doing? Hadn't he just told her he'd take care of the horses? "I'll groom him," Gabriel said in a harsh tone.

Etta stepped away from the horse. "Oh…sorry. I usually help my father in the evenings. It was just force of habit." She replaced the comb on a nearby shelf. "I'll get out of your way." She wiped her palms on her skirt again and headed toward the stable doors.

Gabriel let out a sigh of self-disgust. Why did he snap at people who didn't deserve it? "Henrietta?"

She stopped and looked back over her shoulder.

"If you want to groom the horses…I didn't mean…"

Etta turned to face Gabriel. She tucked a strand of hair behind her ear, took a deep breath, and walked toward him. "I don't want to take advantage of your kindness, Gabriel. I can ask Benito to groom the horses as well as clean their stalls." She rested a hand on the stallion's hip and the horse nickered softly. "The truth is, I'm not going to have as much free time as I did before. Any help you can give us is greatly appreciated."

Gabriel took a step toward her. "Tell you what. I'll come by in the morning and talk to Benito. Between the two of us, we'll make sure your father's horses are happy and healthy."

"Thank you." Etta's gaze was fixed on the pasture until the silence between them became uneasy. Then, the two remaining mares in the pasture neighed loudly. Etta's lovely smile reappeared. "Chara and Vega are feeling neglected. They're getting impatient for their dinner."

Gabriel made sure his reply was lighthearted. "It's not smart to keep a lady waiting, especially when she outweighs me."

Etta's gaze flicked to Gabriel, back to the floor, and then the open doorway. "If you'll excuse me, I need to make sure my father's settled for the evening."

She turned on her heel and strode through the doorway, leaving Gabriel to wonder about the banker's daughter. His mother had described her as an intelligent businesswoman, but she'd seemed nervous while talking to him.

He headed back outside to retrieve the remaining horses. Etta's slight figure disappeared over the rise of a hill and a blessed tranquility filled Gabriel's irritable soul. There was something about Henrietta Davis that soothed his prickly nature. He could do with more of that in his life.

3

Etta took a deep breath before opening the heavy doors of Davis Bank and Trust, but her stomach refused to relax. The granite floors and brass lamps gleamed in the morning sunlight, and a hum of activity vibrated through the dignified building. Both of the teller cages were manned, Etta noticed with approval, and several clients sat with account managers in the smaller offices. Business had carried on in her father's absence.

Etta smoothed her charcoal gray jacket over the matching skirt. When she'd first started working at the bank, her father had advised conservative dress, but that hadn't stopped her from wearing lace blouses beneath the drab jackets or from pinning silk flowers to her hats.

"Good morning, Miss Davis."

As she climbed the stairs to her father's office, Etta smiled at James Walters, the young teller Uncle Carl had hired last month. James was getting married soon. Without her mother to take care of social obligations, it was up to Etta to send a suitable gift to the bride.

"Good to have you back, Miss Davis," Arthur Lewis said.

Etta nodded to the recently hired manager of the loan department. He'd been with the bank for almost two months, but her father had spoken well of Arthur's good judgment and business acumen.

Etta walked into her father's outer office and set her briefcase on her desk. Through the frosted glass door that led to her father's private office, a dark shape moved from one side of the room to the other. No one had the key except her father, herself, and Carolina Swanson, the head teller.

Before Etta could make it to the office door, Carolina walked into the room with a handful of mail. "Glad to see you're back. How's your father doing?"

Etta put a note of optimism in her voice. "He'll be back before you know it." She removed her hat and gloves and took the letters. "Do you know who's in his office?"

"Your uncle." Carolina's voice dropped to a conspiratorial whisper. "He's been in there almost every day since you and your father left."

"You gave him the key?"

"I told him I wasn't allowed to give it to anyone, but he just laughed and snatched it out of my hand. What was I supposed to do?"

"Did he return it?"

"Yes, but he must have made a copy. I make sure the office door is locked every day before I leave, but Carl goes in and out of there as if it was his own." She raised her eyebrows and walked away.

The restlessness in Etta's stomach multiplied. Ever since Arthur Lewis had been hired, Carl's only responsibility was to manage the employees. There was nothing in her father's office that concerned the bank personnel. Etta walked through the door without knocking. "Good morning, Uncle Carl."

A stack of ledgers thundered against the highly polished wood floor as Carl whirled in response to Etta's greeting. "Oh, Etta. You startled me." He squatted to retrieve the books. "I had no idea you were coming in today. How's Henry?"

Several account books lay open on the desk and a stack of receipts were wedged under a marble paperweight.

"What are you looking for? Maybe I can help you."

Carl folded the receipts and shoved them into the pocket of his pinstriped trousers. "Nothing." He closed the ledger books and stacked them. "I was just...uh...just trying to keep on top of things. You know Henry always kept me up-to-date on the bank's investments." He hugged the books to his chest and brushed past Etta on his way out the door. "I'll be by later tonight to pay Henry a visit and to let him know everything's under control here."

Carl's brown and white wingtip shoes squeaked as he hustled through the outer office and out the door. Etta crossed her arms over her chest and studied the top of her father's highly polished desk. Her reflection showed a deep groove between her eyebrows.

In the years she'd worked as her father's assistant, her uncle had seldom had reason to enter any of the second floor offices. But, surely, Uncle Carl had a good reason for taking ledger books.

"Miss Davis?"

Etta glanced up to see a short, wiry man with tanned skin and reddish hair standing by her desk. "Yes?"

"My name's Charlie Simpson." The man nervously fingered a battered hat. "The lady downstairs, a Mrs. Swanson, she told me to come on up."

"Oh, Mr. Simpson. I wasn't expecting you until after lunch."

"Yes, ma'am, I know, and I'll go downstairs and wait if you don't want to see me now." The man's words shot from his mouth like bullets. "It's just that, well, I got a ride from a friend, and he could only bring me this morning. But like I said, I can wait all day if that's what you want."

Etta ducked her head to hide her smile. Did Charlie Simpson always talk so fast or was he just nervous? She walked toward him with her hand outstretched. "I'm glad to talk to you now, Mr. Simpson. Dr. Russell told me you had some experience working with stroke patients."

Charlie took her hand and shook it once. "I sure do. See, I was a medic in the Army for a long time, and then I got a job as an orderly at a hospital in Dallas, but when I heard about my old unit going to France, well, I decided they couldn't go without old Charlie. So I went with 'em. Now the war's over and I'm back to looking for a job. Doc Russell, he told me about your Pa and how you're dead set against sending him away, so I'm here to offer my services."

"I see." Etta took a long breath and blew it out. Even if Charlie didn't need a breather from talking, she needed one from listening. She gestured to a chair next to her desk. "Please sit down, Mr. Simpson."

Charlie sat on the edge of the seat like an alley cat on a fence rail. "I can provide references for you, ma'am." He withdrew a folded sheet of paper from his jacket pocket. "I wrote 'em all down for you. Doc Russell, he knows me from when we were both working in Dallas, and Captain Ross, he's the surgeon I worked with during my last enlistment, and, if you want, I can give you more names." Charlie bit his bottom lip and glanced around the office. "I don't need much in the way of pay, ma'am, but I'd better tell you straight off that I don't have no place to live. I've been staying with an old Army buddy in Austin, but his wife, well, she wouldn't be sad to see me go. Doc Russell said that maybe you would...well, that you might..."

"We can provide room and board, Mr. Simpson. If you're hired, you would sleep in a bedroom near my father, and you'd be welcome to take all of your meals with us."

Charlie smiled and leaned back in his chair. "Oh, ma'am. That'd be perfect. Just what old Charlie needs."

He didn't have gray hair, but the lines around his mouth and eyes suggested Charlie was in his forties.

"Since we'll provide room and board, the pay may not be what you were expecting."

"Whatever you say is fine, Miss Davis. Doc Russell, he said your family was as square as a soda cracker and that's good enough for old Charlie."

Etta had been praying for someone to help her father. Could this short, thin man be the person God had sent in response? "I'd like to check your references, Mr. Simpson. How can I get in touch with you?"

Charlie rubbed his jaw. "Well, ma'am, that's not so easy. See, the buddy I'm staying with, well, he doesn't have no telephone. But I'm going to be in town all day 'cause he can't pick me up until about seven o'clock tonight when he heads back to Austin."

"My goodness. What are you going to do for the rest of the day?"

"Don't you worry about old Charlie. I know how to while away the day. I'll just find me a nice shady tree and take a rest. If it's all right with you, ma'am, I'll check back later this afternoon and see if you've made your decision."

She'd probably be able to talk to the doctor today, but contacting an Army officer might be difficult. "You understand that if I hire you, you'll be providing almost everything for my father. You'll be expected to help him eat, bathe, and dress as well as see to his rehabilitation. That's a lot for one person to take on."

"Maybe. But not for old Charlie." He leaned forward and tapped her desk with his index finger. "I've seen a lot worse than strokes happen to men a lot younger than your Pa. I know how to exercise his legs and arms so that he gets movement back in 'em, and as far as bathing and dressing him…well, that's what I do all the time for those who can't do for themselves."

Etta's heart told her that Charlie Simpson was the right man for the job, but her head told her she'd better check his references. She stood and offered her hand again. "Tell you what, Mr. Simpson. You give me time to talk to Dr. Russell and to locate Captain Ross. I usually leave the bank around five o'clock. Stop back in before then, and we'll talk again."

Charlie's eyes wrinkled with his wide grin. "It's a deal, ma'am." He shook her hand vigorously. "You'll see. Old Charlie's your man, all right."

❧❧

Rosa clucked her tongue as she followed Etta up the back stairs. "Your Papa, he didn't eat nearly enough. I'll bring your dinner on a tray. See if you can get him to eat something."

"What time did the nurse leave?"

"That woman," Rosa answered with a disgusted

tone. "She spent more time in my kitchen than she did with your Papa."

Etta shifted the sewing basket in her arms and knocked softly on his open door. Her father was sitting up in bed, bolstered by pillows. "Good evening, Papa. How are you feeling?"

"Hmph." The stroke had robbed him of speech, leaving grunts and groans in place of words.

Rosa peeked into the room, shook her head, and then hurried down the back stairs.

Etta fixed a smile on her face and entered her father's room. "Your face is almost back to normal, Papa. That's a good sign."

He nodded his head slowly, as though that simple action required forethought.

Etta pulled a chair close to the bed and sat down. "I went to the bank today. Everything's fine there. We're down a little in manufacturing, but that's to be expected now that war production is declining. We're up quite a bit in agricultural futures."

"Hmph."

White stubble covered her father's cheeks and chin. Why hadn't the nurse shaved him?

Etta withdrew two quilt squares from the basket and showed them to her father. "I found these in Mom's sewing room. I'm going to try my hand at finishing the quilt she started."

Henry moved his left arm toward the fabric.

Etta placed the quilt square in his hand. "I don't know much about sewing, but I can put the squares together. Then I'll ask Sara to help me quilt them."

A tear ran down her father's bristled cheek.

Concern and panic tightened Etta's throat. She'd never seen her father cry. Should she comfort him or give him privacy?

He choked on a sob as more tears flowed from his reddened eyes.

Tears sprang to Etta's eyes as well. Her poor, dear Papa. Always so strong. Always so proper. She stood and removed a handkerchief from her pocket. "It's OK, Papa," she whispered as she dried his cheeks. "You'll get better."

He groaned and pushed her away.

Etta bit her lip as she stumbled back. She should have known better than to embarrass him. She resumed her seat and focused on pinning together two of the quilt squares. A sharp pain pierced her throat as she listened to her father struggle to contain his grief. She wanted to embrace him or hold his hand, but he wasn't that kind of man. Even if she meant to comfort, the result might be unintended embarrassment. Perhaps she should step into the hall, but wouldn't that convey the message she found his emotions distasteful? Nothing could be farther from the truth.

She sewed in silence, carefully whipstitching the two pieces of fabric together and removing the pins as she went along. *Please send Papa comfort*, she prayed while she sewed. *Help him endure this illness*. Each stitch was a prayer for her father's recovery.

Rosa called to her from the hall. "I have your dinner, mija."

Etta laid her sewing in the basket and brought a small table to the chair. "Bring it in, Rosa."

The housekeeper entered as though she walked a tightrope. Keeping her eyes on the floor, she set the tray of food on the table and spoke in a low tone. "Let me know if you want something else."

Why wouldn't Rosa look at her father? "Thank

you, Rosa. I'll bring down the tray when I'm finished."

Rosa ducked her head and tiptoed out of the room. Etta scrutinized the food. "Papa, Rosa sent up a bowl of your favorite soup, the kind with the little meatballs. Would you like some?"

Henry moved his head slowly from side-to-side. Whether he had no appetite or simply declined to have his daughter spoon-feed him, Etta decided not to push the matter.

"I have more news for you," she said as she ate from her bowl of soup. "Rosa's nephew, Benito, is coming every morning to clean the stalls and let the horses out. I went to the stable when I got home and everything looks very nice."

"Hmph."

"Do you remember Sara Benson's son?" Etta watched her father for a reaction, but his gaze was fixed to a spot on the wall over her head. "His name is Gabriel. He's volunteered to exercise the horses and to oversee their care."

Her father's gaze didn't waver, but he slowly nodded his head.

"Now, the best news of all. I've hired a man to help you. His name is Charlie Simpson. Dr. Russell recommended him and so did his former commander. He was an Army medic, and according to Captain Ross, Charlie worked as a reconstruction aide." Her father's wooden expression never changed. "I'd never heard that term, but Captain Ross told me it's a new field of medicine aimed at helping people with brain injuries. Reconstruction aides work with patients to help them regain mobility." Etta laid her spoon on the tray and fingered the linen napkin in her lap.

If only her father could tell her what he needed.

He'd always told her what to do, not the other way around.

"Charlie will be here tomorrow morning."

Henry's gaze lowered to Etta's face, and she held her breath awaiting his response. His left eyebrow slanted down and his mouth twisted like a gasping fish. "Arg..doo…nee…" His left arm and leg flung out, overturning the small table and sending the dinner dishes crashing to the floor.

Etta sprang to her feet. "All right, Papa. All right."

He collapsed onto the pillows, his chest heaving from the exertion.

Etta went to his side. "I'm sorry." She wiped his brow with her handkerchief. "I'm sorry, Papa."

Henry exhaled loudly and turned his head away from her.

Rosa's quick footsteps pounded up the stairs. *"Mija! ¿Qué pasó, mija?"*

Etta squatted and began to pick up the dishes. "It's all right, Rosa. You can come in."

As before, the housekeeper sidled into the room, her gaze averted. "What happened?" she asked as she bent to help Etta.

"Nothing. Just an accident."

Rosa clucked her tongue and shook her head but kept her opinions to herself as she reloaded the tray and carried it out of the room.

Etta straightened, closed her eyes, and sent a prayer heavenward. What had she done to upset her father? Was it the bank, the horses, or her plan for helping him recover? "Lead me, Lord," she whispered. "Show me the right thing to do." She took a fortifying breath and turned to face her father.

His eyes were closed, and his chest moved with

steady breaths. Perhaps sleep was the best thing for him now.

Etta lifted her father's leg and placed it on the bed. "If a convalescent home is the best place for Papa, Lord, please let me know. It's hard to see him suffer, but sending him away doesn't feel right." She straightened her father's covers and turned out the bedside lamp.

If only her mother were here.

Her mother had always known the right thing to do.

❧

The gray clouds blanketing the sky matched Etta's mood the next day. The nurse had departed before dawn, leaving Etta to coax her father into eating breakfast. But he'd refused her assistance, pushing her arm away and flinging oatmeal onto the bedroom wall. She'd been near tears when Charlie Simpson arrived, a battered suitcase in one hand and a brown herringbone cap in the other.

Charlie's smile had never faltered. "Looks like old Charlie's arrived just in time," he said with a wink. "You go on now, Miss Davis. Your papa and me will figure things out."

After introducing Charlie to her father, Etta had driven her father's car to town. She hadn't managed to pin down Uncle Carl yesterday, but discovering which accounts he was overseeing was on top of her list today.

The enticing aroma of fresh cinnamon rolls from nearby Hoffmann's Bakery greeted her as she exited the car. Perhaps Papa could be cajoled into eating if she brought his favorite treat. She hurried into the nearby store.

"Oh, Miss Henrietta," Mr. Hoffmann greeted her. "So nice to see you back in town. I heard you returned to work yesterday. How is Mr. Davis? Better?"

"Yes, thank you for asking." Over Mr. Hoffmann's shoulder, Etta saw Carl seated at a small metal table. A woman wearing an emerald green toque and matching dress sat with her back to Etta.

Mr. Hoffmann walked around the counter and patted Etta's shoulder. "Good, good. So glad to hear it. What can I get for you today? Have you had breakfast? We have lebkuchen. I know how partial you are to those."

Etta glanced at the honey cakes she'd favored since her girlhood. "I'll take a few, Mr. Hoffmann, and six cinnamon rolls."

"Your uncle's here having coffee with a lady friend. Shall I pour a cup for you?"

"No, thank you. I'll just say good morning to Carl and then take my pastries with me."

"Fine, fine." Mr. Hoffmann returned to the counter where he began putting the treats into a white box.

Etta approached the table. Who was the stylish woman with her uncle? "Good morning, Uncle Carl."

Carl's cup rattled loudly as he dropped it into the saucer and jumped to his feet. "Oh, Etta. Sorry, didn't see you come in." Her uncle wasn't dressed for work. Instead of his usual three-piece suit, he wore a lightweight linen jacket with matching knickerbockers.

"Sorry to interrupt you," Etta said, "but I wanted to ask if we could meet sometime today."

"Of course." Carl patted his pomaded sandy-blonde hair. "Allow me to introduce my companion.

Miss Florence Edwards, my niece Henrietta Davis."

The pretty young blonde turned blue eyes toward Etta. "How do you do?"

Carl was at least fifteen years older than this girl. Was he meeting with her on bank business or was this a social occasion?

"It's nice to meet you," Etta replied. "Have you recently moved to Burnet?"

"Goodness, no," the young woman answered with wide eyes. "Carl and I are spending the day in the country. Isn't his new automobile simply a peach?"

Etta shifted her gaze to her uncle. "I didn't know you bought a new one."

"A yellow Hudson Super Six," Carl answered.

"Carl got it up to forty miles an hour on the way from Austin," Florence gushed. "It was so exciting." She smiled at Carl. "What a daring, brave man you are to drive so fearlessly."

Carl glanced at Etta, cleared his throat, and then returned Florence's smile.

This definitely wasn't bank business. Etta was as out of place as a prohibitionist at a tavern. "I don't want to disturb the two of you any longer, so I'll be on my way. It was nice to meet you, Miss Edwards."

"Likewise, I'm sure. Perhaps we'll see each other again."

"I look forward to it," Etta replied. "I'll see you later, Uncle Carl."

"If not today, then definitely tomorrow," Carl answered.

With a nod, Etta turned and headed toward the door. Carl was a bachelor, free to entertain whomever he chose, and it was not her place to judge his choice. Her mother had often spoken about Carl's natural charm and easy-going spirit, and if Florence didn't mind the age difference, who was Etta to object?

But she simply must resolve the banking question sooner rather than later. If she was going to be temporarily in charge, she had to know what each employee was doing.

∂∞∽

Later that afternoon, dark clouds cast purple shadows on Etta's desk. Rain was always welcome in drought-prone Burnet County, but the heavy air only intensified her already low feelings. A bolt of lightning illuminated the room, followed quickly by a clap of thunder. Etta jumped in her chair, took a deep breath, and chided herself for being startled. The acting president of a bank couldn't be afraid of thunder. She had to embody confidence and strength, just as her father always had.

She leaned back in her chair and stared at his empty office. It would be a long time before Papa returned. Even if Charlie Simpson worked miracles, Papa had a long road of healing ahead of him.

Hard pellets of rain struck the glass. This was no gentle spring shower. Papa was probably anxious about the horses being caught in the storm and frustrated about his inability to do anything. Perhaps she should call Gabriel.

Etta reached for the candlestick telephone, but her hand stopped in mid-air. She had been grateful for Sara's offer, but now that she'd met Gabriel, she wished she hadn't accepted so quickly. Who knew Sara's son had grown into such a handsome man?

His dark brows framed light blue eyes that made

her catch her breath every time she'd looked into them. His strong jaw was shadowed with dark stubble, and his full lips made her yearn for her first kiss. She'd tossed and turned throughout the night worrying about her father and thinking about Gabriel Benson.

Etta curled her fingers into her palm and rested her hand on the desk. The horses weren't brainless. They'd gather in the three-walled shelter her father had installed in the north end of the pasture if Gabriel didn't get them into the stable. Besides, he might think she was checking up on him.

"Miss Davis?"

Startled by the voice, Etta jerked to attention.

"Sorry to disturb you," Arthur Lewis said with a contrite smile. "But I've come across something I need to show you."

"Of course, Mr. Lewis." Etta cleared her throat. "I'm afraid you caught me daydreaming."

Arthur adjusted his wire-rim spectacles. "I understand. You've got a lot on your mind."

Most of which she'd never share with Arthur Lewis. "What can I do for you?"

He slid a ledger book onto her desk. "I found a discrepancy a few days ago and it's taken me this long to figure it out." Mr. Lewis's brows drew together. "Something's not right, Miss Davis."

Arthur flipped the pages back and forth as he explained his discovery.

Etta's mind slipped away from the tallied columns and returned to the few times she'd seen Gabriel as a boy. He'd been a few years older than she and at least a foot taller, and he'd paid little attention to her. Even when she'd accompanied her mother to Sara's house, Gabriel had been helping his father or working on a neighbor's land. He'd probably thought of her as a bothersome little girl. What did he think of her now?

"So you see, Miss Davis, I'm certain someone has been falsifying the general ledger."

Etta's heart skipped a beat. "What did you say, Mr. Lewis?"

"Over the last few weeks, farmers and ranchers have been coming in about late notices I sent. There's no record of their loan payments, but they had teller receipts. I had no choice but to apologize for the error and to credit their accounts. That made me wonder if any other accounts had similar problems."

"Did you find discrepancies in any of the other loans?"

"Not yet. Normally I would have brought this to your father's attention, but since he's not well, I thought you would be the next logical person."

"Yes. Yes, of course." She steadied herself and reached for the key to her father's office. "My father keeps the general ledgers in his office. Let's compare them to your records."

The desk lamp did little to dispel the gloom brought on by the storm. "Farm and ranch loans are here," she said as she removed an account book from a walnut bookcase, "and here's a copy of the daily cash transactions."

Arthur frowned over the books. "Who's been keeping these up-to-date since you and your father have been gone?"

"Carolina Swanson. She's been working with my father for almost twenty years."

Arthur turned the pages of his ledger until he came to the right page. "Here's where I found the first discrepancy."

Etta found the corresponding page in her father's book. "The entries match, but the handwriting is different. See here," Etta pointed to a column of numbers, "where Carolina wrote her initials?" Arthur nodded. "That shows she's the one who entered the information. But here," Etta tapped the page, "the handwriting is different and no one initialed the entry."

"Someone other than Mrs. Swanson has been entering information."

"And these numbers don't match your ledger." Nausea roiled through Etta's stomach as she stepped away from her father's desk. She had to tell her father about this right away. He'd investigate this matter until the thief was caught. He'd —

Etta rubbed her forehead and sighed. She couldn't lay this at her father's feet. Every ounce of his energy was needed to recover from his stroke.

This was her fight. She straightened her spine and leveled her gaze at Mr. Lewis. "Have you told anyone else about this?"

"No, Miss Davis."

"I'll need to call an independent auditor. It's imperative you tell no one else about your discovery until I've found out more."

"I understand completely. I owe my job and my family's security to your father, and I'll do whatever I can to help. For now, I'll go on as if nothing's out of the ordinary."

"Yes, that would be best. Thank you, Mr. Lewis."

He retrieved his ledger, tucked it under his arm, and left. Etta sank into her father's chair and stared at the rain. Is this why Carl had been in her father's office? The Board of Directors was scheduled to meet in a few weeks. Would she have an answer by then, or would she be forced to admit that a thief had been steadily robbing the bank under her watch?

❧

Gabriel lifted his face to the rain and let the cool water wash away the dust. It had just been thunder. Plain, every day, natural thunder. Not shelling. Not German artillery trained on his platoon. Just thunder.

Thank goodness, no one had seen him dive for cover except the horses. Even they had pricked their ears and huddled in conference about his unusual behavior. When his heart had stopped pounding, he'd rolled over and gazed at the ominous clouds. A simple, spring thunderstorm. Almost every farmer and rancher in the county had probably danced for joy at the first rumble, but not him. He'd hit the ground and searched for his entrenching tool.

Now he sat in the doorway of the stable, letting the rain wash away the last scraps of fear and watching the cats run for shelter. The lead mare, Mira, shook her head and pulled at the rope that tethered her to the grooming post. Gabriel stood and ran his hand down her neck. "All right, girl. I know you're tired of waiting." He retrieved a brush from the bucket of tools and ran it over the mare's muddy belly.

This was supposed to be Benito's job, but there would be plenty to do once the teenager arrived. No use getting worked up about a tardy stable boy. If Gabriel hadn't had the Arabians, he'd have little else to do except stew over the events of the last year. That never led to any good outcomes.

Antares lifted his muzzle above the stall door and

neighed loudly.

Gabriel stopped brushing the mare and listened for what had triggered the stallion's vocalization. Over the sound of the rain hitting the stable's metal roof, he heard two voices speaking Spanish.

Etta entered the stable with Benito at her side. She lowered her umbrella and propped it against the wall. "Hello, Gabriel."

Gabriel nodded in greeting.

"You'll have to excuse Benito for being later than he promised. His aunt made him eat dinner first."

Benito smiled broadly. "Tía Rosa is the best cook in our family." The boy looked down the row of stalls. "What should I do first?"

"Get their feed," Gabriel answered. "Then you can finish the grooming."

"Yes, sir," the boy answered with a wide grin as he jogged toward the tack room.

Etta smiled at Gabriel. "I see you got caught in the rain."

Gabriel used his sleeve to push his wet hair off his forehead. "I'll dry. Looks like the rain's letting up."

Etta turned to look through the open doorway. "You're right." She tucked her arms behind her and stood silently. Something was different about her tonight, as though someone had thrown a rock into her placid surface. "Well…if you don't need anything… I'll let you get back to work."

Gabriel couldn't let her get away that quickly. "How's your father?"

Etta moved closer and gently rubbed Mira's neck. The horse nickered softly, obviously enjoying the soothing touch. "Papa was sleeping when I got home, but his new attendant reported he'd had a good day.

I'm not sure what that means, but I've decided to take it as a blessing. Did you have a chance to ride today?"

Gabriel tossed the brush into the bucket. "I rode Mira over to my parents' house. I tried to talk my mom into going for a ride, but she thought I'd lost my mind."

Etta's smile widened. "I've never seen your mother on a horse."

"She used to ride all the time when I was a boy, but now she says she's as old as Abraham's sandals and climbing atop a horse would do her in."

Etta laughed at the comparison. "That's old, all right. If the weather holds, maybe I can go for a ride on Sunday afternoon."

"Where do you like to ride?"

"Along Hamilton Creek. You know the footbridge that connects your family's land to ours?"

"Sure."

"If you go just a little farther south, there's a nice grove of cottonwoods that makes for a good resting spot."

The same spot where he'd seen her a few nights earlier. "That sounds nice, all right. Would you mind some company?"

Etta's brows drew together. "Do you think your mother would like to ride with me?"

Surely, a young woman as pretty as Etta had her share of suitors, but her confusion seemed genuine. "I doubt it. But I wouldn't mind."

Etta's eyes widened as his meaning sank in. "Oh." She took two steps away from Gabriel. "That would be fine." She picked up her umbrella. "If you're sure."

"I'm sure. Is two o'clock all right with you?"

"Two o'clock is fine," she said as she hurried out

of the stable.

Gabriel watched her hasty exit and laughed to himself.

Etta was almost as jumpy as he, but instead of thunder, she shied away from flirtation.

4

On Sunday afternoon, Etta sat at her sleeping father's bedside and stitched the quilt squares together. Charlie Simpson had only been working with him for a few days, but already she could see an improvement. She smiled to herself as she threaded the needle. Charlie was the most optimistic, good-natured person she'd ever met. Even when she'd come home one evening to the sound of breaking dishes, Charlie had cheerfully swept up the pieces and assured her that no harm had been done.

"Mr. Henry's just frustrated," he'd said with a smile and a wink. "You'd be frustrated, too, if you had to relearn how to hold a fork. But don't you worry, miss. Old Charlie's on the job."

Etta stitched and prayed. *Thank You for sending Charlie to us, Lord. Help Papa be patient in his healing.* A spring breeze ruffled the lace curtains her mother had loved, and doves cooed softly from the oaks. Etta dropped her sewing into her lap and leaned back in her chair.

Everyone had been so kind that morning at church. So many had offered to sit with Papa or to work in her mother's garden until she was ready to take it over. The fellowship of believers was a sweet blessing.

Etta closed her eyes as one of her mother's favorite hymns floated into her memory. *The fellowship of kindred minds is like to that above.*

"Wha…yu…"

Etta's eyes sprang open at the sound of her father's voice. "Good afternoon, Papa. I hope you had a good nap."

"Ahh…waaa…"

"Would you like some water?" Etta stood and offered him a glass.

Henry reached for it with his left hand and curled his fingers around it. Etta held her breath while he moved it shakily toward his mouth. Henry sipped the water, lowered the glass, and looked at Etta.

Relief flooded through her veins. "You did it, Papa! That's wonderful!" Etta used the edge of the sheet to wipe away the drops of water that dribbled down his chin.

"Hmph."

"I don't care what you say," Etta said as she resumed her seat. "It's progress. Remember that fable about the tortoise and the hare? Slow and steady wins the race."

Henry nudged the quilt square on Etta's lap.

"I'm halfway finished sewing the squares together. I saw Sara Benson at church this morning, and she agreed to help me finish the quilt. It will look wonderful on your bed."

"Hor…hors…"

"The horses are doing wonderfully. Rosa's nephew, Benito, comes before and after school to clean the stalls and to feed the horses. And Gabriel Benson is still coming. I believe he rides every day."

Her father's face remained impassive, his jaws slack, and his eyes unfocused.

"I'm going to ride this afternoon. You know how I

love to take Mira out for exercise."

"Yuu..riii…"

"Gabriel said he'd like to go with me. You don't mind, do you Papa?"

Henry shook his head slowly.

"I'll be back in time to fix you some dinner. We all know I'm not as good a cook as Momma, but Rosa left a stew in the ice box. All I have to do is reheat it."

"B..Ban.."

Etta dropped her gaze to the fabric. She mustn't tell her father about her suspicions, but they grew deeper every time Carl sidestepped meeting with her. She'd written to an auditor in Austin who had worked for the bank on a previous occasion. As soon as she heard from him, she'd supply everything he requested and stay out of his way. The less she had to do with his examination, the better. The Board of Directors had to be certain she had no sway over the results. In a few weeks, she'd have an answer about which accounts were affected by the thief, and, if possible, a trail of clues that would lead to the embezzler. "Everything at the bank is functioning as it should, Papa." She stitched in silence, afraid to look at her father. She hadn't lied to him, but she hadn't told him the whole truth, either.

Guide me, Lord. She prayed as she sewed. *Show me the right path to follow.*

The sound of feet hurrying up the stairs pulled Etta's attention away.

Charlie entered the room, his cap in his hand. "Afternoon, miss. Thanks for letting me go to mass with Rosa's family."

"Of course. Papa's been resting."

Charlie winked at Etta and smiled. "Glad to hear

it. It's time for his afternoon exercises."

Henry waved his left arm. "Noooo...don...wan..."

Charlie wasn't dissuaded by Henry's reluctance. "You keep that up, Mr. Henry, and the next thing you know, you'll be speaking in complete sentences. I've seen it happen before. Now if you'll excuse us, miss, I'm going to get your Papa out of bed and started on his strength building routine."

Etta gathered her sewing basket and stood. "I'll check on you after I return from my ride, Papa." She leaned over and kissed his cheek. "Stew tonight for dinner, Mr. Simpson."

"That suits old Charlie just fine, miss. Yes, indeed. What do you say, Mr. Henry?"

Etta scampered out of the room before she could hear her father's reply, but from his dark expression, it was clear he was not pleased about Charlie's plans.

∂∽∾

Gabriel strode into the stable a few minutes after two o'clock and found Etta saddling a mare. Instead of her usual prim, pinned-up hair, today she wore a single braid down the back of her white blouse. She looked much more like the woman he'd seen on his first night home, except today she'd dressed in trousers and knee-high riding boots. There was nothing improper about her clothing, but he couldn't stop looking at what her skirts had previously disguised. He'd seen plenty of women in pants before, especially in the big cities, and he'd agreed with his buddies that most of them looked like peculiarly dressed men. But no one would mistake Etta for a man. She had gentle curves in all the right places.

"I was planning on doing that for you."

Etta turned and smiled. "I've been saddling my own horse since I was ten years old. Back then, I had to stand on a mounting block to do it."

Gabriel took a lead rope from the wall. "In that case, why didn't you saddle my horse, as well?"

Etta laughed at his gentle teasing. "I wasn't sure which one you wanted today. Have you chosen a favorite?"

"They're all fine animals, but the stallion could do with a good, long ride. I'll bring him in."

Etta turned back to her task.

Gabriel walked into the pasture. Already his heart felt lighter, just at having seen her. He'd caught a glimpse of Etta at church that morning, but he'd been surrounded by members of the congregation who'd eagerly welcomed him home. He stole another glance at Etta. Best not think too much about her curves. He was having enough problems sleeping.

Gabriel reached the stallion, hooked the lead rope into his halter, and then returned to the stable to tie Antares to the hitching post.

Etta came out of the stable office with two small crockery bowls wedged in the crook of her arm. "Don't tell Papa," she said with an impish smile as she placed the bowls on the floor.

Gabriel placed the saddle blanket on the stallion's back. "Don't tell him what?"

Etta retrieved a waxed paper package from the office. "Don't tell him I feed the cats. He says barn cats aren't pets and that if I feed them, they'll stop hunting the rodents that steal the horses' food. Besides, I'm just giving them a little leftover chicken."

"Your secret's safe with me. Besides, I haven't seen

your Papa since before I went away."

Etta bit her bottom lip. "I'd bring you to visit, but now isn't a good time."

"Of course not. I'll pay my respects when he's feeling better. How's he doing?"

Etta gazed out the open stable door toward the house. "I hired a former Army medic to help him. Dr. Russell said Mr. Simpson was trained as a reconstruction aide in the Army. Have you heard of that?"

"There were several medics who did that kind of work in the hospital in France. They help men with head wounds."

"Hospital? Were you wounded?"

Gabriel shrugged one shoulder. "It wasn't much of anything. Especially when you consider what some men are going through. But that's why I got discharged early. The rest of my division will probably be home this summer."

"Lots of mothers will be glad when that day comes."

And others would grieve for sons who would never return.

Etta mounted her mare and rode through the open doorway.

Gabriel finished saddling Antares and led him into the afternoon sunlight.

Etta twisted in her saddle and patted the canvas saddle bags that rested behind her. "I brought some lemonade and sandwiches in case we get hungry."

"Good thinking. My mother used to say I ate more than Sam Houston's army." Gabriel straightened in the saddle and lifted his face to the sun as a gentle breeze ruffled his hair. It seemed as though every part of nature had joined together to form the perfect spring day. He lowered his head and looked at Etta. She watched him with a mixture of curiosity and anticipation. "Take the lead, Miss Davis, and I'll follow."

Etta directed her mare down a well-worn path. Gabriel let her set the pace, keeping his horse close, but not interfering with her. She was an expert rider, commanding the horse with subtle movements. Her braid bounced in rhythm as the mare traveled across the sloping terrain that led to Hamilton Creek.

How often Gabriel had thought of such a day when he'd been in the hospital. He'd will himself away from the smells and noise of wounded men and into the clean, refreshing countryside of his boyhood. He pulled his mount to a stop and breathed in the scent of wild cedar. This was no dream.

Etta turned and rode back. "Is everything all right?"

Gabriel leveled his gaze at the lovely young woman. "Better than it has been in a long time."

A daring glint lit her eyes. "How about a race?"

"Are you prepared to lose?"

Etta's face shone with humor. "You may have the bigger horse, but Mira can hold her own." Etta pointed to the right. "See that live oak standing by itself? Last one there has to clean the boots of the winner."

Gabriel squinted into the horizon. The finish line was at least five hundred yards away, far enough for Antares to work up a fast gallop. "You're on," he said as he slapped the stallion's sides.

"Hey!" Etta laughed and urged her mare to follow.

Within seconds, Etta was at his side, her head level with her horse's neck, the wind rippling her blouse.

Gabriel knew his stallion could win, but he kept the pace steady. Cleaning Etta's boots was a small price to pay in return for watching her. She was joy and purpose and pleasure all wrapped up in one.

But fifty yards from the finish, Gabriel rose slightly and gave the stallion its head.

Antares bolted forward, his hoof beats striking the hard ground like chisels into stone.

Etta turned her head and smiled as Gabriel passed her then urged her mare to accelerate across the imaginary finish line.

Both horses flew past the tree together.

"Who won?" a breathless Etta asked as she walked her horse back to where Gabriel waited.

Gabriel loosened the reins and allowed Antares to prance with excitement. "I guess it's a tie."

Etta looked at him from the corner of her eye. "You didn't let me win, did you?"

"Did it look like I was holding back?"

"No. Not at the end anyway." Etta leaned over and patted the mare's neck. "Let's go to the creek now. I imagine Antares needs some water."

"My horse is tired, but yours isn't?"

"Mira is part falcon. Did I forget to tell you that?"

Gabriel grinned at her joke and let her set a gentle pace, allowing the horses to cool down. How long had it been since he'd felt so comfortable in someone's company? Even though he was just getting to know her, riding beside Etta in companionable silence felt as right as putting on his favorite boots.

"I saw you and your parents at church this morning," Etta said. "Did you enjoy the service?"

He'd woken before daylight, his sheets twisted around him like a shroud and his mouth as dry as cobwebs. "I didn't really want to go, but my mother talked me into it."

"It's a good thing you did. Otherwise, your circle of admirers would have been disappointed."

Circle of admirers?

"Just my parents' friends wanting to say 'welcome home.'"

"I wasn't referring to them. I was talking about all the young women who flocked to you like hummingbirds to nectar."

He smiled at the realization that Etta was teasing him again. "Oh, I see. Jealous, were you?"

"Did you accept Mary Henderson's invitation to dinner? Or Juliet Franklin's hint about needing a partner for the dance contest in San Antonio?"

Gabriel narrowed his eyes. "Mary Henderson's mother invited my whole family to dinner, and I told Juliet I don't dance. What about you? Didn't I see William Clark paying you special attention?"

Etta pursed her lips. "William was just asking about Papa."

"Uh-huh. He didn't look like he was thinking about your father. What's William doing these days?"

"He's the county prosecutor."

"Awfully young for such an important position."

"He took the position last year. He's one of the men on the bank's Board of Directors."

Gabriel leaned across his saddle toward her. "I'd watch out if I were you, Etta. Mr. Clark has more on his mind than bank business."

"Now you sound like the jealous one."

"Maybe I am."

Etta's cheeks reddened, and she looked away.

Their good-natured bantering disappeared and

tense silence wormed its way between them.

Of all the lamebrain things to do. He'd been in the company of men so long, he'd forgotten how risky it could be to tease a woman. Hadn't he'd seen his mother dissolve into tears over some off-handed remark his father had made? "I'm sorry if I embarrassed you, Etta."

Her gaze flitted from the ground to him and back again. "I, uh...I'm not very good at..."

If he didn't change the subject, she'd be as red as a radish, and he'd be in more trouble than Mrs. O'Leary's cow. "I'm ready for some of that lemonade. How about you?"

Etta smiled, and he knew he'd been forgiven. "There's the spot I was talking about," she said with a nod of her head. "Shall we give Antares and Mira a rest?"

Gabriel tied the horses to a low branch where they could drink from the pristine waters of Hamilton Creek.

Etta took out a bundled sheet from her saddlebag, unwrapped two jars of lemonade, and spread the sheet over the shaded grass. She handed one jar to Gabriel. "I don't imagine it's still cool, but at least it's wet."

Gabriel unscrewed the lid of the jar and drank the sweet, tart refreshment. "It's been a long time since I had lemonade. The Salvation Army gave it to us sometimes in France, but mostly they had coffee."

"I imagine lemons were hard to find during a war."

"Not to mention sugar." Gabriel dropped to the ground beside Etta. "One of the men in my platoon hated drinking straight coffee so much he stole sugar from the Germans."

Etta's eyebrows shot up. "He what?"

"Believe it or not. We overran a German camp near the Argonne Forest, and they'd left their provisions. Nichols was running around, opening tins trying to find sugar. Finally, Sergeant Schmidt told him the German word for sugar was *Zucker*. Nichols found four tins that day. Now, you might think he'd hoard it, but he didn't. He shared it with everyone in the squad. Funny how a little thing like that could make ten men so happy."

"Ten men in a squad?"

"Usually. And four squads in a platoon."

"Did you like being in the Army?"

Gabriel braced his hands on the ground behind him and leaned back. "It's not a simple answer. I liked being with my men, but I hated almost everything else." Gabriel's thoughts floated back to the smoke-filled battlefield and the cries of wounded men. So much confusion. So much desperation. Death could come in an instant or linger for months, but once it came, there was no escape.

"Don't you think?"

Gabriel focused on Etta's lovely face. "Sorry. I was daydreaming. What did you say?"

"I said, the bluebonnets are beginning to leaf out. We'll have a lot this year, don't you think?"

Fields of bluebonnets. Another thing he'd dreamed of during his mental forays back home. "That rain we got last week will help. Did you know they have bluebonnets in France?"

Etta's voice took on an accusatory tone. "I don't believe it. Everybody knows they don't grow anywhere except Texas."

"Captain Brooks said they were called lupines,

and I'll admit they were taller than our bluebonnets, but they looked almost the same."

"You'd better not tell anybody else that story or you'll be drummed out of the state."

"Oh, I'm scared now."

She tilted her head to the side and laughed. "Tell me more about France."

What would he tell her? About the dead horses that lay in the streets still harnessed to carts and wagons? About the civilians who'd been unable to escape impersonal artillery barrages? Or should he tell her about his failure that led to the deaths of his friends? "How are things at the bank?"

Etta blinked but allowed the thread of conversation to drop. "Actually, things aren't going so well."

"How can things go bad at a bank? Jesse James didn't show up, did he?"

Her voice grew quiet. "In a way...yes."

Gabriel's brows drew together in concern. "Someone robbed the bank?"

The color of Etta's eyes deepened as she gazed into his. "I'd like to talk about it. I've been keeping it inside for a while, and I can't decide what's worse, the guilt at not telling my father or the worry about who I suspect." She was too delicate to have so much on her shoulders.

First her mother's death, then her father's illness, and now a problem at the bank.

"Go ahead. I'll listen."

Etta drew her knees up to her chest and wrapped her arms around them. "Will you give me your word to keep it a secret?

"You have my word."

Etta looked into his eyes as though trying to assess his trustworthiness. Although they'd known of each other for many years, she couldn't know what kind of man he'd grown to be.

She withdrew two sandwiches wrapped in waxed paper. She passed one of the sandwiches to Gabriel. "I have to collect enough evidence to catch an embezzler without him knowing."

A piece of the darkness that shadowed Gabriel's soul broke off and floated away. Etta trusted him. His word was good enough for her.

"All of the loans our bank makes are overseen by one person," Etta continued. "Do you know Arthur Lewis?"

"His youngest brother went to school with me. Didn't Arthur remarry recently?"

"About two years ago. After his wife died, he married a girl from Belton. They have a baby now."

"There was something unusual about his wife's death, as I remember."

"The gossips went wild with rumors, but nothing ever came of it. The newspaper account listed her cause of death as heart failure."

"Then why all the gossip?"

"Because she was relatively young. William Clark had just become county prosecutor and, if her death had been suspicious, I'm sure he would've brought charges against Arthur."

"Did Arthur gain financially from his wife's death?"

"Not that I know of. My father hired him despite the gossip. Being in charge of loans is one of the most responsible positions at the bank."

"Are you saying Arthur Lewis is involved with

embezzlement?"

"No. Not yet, anyway. He discovered a discrepancy in the books, and it's not a bookkeeping mistake. Someone is making false entries in the ledgers. Whenever there's a problem like this, the best thing to do is call an outside auditor, someone who's not affiliated with the bank in any way."

Gabriel bit into the ham sandwich. "Have you already contacted this guy? The auditor?"

"He'll be here in a few days."

"Will you have to inform the Board of Directors?"

"Yes, eventually. We're a privately owned bank, but we have a Board of Directors as a way to create trust between the bank and our clients. Everything we do is open to inspection by the board members."

"How long do you have before you have to inform the board?"

Etta pulled her legs up and laid her cheek on her knees. "I need to get all the facts first. The next meeting is in mid-April."

"And in the meantime? You're going to just let the thief keep taking money?"

"I know it sounds wrong, but I need him to keep stealing. He'll be easier to find if he keeps it up."

"Do you have a suspect?"

Etta bit her bottom lip and looked into the horizon. "This is the worst part, Gabriel. I think it could be my Uncle Carl."

"Your own family?"

"My mother's brother. He took a key to my father's office without permission, and I found him going over some account books. I don't know this for sure, but I think he's falsifying the ledgers."

Gabriel let out a low whistle. "You're in a tough

spot, that's for sure. But it sounds like you're doing the right thing."

"I hope so. But if the evidence points to Uncle Carl how will I ever confront him? Every time I think about having to file charges against a family member, my stomach doubles over."

"You can't let him get away with embezzlement."

"I know. I know, but..." Etta reached for her braid and fingered the small bow at the end. "I wasn't raised to do this kind of thing. I was taught to be a lady."

"What does that mean?"

"You know. Quiet, demure, sweet, helpful. I like working with my father at the bank, and he's taught me a lot about business, but I never thought I'd have to hold my own in a man's world." She was in her own kind of battle. The kind that helps a person find out what they're made of.

"I know what you need, Henrietta Davis."

"What's that?"

"You need to be more of a man."

Etta rolled her eyes. "How am I supposed to do that?"

"Toughen up. Ask yourself, 'What would a man do?'"

"Easy for you to say."

"What's your other choice? Sit back and smile sweetly while someone steals from you?"

Her eyes flashed. "You know I can't do that. I *won't* do that. But I wish I could talk it over with Papa."

She was protecting her father and fighting for her family's good name, but there was no way Gabriel could help. "Tell you what, Etta. I'm not your Papa, and I don't know a whole lot about banking, but I'll be around when you want to talk."

She nodded slowly and got to her feet. "I'd like to take a walk." Gabriel started to stand, but she put a hand on his shoulder to stop him. "I want a few minutes to think things over."

Etta had a lot on her mind, and maybe a walk alone would help her sort things out.

"Go ahead. I'm going to stretch out and relax. If I hear any screams, I'll rescue you from the terrible snake you've stumbled across."

She rolled her lovely blue-gray eyes again. "There are only four kinds of venomous snakes in Texas, and I know how to recognize them. You won't hear any screams from me."

"I like that tough talk. You sound like a man already."

She shook her head as if to dismiss his preposterous suggestion and headed toward the creek.

Gabriel laid down on the sheet, one arm under his head for a pillow. He closed his eyes and listened to the soothing sounds of a Texas spring. Was that a mockingbird singing nearby or a catbird? A breeze ruffled his hair as he released a bit of his ever-present restlessness. It was good to be home. To lie in the shade and listen to the creek, and to know that battlefields and violent death were far away. He'd spent many afternoons daydreaming when he'd been a boy, wondering about his future and constructing imaginary bridges across incredulously deep gorges. He'd come back as an older and warier version of that boy. He'd come back while others rested in French cemeteries for eternity.

Nichols motioned for him to follow.

But Nichols was dead. He was having a dream. Wasn't

he? Nichols held out a tin with black letters. "Have some, Lieutenant. Have some Zucker."

Gabriel sipped his black coffee. "No, thanks. Save it for yourself."

"I ain't got no use for it, Lieutenant. You take the sugar." Nichols poured the white crystals into Gabriel's cup. "Take it all." He emptied the container, causing Gabriel's cup to overflow.

Gabriel watched the white grains fall slowly into the mud. "You're wasting it, Nichols."

The soldier smirked. "Don't matter now. Nothing matters now." He laughed and then climbed out of the foxhole and ran into clouds of yellow gas.

"Stop!" Gabriel shouted. "Come back!" The private looked back and shook his head. "Get back here!" Gabriel commanded.

Nichols ran ahead, heedless of Gabriel's commands. Shells hit nearby, turning clods of dirt and stone into showers of shrapnel, but Nichols advanced steadily toward the line of fire.

"Nichols!" Gabriel's shout was useless in the barrage. He threw his metal cup on the ground and grabbed his rifle.

Someone shook his shoulder. "Gabriel?"

Gabriel sprang to a standing position, his hands fisted at his waist. Where was he? What had happened to Nichols? Why was Etta kneeling beside his feet? His rapid pulse roared in his ears. He rubbed a hand across his face and commanded his heartbeat to slow. He wasn't in France. It had been another dream. One more chapter in the ongoing saga of his futile quest for peaceful sleep. "Sorry," he muttered.

Etta sat back on her heels. "I wanted to let you sleep, but it sounded like you were having a nightmare."

"Yeah." Gabriel shoved his hands through his hair and rubbed his eyes, trying to banish the dream into the land of nightmares. "Sorry I drifted off. I haven't been sleeping very well."

"It's all right." Etta returned to her spot on the sheet and picked up a blue and white cloth. "Go back to sleep if you'd like. I was sewing while you napped."

Gabriel scanned the landscape as he searched his mind for remnants of the nightmare. But there was no danger. Nichols's scornful laugh was safely tucked into the compartment where Gabriel hid his bitterest memories.

He drank the last of his lemonade, sat down, and watched Etta. Her needle moved rhythmically through the cloth, in and out, in and out. Even though she had her share of problems to overcome, Etta's inner serenity shone. "What are you making?"

"I'm piecing together quilt squares my mother made. See?" She held out the cloth. "Your mother's going to help me make this into a real quilt."

"Do you like to sew?"

"Goodness, no. I'm basically teaching myself as I go along. But my mother left it unfinished, and I..." Etta's voice trailed off.

Gabriel's heart winced to hear grief shadow Etta's usually peaceful voice. "My mother will enjoy spending time with you. She thinks you're one in a million."

Etta cleared her throat and returned to her stitching. "Sara's been a lifesaver these last few weeks."

What should he say? He didn't have the right words to ease Etta's heartache any more than he had the solution to her problem at the bank. Perhaps it was time to lighten the mood. "What else do you have in those saddle bags?" he asked, making his voice as cheerful as possible. "I was hoping for cookies."

"If you like ginger, you're in luck." Etta retrieved a checkered napkin and passed it to Gabriel.

He took two cookies and passed the napkin back to her. "Did you bake these?"

"I'm a much better banker than a baker. The credit goes to our housekeeper, Rosa."

He chewed the cookie slowly. Although he would have never predicted it, Etta Davis, daughter of the richest man in town, was becoming important to him. He'd left faith and hope on the battlefield, but whenever she was near, a calm reassurance surrounded him. "I have a confession to make."

Her eyes twinkled with humor. "Sounds serious."

She thought he was teasing, and for a moment, he reconsidered his words. But he wanted her friendship, and keeping secrets wasn't the way to make a friend. "I walked by here during my first night home. I saw you that night."

Her smile melted and concern filled her eyes. "I didn't see you."

"Didn't want to startle you, so I kept to the far side. I overheard you praying."

Etta folded the cloth and tucked it into the saddle bag. "That was right after my father's stroke."

"I didn't know who you were then. Now that we're becoming friends, it doesn't feel right to keep it a secret."

She walked toward her mare and threw the saddle bags over the horse's back. When she returned, her eyes were serious and her voice soft. "If you see me here again, will you let me know? I understand you didn't want to frighten me that night, but I don't like the idea of someone secretly watching me."

Gabriel stood and folded the sheet. "That's a fair request. One more thing. Don't tell my mother about my bad dream or that I'm having trouble sleeping. I don't want to worry her."

"I'll keep your secret. After all, you're keeping mine." She held out her hand as if to shake on the deal.

Gabriel took her hand and looked into her eyes. There was something special about Etta. Despite her anxieties, a calm presence permeated her spirit. She seemed to have that intangible characteristic of certainty that everything would turn out all right with the world.

What a blessing it would be to have more of that in his life. But if Etta knew what he'd done in France, she'd turn her back on him.

Gabriel dropped Etta's hand and held her horse's bridle while she swung into the saddle. He'd have to make sure she never learned the secret that plagued him.

5

Etta spread out the account books on the kitchen table. The CPA would be in Burnet soon. If she could find a pattern in the accounts, something that didn't make sense or couldn't be verified, she'd at least have a lead when he arrived.

A soft breeze ruffled the white voile curtains over the sink. Perhaps she should work in her father's library, but the lamplight made that room dark and lonely. It was filled with her father's books and mementos, and smelled of her father's cologne. In contrast, the kitchen was bright and cheerful. Her mother had painted the walls a pale yellow and the cabinets a pristine white. Cheerful prints of ripe cherries decorated the walls and cherry-themed dish towels hung from a peg rack near the ice box.

Rosa shuffled into the kitchen and clucked her tongue. "I hope you don't plan to stay up all night with those books."

"I'll go to bed soon," Etta promised as she sharpened a pencil. "Papa ate all of his dinner tonight."

Rosa sat down across from Etta. "When a sick person starts to eat, it's a sure sign he's getting better."

"But he's so grumpy. I've never known Papa to be so ill-tempered for so long."

"Well, mija, you got to remember who your Papa is. He's Mr. Big Boss. Always in charge. Always giving orders. And then, just like that," Rosa snapped her fingers, "he can't do nothing for himself."

"I telephoned Dr. Russell today. He said Papa was making slow progress, but he still thinks Papa should go to the hospital in Dallas."

"You did what was best for your Papa. Don't you know that?"

"I hope so. If Momma were here, she'd know what to do."

Rosa reached across the table and patted Etta's arm. "If your momma were here, maybe she'd help Mr. Henry, but she couldn't help with the bank. You're the only one who can do that." Rosa stood and poured cups of tea for herself and Etta. "I saw you're almost finished sewing the quilt squares together."

"It gives me something to do while I visit with Papa every evening. Every stitch is like a little prayer to God." Etta mimicked sewing with a needle and thread. "Please help Papa get better. Please help me do the right thing at the bank. Please help Papa get better. Please help me do the right thing at the bank. Over and over and over."

Rosa nodded her head slowly. "You're making a quilt full of prayers."

"Maybe. I hadn't thought of it that way."

Rosa sipped her tea in silence while Etta perused the account book for farm and ranch loans. After several minutes, Rosa broke the silence. "How's Benito doing?"

Etta looked up from the column of numbers she'd been adding. "As far as I know, he's doing fine. I'm sure Gabriel would have said something if Benito wasn't doing a good job."

"What do you think about asking him to take care of your momma's flowers?"

Etta frowned. "Aren't some of the ladies from the church coming by to work in the garden?"

"Not really. Two ladies came yesterday, but they didn't do very much. They watered the plants and they cut a lot of your momma's flowers, but I don't think that's what you meant when you asked them to work in the garden."

"They cut Momma's flowers?"

"They put them in baskets and carried them away."

"Maybe they're going to use them in the sanctuary."

"Maybe." Rosa's frown made it clear that she didn't believe the ladies had such charitable intentions.

"Does Benito have time? He's still in high school, isn't he?"

"He's graduating in a few months, and then he's going to college. He's trying to save money for his education."

"I didn't know he wanted to go to college. What's he going to study?"

"He wants to be a teacher. First one in our family to go to college." Rosa's pride shone in her dark eyes.

"Well, of course he can take over the garden. I'll put some extra cash in his pay envelope. And the next time I see him, I'll have to tell him how proud I am of him, too."

Charlie Simpson pushed through the kitchen's swinging door. "Evenin', everybody. How's it going?"

Etta couldn't help but smile at Charlie. How in the world did he maintain such a cheerful disposition? No matter how her father treated him, Charlie was always chipper. "Is Papa asleep?"

"Snoring like a tuba in an oom-pah-pah band. I'll

check on him before I turn in."

"How much longer before he recovers his speech?"

"Hard to say, Miss Davis. He's regaining some of his muscle strength, and he can stand for about a minute, but relearning how to talk usually takes longer. But don't you worry. Old Charlie's on the job. Before you know it, your Papa will be reading the Sunday newspaper to you."

That will be a wonderful day. "And what about you, Mr. Simpson. Is there anything you need?"

Charlie cut his gaze to Rosa. "Actually... there is something I was hoping for..."

"I know what you want," Rosa said. She stood and removed a pan of bread pudding from the warming box atop the stove. "How do you stay so skinny with all the food you eat?"

"Just lucky, I guess," Charlie answered with an impish grin. "I knew living and working here was the answer to my prayers, but I didn't know the Lord had a bonus in store. Rosa is a great cook."

"Such a smooth talker," Rosa said as she spooned bread pudding into a bowl. "You want some, mija?"

Etta shook her head.

Charlie tasted the dessert and waggled his eyebrows. "Mmm...best cook in Texas, that's what I say. If you don't watch out, Miss Davis, somebody might steal Rosa."

Rosa clucked her tongue as she placed a glass of milk in front of Charlie. "I'm not going nowhere. I got my own room, my own kitchen, and my family only a few miles away. *Voy a quedarme aquí hasta que voy a la gloria.*"

"Ah, Rosa, come on," Charlie protested. "You

know I don't speak Spanish."

"She said she's going to stay here until she goes to Glory," Etta translated.

"Is that right?" Charlie asked. "Well, that suits me. I don't have no other plans."

Etta looked at Rosa, but the older woman quickly looked away.

Charlie couldn't have been much clearer about his intentions.

Rosa muttered something in Spanish as she cleared the table and returned the bread pudding to the stove. "You two can stay up all night, but I'm going to bed." She patted Etta's shoulder. "Goodnight, mija."

Etta covered Rosa's hand with hers. "Goodnight."

Rosa walked up the back stairs.

Etta returned her attention to the account books while Charlie ate in silence. But being quiet was not in Charlie's nature, and after a few minutes, he interrupted Etta's concentration.

"How long has Rosa been living here?"

"About fifteen years. Why do you ask?"

"Has she ever been married?"

"She's a widow, and I'm not volunteering any more information, Mr. Simpson. You should be asking Rosa these questions instead of me."

Charlie grinned again. "I've been to mass with her family several times, and they seem like a nice bunch of folks, but they won't tell me a thing. Their mouths are closed tighter than a jelly jar."

"Maybe they're protecting Rosa."

"I understand that. Really, I do. But how's a man supposed to court a woman when nobody'll lend a helping hand?"

Etta narrowed her eyes. Rosa was much more than

a housekeeper, and Etta wasn't about to let Charlie Simpson hurt someone as dear as Rosa. "Does Rosa know your intentions?"

"I imagine she's got the idea by now," Charlie replied. "I haven't been exactly secretive about my interest in her. I'm going to talk to her older brother next Sunday after mass. That'd be the right thing to do, don't you think?"

Etta held up her palm as if to ward off the question. "Don't ask me, Mr. Simpson. What I know about courtship and marriage could fit inside the eye of a needle."

"That's because you're still young, Miss Davis. Your turn'll come. You'll see."

Etta didn't respond. What could she, a twenty-five-year-old woman who'd never had a serious beau, possibly say in reply?

Charlie carried his dishes to the sink. "Well, that does it for me. I'll take one last look at your papa before I turn in, and then I'm off to dreamland. Goodnight, Miss Davis."

"Goodnight." Etta listened to Charlie's footsteps on the back stairs as she thought about all the changes that had come into her life. Her mother was gone, her father was fighting for his health, and now Rosa might leave, as well. Good thing she'd been praying so much lately, but now she'd have to add another concern to her list.

❧❦

It was past midnight, but Gabriel couldn't sleep. He'd left his hostile bed, pulled on his boots, and headed toward the hill that overlooked the Davis property.

Etta would be safely tucked into bed by now.

Gabriel would never again take untroubled sleep for granted. Before the French battlefield, he'd slept like a hibernating bear. His mother had resorted to banging a metal spoon against a skillet as an alarm clock, and Captain Brooks had once thrown water on Gabriel to rouse him. But peaceful dreams and easy sleep were things of the past. No matter how hard Gabriel worked during the day, he couldn't close his eyes and ease into sleep. Memories crept into his mind like termites into rotten wood.

The look in his men's eyes when they realized he'd led them into danger, their courage despite their narrowing chances of escape, their mangled and bloodied bodies. Would time really erase those images from his mind? Would their voices ever stop whispering to him in the dark?

Gabriel climbed to the top of the hill and looked at the Davis's house. One light shone from an upstairs room that overlooked the courtyard. Was that Etta's room? Did worry keep her awake or was she ill?

If he could, he'd bundle all her concerns and throw them into the sky. Her worries would scatter into stardust and disappear into God's immense cosmos. If he could, he'd gather her into his arms and kiss her forehead, easing her troubles until laughter lit her lovely face and smiles banished all her cares.

The light blinked out, leaving Etta's house illuminated by pale moonlight. "Watch over her, Lord," Gabriel whispered. "Send Your angels to protect her and keep her in the palm of Your hand."

Gabriel lay on the slope of the grassy hill and stared at the darkened window. Maybe he could fall asleep now. He'd think about Etta, her goodness and her loveliness, and chase away the insidious memories that plagued him so.

∂∞⌐

A few days later, Etta led the auditor into her father's office. "I thought this would be the best place for you to work, Mr. Owens. You'll have access to everything you need, plus you'll have privacy. My desk is right outside."

George Owens laid his briefcase on the desk and looked out the window. "I've always liked it here in Burnet. Such a nice little town, far enough from the hustle of the state capital but close enough to go there when needed." He sat on the corner of the desk and smiled at Etta. "It's nice to see you again, Henrietta."

She'd seen George Owens occasionally over the years at one social gathering or the other. He was only in his early thirties, but a bald spot already shone through the thin hair covering the crown of his head. "Do you need me to make arrangements for you to stay in Burnet, or will you be driving back to Austin every day?"

"I recently bought a brand new car, so driving back and forth is pure pleasure. Maybe you'd like to go for a drive one day."

Etta wouldn't call her acquaintance with George anything more than casual. A few receptions and chit-chat over coffee certainly didn't equate to an intimate connection. But alienating him before he started his work wouldn't get results. "Maybe when you've finished your investigation." She made sure her words were accompanied by a pleasant smile. "I don't want to be seen to have influenced your findings in any way."

"I don't think that would be a problem. You did the right thing by calling me. If anyone from the State Department of Banking gets wind of this before I've found the problem, your worries will double."

"We're a family-owned bank, Mr. Owens. The State Department doesn't have a lot of say in the dealings of privately held banks."

"That's true for now, but things are changing all over the country." He removed his suit jacket and hung it on the coat tree in the corner. "Since I have experience with the way your bank is organized, I already have an idea where to begin." He fingered the ledgers on the bookcase near the desk. "But before I lose myself in these books, please tell me you'll join me for dinner this evening."

"Are you sure it wouldn't be better to conduct your investigation without a hint of influence from me?"

"You couldn't possibly sway my findings one way or the other, Henrietta. I'll ferret out the root of your problem and that will be that." He stepped closer to Etta and lowered his voice. "I'd hate to lose the opportunity to get to know you better while I'm here."

"I'm not free in the evenings, Mr. Owens. I—"

"Please call me George."

"I have to check on my father once I close up the bank. As I told you, he had a stroke and—"

"You don't mind me calling you Henrietta, do you?"

"Uh, no…if you'd like, but—"

"What about this Sunday? I'll put the top down and we'll drive out to the lake."

Etta backed out of her father's office. "Can I let

you know later? I should ask my father." The telephone on her desk rang, and Etta sprinted to take the call. She tried to listen, but her mind flitted from one concern to another like a June bug trapped against a window screen.

"Yes, Carolina, I'll be right down to look at the transactions." Etta pushed away from her desk and headed downstairs without glancing into her father's office. Best to leave George Owens and the audit to themselves.

Carolina Swanson and James Walters had their heads bowed over a stack of papers when Etta walked into the tellers' workroom. Etta still hadn't bought that wedding gift for James and his new wife. She'd take care of that today.

"Here she is now," Carolina said with a nod toward Etta.

James moved out of the way, and Etta stood next to Carolina. "What's the problem?"

"There's a shortage of five hundred dollars, but there's no teller's receipt to match. It's almost as if someone helped themselves to the money."

"When did this happen?"

"I reconciled the amounts in the cash drawers last night before I left," Carolina explained. "But this morning, I discovered the amounts were different."

"Which of the cash drawers was short?"

"Both of them. James is missing two hundred, and I'm short three hundred."

"Have you checked the teller's log books?"

James picked up a black book with red binding. "I checked them both. There isn't any notation about withdrawals of those amounts."

"Normally, this would point to the teller helping

himself to an unauthorized pay raise," Carolina said. "But both of us are missing cash."

"Someone is trying to make us look guilty," James said. "But one of us is always on duty when the bank is open, and our cash drawers are locked when we step away."

Etta laid her hand on the stack of tellers' receipts. "Where did you put the cash drawers when you left yesterday?"

"In the vault room, just as I always do," Carolina answered.

But not in the vault itself. That's where the majority of the bank's cash was kept and it remained closed and locked. Etta and her father were the only ones who knew the combination.

"And before you ask," Carolina said, "I've started keeping my keys with me at all times." She pulled a black grosgrain ribbon from beneath her blouse. Three brass keys were suspended from it.

Etta had ordered the lock on her father's office door to be changed, but she hadn't thought about the vault room. She patted Carolina's arm. "All right. You've reported the matter to me, and that's where your responsibility ends. Send the log books up to me tonight before you leave. I'll look into it."

Carolina's eyes grew moist. "I'm so sorry, Etta."

"Don't give it another thought. But starting tonight, we lock all cash drawers in the vault."

Carolina nodded and wiped her eyes while James mumbled his agreement.

Etta stepped out of the workroom and into the lobby. Her mind shuddered with the realization that someone had blatantly robbed the tellers' cash drawers. Only three people had keys to the vault room.

Etta's keys were in her pocket, her father's keys were on his dresser, and Carolina's keys were nestled somewhere close to her heart.

Etta would have to report this discrepancy to the auditor, but she wasn't prepared to face his persistent invitations again so soon. As though summoned by her thoughts, George paraded through the lobby and made his way to Arthur Lewis's desk. Talking to the account manager could take hours. What better time to pop over to Moore's Department Store and buy that wedding present?

The store owner's wife greeted Etta as she walked through the door. "Good morning, Henrietta. You look lovely today."

Etta smoothed her hands down her light wool brown skirt. There was nothing special about the ensemble she'd chosen that morning. "Thank you, Mrs. Moore."

Cassandra Moore glided from behind the counter like a swan on a smooth lake. "What can I show you this morning? We have some lovely new hats."

Etta touched her hair. She'd left in such a hurry she'd forgotten her jacket and hat. "Actually, I need to buy something for James Walters and his new wife. I don't suppose you know what they need?"

A gleam lit Cassandra's eyes. "The bride was in here just a few days ago admiring some silver candlesticks. May I show them to you?"

Etta followed the store owner's wife to a back corner. Very few people bought silver candlesticks in Burnet, but Cassandra had jumped at the chance to sell an expensive item to the banker's daughter. This was another task her mother had done with her usual grace and efficiency. She wouldn't have been so easily persuaded.

"Here they are." Cassandra placed the candlesticks on a piece of black velvet that stretched across the counter. "These are sterling silver, of course. Aren't they exquisite?"

Overdone was the word that sprang to Etta's mind. They looked like balusters entwined with boughs of roses. Would her mother have spent this much for an employee's gift? "Do you have anything else that the bride might like?"

Cassandra's cheeks paled slightly. "Oh. Well..." She moved to a display of china. "Perhaps you'd like to give a serving dish. Very few people think of that, but every new bride needs one."

Etta examined the pieces and the price card. A platter would be one-fourth the cost of sterling silver candle sticks and much more practical. "I'll buy one platter, Mrs. Moore. Will you have it delivered?"

If Cassandra was disappointed, she hid it admirably. "Of course. And I'll gift wrap it for no extra charge. Shall I put this purchase on your account?"

She hadn't brought money either, Etta realized. "Yes, please. I'll be sure to settle my account at the end of the month."

"Oh, I'm not worried about that," Cassandra said as she carried the platter toward a back room. "If you'll wait a few minutes, I'll bring you a card to sign."

Etta wandered aimlessly through the store until she came to a display of spring clothing.

At the sight of pastel linen and silk, grief climbed out of its hiding place and encircled her throat. She and her mother wouldn't be shopping for Easter ensembles this year. Neither would they help with the Fourth of July community picnic nor host their traditional

Christmas open house. Years and years of motherless holidays stretched before her. Etta blinked back tears and strode away from the display. As soon as she was alone, she'd give in to the tears, but not now. Not here.

"You know it's for the best, Mr. Moore," a familiar voice said.

Etta peered through a rack of men's jackets.

Uncle Carl leaned in the doorway of James Moore's office, his hands in his trouser pockets. "It's just not fair."

James Moore rubbed the back of his head and frowned. "I don't know, Carl. This is a decision for the bank's Board of Directors to make. I can't give my permission without the others' consent."

Etta's heart danced a quick step. What was Uncle Carl up to? It obviously had something to do with the bank.

Carl's voice sounded like butter on a hot biscuit. "Of course, of course. But I'm willing to do what I can. Can I count on your support?"

James stood and walked Carl out of his office. "The Board will be meeting in a few weeks. We'll talk it over then."

"That's fine, James, just fine." Carl shook the storekeeper's hand and walked toward the exit. "I only hope nothing unfortunate happens before then."

Etta clenched her fists.

Uncle Carl had been working with ledgers in her father's office, taken Carolina's keys, and now was talking to members of the board. Perhaps there was an innocent explanation for his actions, but what was it?

"Here you are," Cassandra Moore said from behind her. "My goodness, Henrietta, are you all right? Your face is as red as a chili pepper."

Etta struggled to keep her voice calm. "Please sign the card for me, Mrs. Moore. I need to get back to the bank." She forced herself to walk slowly through the store, but once outside, she took a deep breath and concentrated her thoughts on what she should do next. She couldn't go back to her desk while her mind reeled with this latest development. She needed time to think.

She turned right and strode past the row of shops. What would the auditor find? How long would it take? She couldn't close the bank, too many people depended on it, but someone was siphoning off the funds. Was it her uncle? She had no real evidence. Except for the missing cash, the other problems could be accounting mistakes.

She crossed the street at the corner and headed back toward the bank. Her heels tapped loudly against the boardwalk, matching the pounding of her heart. Why did she have to be the one to sort out this mess? Handling these kinds of problems was her father's responsibility.

Her skirt swished around her ankles as her steps came to a sudden halt in front of Adler's Hardware Store. Shame darkened her heart. How could she be so selfish when her father was fighting for his life? She covered her face with her palms and moaned softly.

A warm hand touched her shoulder. "Etta? Are you all right?"

She lowered her hands and lifted her gaze to Gabriel's concerned face. Relief weakened her knees, and she reached out to him. How she wanted to wrap her arms around him and rest her head on his chest. Gabriel would know what to do.

Instead, she folded her arms across her abdomen and swallowed hard. "What are you doing here?"

He nodded toward the hardware store. "I came into town with my dad. Is something wrong?"

Etta stepped away, forcing his hand to drop. "I was at Moore's Department Store and…" She glanced at the other people nearby. What if someone overheard her?

"And what, Etta?"

She shook her head and cast her gaze to the ground. "I can't talk about it now."

Gabriel's father stepped out of the hardware store. "Morning, Etta. How are you today?"

Etta tried to smile. "Fine, thank you. And you?"

Ethan slapped Gabriel on the back. "Much better now that my boy is home. We need to get going, son. Sorry to run, Miss Davis, but we've got a delivery to make."

A strong breeze blew a lock of Etta's hair across her face, and she tucked it behind her ear. If she'd remembered her hat, she wouldn't have this problem. "That's quite all right, Mr. Benson."

Ethan Benson walked down the narrow alley at the side of the store, and Gabriel touched her elbow. "Would you like to talk later? I can meet you at the stable."

Her heartbeat eased as her spirit lifted. "Yes. After work."

Gabriel gently squeezed her arm, sending encouragement and support in the simple gesture. "I'll be there."

Etta watched him trail after his father. In the midst of grief and worry, she'd found a new friend. A genuine smile crossed her lips for the first time that day, and she headed toward the bank with renewed determination. She'd solve the problem of the missing funds, even if it meant her uncle was a thief.

∂∘∾

The truck's front right wheel dropped into a hole, bouncing Gabriel's head into the roof.

"Sorry," his father said with a chuckle. "These roads were built for horse and wagon. Who knows when they'll get around to improving them?"

Gabriel rubbed the sore spot on his head. The Army doctor in France had commented on how lucky Gabriel had been to have a thick skull, but Gabriel never imagined his father's driving could endanger him.

"I heard you go out last night," his father said. "Around two o'clock. Everything all right with you?"

"Just having trouble sleeping. I went for a walk."

"Uh-huh. Have you thought about what you're going to do with your life, now that you're finished with the Army?"

"I have three more months of Army pay. Thought I'd use that time to think about it."

"There's lots of opportunities for civil engineers. Think you'll use that degree of yours?"

"Probably. Maybe I'll ride over to A&M and talk to my old professors about it."

"I bet you're not the only soldier who'll be looking for a job."

But so many would never return. Suddenly Gabriel didn't want to talk about his future. "If you can manage to drive around the holes, I'm going to close my eyes and catch a nap."

His father grinned and nodded.

Gabriel slid down and rested his head against the

back of the seat. He still didn't feel as though he was truly home, despite the fact he slept in his childhood bedroom and ate his mother's cooking every day. But maybe it was time he thought about what he'd do with the rest of his life.

He didn't deserve to be alive when better men than he had perished, but for reasons he couldn't understand, he'd survived. The hospital chaplain had said that God had plans for Gabriel. But what were they? To return to Burnet in order to help Etta with her father's horses? Not likely. But so far, that summed up his contributions.

The thought of Etta brought a smile to his lips and a new worry to his mind. Something had upset her. She'd always projected calm assurance, but today she'd been troubled. Perhaps it was his turn to offer comfort, though he couldn't imagine what his prickly personality could do for her.

6

Etta threw her hat and satchel on her bed and hurried to the stable. All afternoon she'd looked forward to seeing Gabriel to tell him about her latest discoveries. He'd probably advise her to stand up to her uncle, but how did one do that? If she confronted Carl, he'd deny her suspicions or explain them away. But if Carl was behind the bank's missing funds, she had to find a way to stop him.

An orange striped kitten dashed past her as she stepped into the shaded stable.

Etta paused to watch the small animal pounce on a butterfly then smiled as the insect rose above the wildflowers and fluttered away.

A horse neighed from inside the stable, calling her attention back to the reason she'd come.

Gabriel was inside, carrying a bucket of food from the feed room toward a stall. "There you are," he said. "I've been waiting for you."

Etta's heart smiled at his warm greeting. He was becoming an important person to her—a good friend and confidante. "I got held up just as I was leaving work." Etta stroked Mira's neck and the horse nickered in reply. "The auditor came today."

Gabriel emptied the pail of feed into Mira's trough. "What's he like?"

Pushy, Etta thought.

George Owens had detained her after the bank

closed, trying to persuade her to join him for dinner.

"He's all right, I suppose. He's worked for us before, and he knows how we do business, so I expect he'll find the problem."

Gabriel set the empty bucket on the floor and looked at her closely. "I think you're not telling me everything."

Etta's cheeks warmed. How could she explain George Owens's actions to Gabriel? "What do you mean?"

"When I saw you this morning you were obviously upset. What happened?"

Etta blew out a breath. "Oh, that." She walked to the stable door and looked out. Benito had Vega on a lead rope and was walking toward Gemma. "Someone took five hundred dollars from the tellers' cash drawers. Unlike the loan accounts, cash is hard to track. But that's not the worst part."

Gabriel moved behind her. "Tell me."

Etta turned to face him. "I was in Moore's Department Store this morning just before I ran into you, and I overheard Uncle Carl talking to James Moore. I think he's up to something, but I'm not sure what."

Gabriel's dark eyebrows drew together. "What did he say?"

"Nothing I can put my finger on. Uncle Carl asked for Mr. Moore's support, but I didn't hear more. But I know it's about the bank because Mr. Moore wouldn't commit to anything without talking to the other members of the board."

Gabriel rested his hand on Etta's shoulder. "You're in a tough spot, all right. What are you going to do?"

Etta tilted her head toward Gabriel's hand. How

she wanted to lay her head there, to let his reassuring touch seep into her soul. She wanted to soak up his strength, to rest in the protective circle of his arms until she was certain of her ability to fight.

Over Gabriel's shoulder, a gray cat leaped atop a stack of galvanized steel stock tanks. One second later, the pile tilted ominously. Etta pointed toward the impending accident. "Watch out—"

She was interrupted by a high-pitched screech and a thunderous metallic crash. She caught a glimpse of the cat jumping to the windowsill just before she was thrown to the dusty stable floor. She struggled to catch her breath while pinned beneath a heavy masculine weight.

Gabriel's breath came in quick pants, and his heart pounded against her chest. His calloused hand covered her mouth. "Quiet," he whispered.

Above her, Gabriel's wild eyes searched the barn, and his nostrils flared with each shallow breath. His muscles were taut, his body primed to fight. Didn't he realize the crash had been caused by a harmless cat? Should she wait for him to calm down or try to reason with him? She touched the hand that covered her mouth.

He removed his hand, but continued to scan the area. He was like a wild animal alerted to a nearby predator. But there was nothing in the stable that could harm them.

Etta gingerly laid her palm against his chest. "Gabriel," she whispered, "it was just the cat."

He looked down at her and blinked, as though trying to focus. The fierce gleam in his eyes gradually faded.

"It's all right, Gabriel. A cat knocked over the

stock tanks."

He blinked, swallowed, and then glanced at the fallen tanks. He used his fingertips to move wisps of hair away from her face. "Are you all right?"

"I'm fine. Are you all right?"

He rested his forehead on hers and let out a long breath. "The noise. I thought..." His warm breath against her cheek caused her heart to stumble. "Did I hurt you?"

"No. Of course not." He smelled of leather and spring breezes. If she were pinned beneath another man, she'd be panicked by now. But every part of her body knew she was safe with Gabriel.

The clip-clop of horses' hooves sounded nearby. Gabriel tensed at the noise just as Benito lead in the two mares. Gabriel scrambled to his feet, pushed past Benito, and strode through the doorway.

Etta stood and brushed off her skirt.

Benito walked toward her. "Are you all right, Miss Etta?"

"I'm fine."

"What happened?"

"Nothing." She had to catch Gabriel, to assure him that he hadn't hurt her. Etta hurried toward the doorway. "Stop by the house before you leave," she said over her shoulder. "I have your pay."

Etta rushed to the footbridge that connected her family's property to the Bensons' farm. She needed to catch Gabriel, to tell him she'd never been afraid. Even when he'd pushed her to the floor, she hadn't questioned his actions. But Gabriel must have been embarrassed. Why else would he have left so quickly? At the creek, she caught sight of his chambray shirt just before he disappeared behind a hill.

Etta shoulders dropped and heaviness settled around her heart. Why had Gabriel been so frightened? He'd always been so strong. So solid and steadfast. But today he'd been startled and terrified. All because of a sudden noise?

She turned and headed toward her house. She didn't know how, but she'd find a way to reassure Gabriel the same way he'd reassured her.

∽∾

Gabriel grumbled under his breath as he trudged up the low hill. "Of all the idiotic, lamebrain things...a cat, a harmless cat...I could have hurt Etta..." His hands fisted at his sides and a sharp pain rammed its way through his tight neck muscles. How much longer would the St. Etienne battlefield haunt him?

As he neared his parents' house, the fragrant aroma of his mother's cooking reached him. It would be so easy to go inside, give his mother a squeeze, and let her take care of him. If only he could push his memories aside and bury them where dreams and curious cats couldn't disturb them.

He stopped outside the kitchen door and listened to the clanging of pots and pans. His mother was humming, her lilting voice inviting him into the comfort of home. But Nichols's mother would never make dinner for him again. Neither would Blake's mother, nor Tillman's wife. Spencer had two sons who would grow up without a father. Gabriel's mistake had brought grief and pain to so many. Why should he accept comfort when so many would never experience it again?

He turned his back and walked into the darkness.

ॐॐ

Dr. Russell's car was in the driveway when Etta returned to her house. She hastened up the back steps and burst into the kitchen. "Is something wrong with Papa? Why is Dr. Russell here?"

Rosa turned from the stove. "There's no change in your Papa. Dr. Russell came to check on him. What happened to you?"

Etta brushed her hair back. "There was an accident in the stable, but I'm fine." She headed toward the stairs.

Charlie Simpson stood in the hallway outside of her father's bedroom. "Mr. Simpson, is everything all right?" Etta asked.

He beamed a warm smile at her. "Your father's complaining so much the air is turning blue. Believe it or not, that's a good sign."

Etta peered into her father's bedroom. He was sitting in an upholstered chair near the windows while the doctor examined him. "Da man...no res...don like..." Her father shook his head and gestured toward Charlie with his left hand.

Dr. Russell took her father's hands. "Now squeeze my hands, Henry. Is that as hard as you can squeeze them?" The doctor wrote a few notes and packed his bag. "I'll be back in a few days. In the meantime, keep doing your daily exercises. You're getting better, Henry. I know you're frustrated at how long it's taking, but you're improving."

Etta's father shook his head and waved his arm in a dismissive gesture.

Dr. Russell stepped into the hall and gestured with

his head for Etta and Charlie to follow him downstairs.

In the parlor, Etta braced herself for the doctor's prognosis.

"You're doing a good job, Charlie. Mr. Davis's motor skills have improved, and his speech will gradually return. Although..." Dr. Russell dipped his head and looked over his glasses, "you may be sorry you ever helped Henry recover his speech. He's certainly in a foul mood today."

Charlie laughed. "It's not just today, Doc. But we both know how aggravated a patient feels when he's suddenly incapacitated the way Mr. Davis is. He still hasn't accepted the fact he's not going to wake up one morning and be magically healed."

"Keep following the reconstruction plan I gave you. Do you have any questions for me before I leave?"

Charlie shook the doctor's hand. "Nope. But I'll give you a call if anything comes up. Right now, I need to get Mr. Davis's dinner." Charlie headed toward the kitchen.

Dr. Russell pursed his lips and turned to Etta. "Now, Miss Henrietta, I hope you understand why I said your father needed a convalescent home."

"But you said he was doing better."

Dr. Russell put on his hat. "He's improving, but he could have made much more progress if he'd been in a facility where he'd get round-the-clock care. The convalescent home in Dallas I spoke to you about has nurses and aides who are specially trained to work with stroke victims. Charlie Simpson is a good man, but he can't provide the same level of care a team of professionals can."

"Are you saying I should send Papa to Dallas?"

"It's your decision, Henrietta. All I can do is make

a recommendation."

"What will happen if I don't follow your advice?"

"I'm no soothsayer, but I'd be a lot more certain of his recovery if he were in the hands of trained medical staff. I'll be back in a few days. Call me if you need me before then."

The doctor walked to his car and drove away.

What was she supposed to do now? Send Papa to Dallas where strangers would be in charge of his care or keep him home? She couldn't go to Dallas with him, especially with problems at the bank. Where was her mother when she needed her?

Etta rubbed her forehead and blinked back tears. Her mother wasn't coming back, and her father couldn't solve the bank's problems. Whether she was ready for it or not, this was Etta's fight. She took a deep breath, squared her shoulders, and walked into the kitchen.

Charlie was setting a plate of food on a wooden tray. "Don't let your papa's sour disposition upset you, Miss Davis. Stroke victims often have a difficult time controlling their emotions."

Etta picked up the tray and headed toward the stairs. "I'll help him with dinner, Mr. Simpson. You stay down here and have a bite."

"Don't mind if I do," Charlie said with another broad smile and a wink. "I'm sure Rosa will fix me something mighty tasty."

Rosa waved a dishtowel at him. "What nonsense. You'd eat anything put in front of you."

Charlie rubbed his chin and looked at the ceiling. "That's not quite true. I once turned down fried crickets."

"Then don't eat the rice I made tonight," Rosa said

with a straight face. "I put grasshoppers in it."

Charlie's eyebrows shot up.

Etta followed Rosa's lead. "Haven't you ever wondered about that crunchy stuff in Rosa's food?"

A beat of silence passed before Charlie shook his head and chuckled. "Oh, you're both pulling my leg. Aren't you?"

Rosa crossed her arms and cocked her head, but Etta couldn't hold in her laughter. "Rosa has more power than anyone else in this house, Mr. Simpson. I wouldn't make her mad if I were you."

"No ma'am," Charlie said as he pulled out a chair at the kitchen table. "Why, I would do anything for Miss Rosa. Yes, I surely would."

Rosa shook her head but smiled.

Etta headed up the back stairs.

Her father was still in his reading chair when she arrived with his dinner. He was gazing through the window, his face an impassive mask, but tears rolled quietly down his cheeks.

"Oh, Papa." Etta set the tray on the side table and hurried to his side. "What is it, Papa?"

He gestured with his left hand. "Nnn...Nito...he..."

Etta glanced through the window and saw Rosa's nephew bringing Antares into the stable. "Benito? Yes. He's feeding the horses and brushing them. I was just in the stable. Everything's fine there." She took a handkerchief from her pocket and blotted her father's tears, but he did not seem to notice. "Are you ready to eat? Rosa made one of your favorites—beef tips with rice and gravy."

Etta moved the table in front of her father's chair and tucked a large white napkin into his collar. She speared a chunk of meat with the fork and held it to her father's mouth.

"Nnn…No." Henry grasped the fork in his left hand and brought the food to his mouth. He could feed himself!

A long breath passed through Etta's lips and her shoulders dropped in relief. Her father was getting better. She'd spent time with him every evening after dinner, but he'd usually slept while she sewed. This was the first time she'd seen real progress. Etta pulled a stepstool close and sat at her father's side.

His hand shook, and he chewed slowly and deliberately, but he managed to get the food where it belonged. So what if his recovery took longer at home? Mr. Simpson obviously knew what he was doing or her father would still be bedridden. But perhaps he could make the decision for himself.

"Papa," she began slowly. "Dr. Russell thinks you should go to a convalescent home in Dallas."

"Hmph."

"He says the convalescent home has experts who could help you recuperate faster. If you want to go there, I'll let the doctor know."

For the first time that evening, Henry looked Etta in the eye. "No." He shook his head for emphasis. "No go."

Etta's chest warmed with relief. She placed her hand on his forearm. "All right, Papa." Then she closed her eyes in prayer. She had a lot she wanted to talk to the Lord about, but at that moment, she needed to send her gratitude heavenward.

Gabriel crossed the footbridge that led to the Davis's land. He'd been walking for three hours. He was hungry and thirsty, but he owed Etta an apology and an explanation.

He strode past their picnic spot and entered the stable. As he'd expected, the Arabians were bedded down, safe, and well-cared for. Now that Benito was helping out, Etta didn't really need Gabriel to tend the horses. But he'd miss his daily rides, not to mention the opportunity to see her. Just a glimpse of Etta could lighten his mood and kindle that last spark of hope that lay in his heart.

He had so little to offer her. What could she possibly want with an ex-soldier who spent every night with the ghosts of his fallen comrades? Gabriel had gone to college with dreams of an engineering degree. It was clear that automobiles would change the way people lived, and the state would need roads and bridges. His future had seemed secure. Until he'd decided to join the Army with his college buddies. They'd planned to serve together and come home as heroes, but France had changed all of them in one way or another.

Gabriel closed the stable door and walked slowly toward the front door of the Davis's house. What kind of man built such a huge place for a family of three? Henry Davis must have been proud of his riches and determined to show everyone just how successful he was.

Gabriel's family lived in four rooms. Their home was comfortable, and he and his father had installed indoor plumbing a few years earlier. But the Davis house probably had several bathrooms, each with a marble tub and gold faucets. What could he ever offer

Etta?

Gabriel knocked loudly on the front door. Maybe it was too late to bother her. He had no idea what time it was, but the lights were still on.

A dark-haired middle-aged woman dressed in a white blouse and dark skirt opened the door. "Yes?"

Gabriel removed his hat. "Evening, ma'am. I'd like to see Etta."

The woman squinted into the darkness. "Is that you, Gabriel Benson?"

"Yes, ma'am. Is Etta still awake?"

The woman stepped aside, allowing Gabriel to enter. "She's upstairs with her father. I'll call her."

"Thank you, ma'am."

The woman headed up the stairs, and Gabriel looked around the foyer.

It wasn't just the size of the house that bespoke of Henry Davis's wealth. Highly polished wood paneling covered the walls and stained glass windows were situated along the staircase to catch the morning sunlight. Thick rugs covered the tile floors and a white caisson ceiling towered overhead. In the adjoining parlor, the furniture was deeply upholstered and gathered around an ample fireplace.

If Gabriel saved every penny he earned for the rest of his life, he could never buy a palace like this.

"Gabriel?" Etta hurried down the stairs. "Is everything all right?"

She was so lovely. Her cheeks were the color of peaches and her skin as fair as lilies. Would she ever let him kiss her?

Etta laid her hand on his sleeve. "Can I get you something? Have you had dinner?"

"I wouldn't say no to a glass of water."

"I'm sure I can do better than that." She turned and headed toward the back of the house.

He followed her into the brightly lit kitchen. White tile and glass-fronted cabinets set off the latest appliances.

Etta removed a pitcher from the ice box and poured water into a glass. "Sit down. What else can I get you? There's some cheese in here and Rosa's homemade tortillas. I could make something for you."

"Don't go to any trouble, Etta. The water's enough for now. Knowing my mother, she's kept my dinner warm." Gabriel emptied the glass of cool water in one long drink.

Etta refilled the glass. "Remember that quilt I was working on? Your mother and the ladies from the church sewing circle are going to finish it for me."

"Mom loves to get together with the ladies from the church for sewing circles. I learned to avoid going inside when she had the ladies over to our house."

"Why? Don't tell me they were mean to you."

"No, but there's only so much pecking a young rooster can take from a group of hens."

Etta smiled broadly, lifting Gabriel's mood and encouraging him. She obviously wasn't angry, and she bore no visible injuries from the incident in the stable. "Would you like to go for a walk?" he asked.

Etta glanced through the window.

"I know it's late," Gabriel said, "but…"

"Actually, I was planning on going to my spot by the creek tonight. I have some praying to do."

"Do you mind some company?"

"Not at all. Just give me a minute. There's a lantern on the back porch."

"I'll take care of the lantern and meet you

outside."

She nodded and headed up the back stairs. Gabriel found the kerosene lantern and lit it. Despite her reassurance, Etta must think him half mad for jumping on top of her in the stable. But how should he broach the story of what he'd done in France? Etta's good opinion was important to him, and once she knew how costly his mistake had been, there was little chance she'd ever look at him the way she did now.

"I'm ready," Etta said as she re-entered the kitchen. Gabriel opened the back door and followed her outside.

The moonless sky was awash with stars. They both stopped and tipped their heads back to take in the sight.

"The heavens declare the glory of God," Gabriel said.

"And the firmament showeth His handiwork," Etta concluded.

"Did you see Halley's Comet when it came through?"

"Of course. The science teacher at Bennett's Schools for Girls brought a telescope, and we all had a look at it. What about you?"

"I saw it while I was in college. What did you think about it?"

"I thought it was amazing. I expected it to streak across the sky like a big meteor, but we couldn't see it move. Could you?"

"No, but my physics professor showed us how to chart its movement, and then it made sense. Remember all the silly things people did?"

"My roommate's mother sent anti-comet pills and a gas mask."

"Roommate? Were you at a boarding school?"

"In Philadelphia."

"I thought you were living with an aunt up there."

"My father's aunt, actually. She visited me often while I was in school, and I spent the holidays with her."

Gabriel held out his hand to Etta. She accepted the unspoken invitation without hesitation, and he curled his fingers around her small hand, which fit his like gears in a finely-made clock. She was everything he'd ever wanted, but she deserved so much better than what he could offer her.

They strolled toward the creek in silence, as though words were unnecessary in the starry sanctuary, and sat across from each other on large flat rocks near the bank. The water flowing over the limestone rocks and the low, sad call of a night bird should have lulled Gabriel into a peaceful reverie, but his pulse quickened every time he thought about telling Etta about St. Etienne.

Etta closed her eyes and folded her hands on her knees. She was praying. Talking to their Lord about her troubles. Goodness knew, she had enough on her plate. Etta was small in comparison to him, but she must have a spine of steel to withstand everything she was going through.

Gabriel gazed at the sky. Praying was a good idea. But what would he say to his Creator? *Thank You for my life?* He still didn't know why he'd been spared when so many hadn't. *Please help Etta?* She was one of those people the Lord held close to His heart. Anyone as good and kind as she need never worry about her future. Of course, the preacher said that God loved all his children, but surely the Lord had special regard for sweet souls like Etta.

Gabriel would need help to find the words to tell Etta about his mistake. He lowered his head and found Etta smiling at him. The lantern light shone on her lovely face, highlighting her strawberry-pink lips.

"Dr. Russell came by this afternoon," she said in a quiet tone. "Papa's getting better. It's slow progress, but at least he's improving."

"Glad to hear it."

Etta placed her palms behind her and tipped her head toward the sky. "Rigel is shining brightly tonight. Orion is the first constellation I learned as a girl."

"Etta," Gabriel began. "This afternoon…in the stable…"

"I wasn't afraid, you know."

"What?"

"When you knocked me down. I wasn't afraid. Not once."

"I could have hurt you."

Etta lowered her head and looked him squarely in the eye. "No you couldn't. It's not in your nature. You were protecting me."

"You must have thought I'd gone crazy."

"Not crazy. Just startled. The newspaper accounts of the battles in France describe horrific violence. They tell of artillery barrages and machine guns that can kill fifty soldiers in a matter of seconds. You were conditioned to dive for cover whenever you were threatened. This afternoon, those reflexes took over." She was letting him off easy.

He could just accept her kindness and go on. But if he didn't tell her everything, his secret would be like a slow-acting poison, destroying the bond he hoped to make with her. "I appreciate your understanding, but there's more I need to tell you."

Etta patiently waited for him to continue, her gaze never faltering.

Gabriel unclenched his fists and took a deep breath. "Do you remember when I told you I'd been injured?"

"Yes."

"I want to tell you what happened. I don't know what you may think about me after I tell you this story, but...well, I'm hoping it'll help you understand why I may not be the most easy-going person to be around. At least, not for a while."

"Were you easy-going before you joined the Army?"

"That's what most people said. Now I'm a bundle of nerves tied up in barbed wire."

"I haven't seen you that way. Except for this afternoon, that is."

"When I'm around you I feel calmer. But I don't sleep more than a few hours at a time, and I've stayed away from my parents because they irritate me so much. Taking care of your horses is about the only thing that doesn't aggravate me."

"How do your parents annoy you?"

"It's not my parents who have the problem. It's me. Things that never bothered me before I joined the Army almost make me scream now. Like this morning during breakfast, my mother put the kettle on the stove, and it started to boil over. I sat at the table and waited for her to turn off the heat, but she was busy with something else. I kept sitting there, watching steam spew from that kettle and wondering when she was going to take it off the fire. Finally, I got up to do it myself, but she blocked me and said, 'I've got it. Go

120

finish your food.' I sat down and tried to eat, but she still didn't take the kettle off the stove." Gabriel shook his head. "It's such a silly thing to get upset about, but I had to leave the house. I felt like my body was going to explode just like the kettle."

"What did you do?"

"I went for a walk. That's what I do whenever I'm feeling tightly wound. I bet I've walked every square yard of Burnet County. Riding every day has helped, too. Antares loves to run."

Etta looked toward the creek. Her face retained its usual placid, open countenance, giving Gabriel no clue about what she was thinking. After several minutes of quiet, she turned back to him. "You were going to tell me about being injured."

Gabriel took a deep breath. He'd started this. He may as well finish it. "What did you read about the Battle at St. Etienne?"

"Not much. All I remember is that it happened last October."

"That's right. It was the first and only time I saw action. Our regiment got there in late September. The Germans had plenty of time to place their artillery and machine guns in the most advantageous locations. As we made our way to our new camp, we came across unexploded shells, broken and discarded equipment, graves, and dead horses. The artillery bombardment had left jagged tree stumps and hills without tops. Observation balloons floated above the horizon, easily relaying our position to the German guns. It didn't take long for us to discover snipers in the trees and on rooftops. Barbed wire was stretched throughout the forest, so the only way to advance was straight on."

"It sounds terrible."

"It was. When the men saw what they were up against, all their bravado disappeared. The machine guns were the worst. The Germans had set them up with overlapping fields of fire, so when one gun was taken out another was already firing on the men. Have you ever seen a farmer using a scythe?"

Etta nodded.

"That's what it reminded me of. Men fell like blades of grass, crying out in pain and bleeding uncontrollably."

"Is that how you were hurt?"

"No. The second day, Captain Brooks ordered me to take Sgt. Schmidt's squad, equip them with wire cutters, and scout out a way through the woods on the east side of the battlefield. Another squad took the west side. We left before dawn, easing our way through the trees and marking the trail with red paint. Then the shelling started. We were surrounded by thick trees and brush, but we could tell both sides were letting loose with everything they had."

Gabriel shifted his gaze to the ground. He'd reached the part of the story that was the most difficult to tell, and, even though he'd relived it every day since, he hesitated to burden Etta with it.

"You don't have to tell me, Gabriel."

He swallowed hard and looked at her. Telling her the rest of the story felt like betting his life on a hand of cards. What would she do once she knew?

"We kept working our way north, toward the village, and the smoke from the artillery bombardment grew thicker by the minute. We went another hundred yards or so when we came to a ravine that was too deep for our company to cross. I was doing my best to make a crude map as I went, but the heavy smoke was making it impossible to see what lay ahead of us. Sgt. Schmidt wanted to return to camp." If only Gabriel had taken that advice.

His mind traveled back to that ravine. The pale morning sunlight had streamed through the smoke-laden treetops as the smell of gunpowder filled his nostrils. Schmidt and the others had looked to him for guidance, and he'd lead them to their deaths.

"So you decided to head east?"

Gabriel blinked at Etta. His mind had been trapped in the forest outside St. Etienne, and he'd forgotten she was there. "Yes," he said slowly. "But I made the wrong choice." He wiped his sweaty palms on the legs of his trousers. He had to tell her the rest.

"I thought if we followed the edge of the ravine, we might find a spot where the company could cross. The shelling was constant, one blast on top of another, both sides firing nonstop."

He rested his elbows on his knees and covered his eyes with the heels of his hands. He mustn't cry in front of Etta. He mustn't be shamed any worse than he already was. "That's all I remember."

He felt a gentle touch on his knee and lowered his hands. Etta knelt in front of him, her fingers barely touching him. "That's when you were injured?"

He nodded his head and swallowed. "My squad took a direct hit."

"An artillery shell hit your men?"

He nodded. "There were non-stop explosions. I didn't even hear the one that hit us. But when I came to, we were lying in a crater."

"Were any of your men killed?"

"Everyone except me."

Etta gasped and widened her eyes.

"The blast knocked me out. The doctor told me I'd suffered a cerebral concussion, but after a few days, I was fine. The battle was over by then, and the armistice declared a few weeks later. I'd led my men to their deaths for nothing. Ten men dead because of me."

A deep line appeared between her brows. "That's not true."

"Yes, it is. If I'd turned back toward camp, they'd all be alive."

"You can't know that for sure."

"It was *my* decision, Etta. I'm responsible for their deaths."

Etta frowned and sat on her heels. "Perhaps you would have been shelled in another spot on the way back. There's no way to know."

"I was in charge. Those men trusted me to lead them safely through the woods and back to camp. I got lost, Etta. Lost in the smoke and noise." A traitorous tear rolled down his cheek, and Gabriel closed his eyes.

A pair of lips as soft as dew kissed his tear away. Gabriel's breath caught in his throat.

"Sh…" Etta's warm breath caressed his skin. "It's all right."

Gabriel hid his face in his sleeve. What kind of man would let a woman see him cry?

Etta stroked his hair and kissed his other cheek.

He couldn't take much more of this. If she continued to show him kindness and understanding, he'd break into childish sobs. He wrapped his hands around her upper arms and nudged her away. "Stop, Etta. I can't…I don't want to…"

She retreated slowly and sat beside him. Did she understand why he'd rejected her tenderness? He fought for control, took a ragged breath, and reached for her hand. "Thank you."

Etta rested her forehead on their joined hands. After a few seconds, she closed her eyes.

What must she think of him now? He'd failed his men and cried like a baby. Surely, this was the end of their friendship. How could a woman like Etta want a man as incompetent as he? A man who got lost in the woods and caused the death of every soldier in his squad?

"Amen," Etta whispered.

"You were praying?"

Etta raised her head and nodded. "I didn't know what to say to you, so I prayed for guidance."

"Did you get an answer?"

"I did. You need to forgive."

"Forgive? Sorry, Etta, but I think you might have misinterpreted that answer. Maybe I need to seek forgiveness for my mistake, but there's no one I need to forgive."

"Then you pray, and see what answer you get."

"You think I haven't prayed?" He immediately regretted his strident tone. The truth was he hadn't really talked to the Lord for a long time. He let out a long, troubled sigh. "I'm so mixed up right now. I can't figure out what I should do or where I should go. I walk all night until I'm exhausted, and even then, sleep eludes me. When I'm awake, I feel like a lit stick of dynamite."

"Would you like to pray about it?"

"What? Now?"

"That's the idea."

He rubbed the back of his neck. What had he gotten himself into? "I guess so. If you want to."

Etta bowed her head. "Heavenly Father, thank

You for bringing Gabriel safely through the war. Thank You for the divine comfort You offer the families of the men who didn't return." Etta was quiet for a few moments.

Did she expect Gabriel to chime in? He watched her from the corner of his eye.

"Tonight, I bring Gabriel to You. He feels lost and is unsure what he needs to do. Help him, Lord. Show him Your plan for the next part of his life. In Jesus's name I pray, Amen." Etta opened her eyes and smiled at Gabriel. "Rev. Martin says the hardest part about praying is listening for God's answer."

"I remember. He said people like to talk more than they like to listen. Maybe I do need to seek forgiveness. Did you know the men in that squad were all from Texas?"

"That's a coincidence."

"Not really. The Thirty-sixth Division was made up of men from Texas and Oklahoma. My platoon was made up of men from Austin and its surrounding counties."

"You must have gotten to know each other quite well."

"That's how it is in the Army. I was stuck with the same people, day in and day out, and I soon learned everyone's story. Sergeant Schmidt was from Llano and Nichols, the guy I told you about who craved sugar so bad, he was from Seguin."

"Practically neighbors."

"If I wanted to, I could visit all ten of the men's families in about two weeks."

Etta looked at him expectantly.

"You think that's it?"

"That's not for me to say."

"It might help if I visited the men's families. I could tell them how their sons and husbands died. But, Etta..." A ponderous weight settled in Gabriel's chest as the enormity of the challenge crystallized in his mind. He'd have to admit his culpability to every father, mother, wife, and sweetheart his men had left behind. He'd have to confess his mistake over and over. He raised a hand to his head. "I don't know if I can do this."

"Are you sure that's what the Lord asked you to do, Gabriel?"

Of course, he had to own up to his mistake and take whatever censure the families thought appropriate. He'd never be able to live with himself if he didn't accept their retribution. "I owe the men's families that much. If I hadn't come back, my parents would want to know what had happened to me. I'm the only one who can tell the families."

"How will you find out where they all live?"

"I'll go to Fort Worth first. They'll have all the records at Fort Bowie."

"When do you think you'll leave?"

"As soon as possible." Gabriel snapped his fingers as he remembered his one responsibility. "Your horses. Do you think Benito can take over for me until I get back?"

"Don't worry. I'll make arrangements."

"It's a bad time to leave you, isn't it? You've got your father and the mess at the bank."

"My father's getting better, and that mess at the bank will probably still be there by the time you get back." She touched his sleeve. "But come back soon, Gabriel. I'll miss you."

Gabriel lowered his brow until his forehead

touched hers. "When I come back, I'll be whole again. There's so much I want to do, but...something's holding me back."

"I'll be praying for you."

"I'll think of you, here in our spot." Was it too soon to kiss her? Their friendship was new but not weak. Etta would be waiting like a steadfast sentinel while he undertook this challenge.

Before he could act on his desire to kiss her, Etta stood. "How long do you think you'll be gone?"

"Hard to say. A few weeks, I suppose. I wish..."

She looked at him expectantly, but the words eluded his grasp. There was so much to say, but it was too soon. His feelings for Etta were tangled in the confusion, guilt, and irritation that burdened every minute of every day.

"Will you be all right while I'm gone?"

"Of course," she answered with a reassuring smile. "I'm not facing this fight alone and neither are you. But I'll be counting the days until you come back."

Gabriel brushed his fingertips over her cheek and down the line of her jaw. Could someone as dear as Etta truly be his someday? "You do that."

7

The train traveled relentlessly south, its rhythm lulling most of the passengers into peaceful slumber. Gabriel stared into the darkness and tried to plan what he would say to Anthony Blake's parents. Blake had celebrated his twentieth birthday on the Atlantic Ocean. How he'd bragged about being the only member of his family to travel beyond Texas. He couldn't have known he'd never return.

The commanding officer at Fort Bowie had welcomed Gabriel. He'd even offered a bed and warm meals.

But Gabriel's skin had itched to get away from the regimented lifestyle he'd once embraced. After entering the families' addresses in a cloth-bound notebook, he'd hurried back to the depot. There, with the help of a timetable and wall-mounted map, he'd planned the rest of his trip.

From Fort Worth he planned to travel to Waco, and then head east to Caldwell. Eventually, he'd work his way back to Burnet to where Etta waited for him. At this time of night, she'd be getting ready for bed. Perhaps she was saying her prayers or brushing out her hair. He hoped she wasn't fretting over ledger books or losing sleep about the bank's problems. Despite her worries, Etta cloaked herself in tranquility.

Gabriel closed his eyes and sent a prayer heavenward. *Watch over Etta and uphold her with Your mighty right hand.*

When Gabriel finished this trip, when he had looked into the eyes of widows and grief-stricken parents and explained his responsibility for their sorrow, perhaps his soul could find peace. Bearing the brunt of their anger and heartbreak was the only way he could atone for his disastrous mistake. Then he'd return to Etta. He'd wrap his arms around her and never let go.

As dawn broke, the train passed Camp MacArthur. It had shrunk in size from the tent city Gabriel had first seen two years earlier. Now the infantrymen had either been deployed or discharged. How many of those soldiers had returned to their homes and families? Was there another officer traveling around another state on a mission such as his? The number of casualties from the Great War was staggering, and the Army was still counting.

When the train finally pulled into the MKT Station, Gabriel waited while the sleepy passengers gathered their belongings and filed out. Then he retrieved his battered brown leather suitcase from the overhead luggage rack. After a quick breakfast at the depot's canteen, he checked his suitcase at the baggage locker and got directions to the Blake house. He'd be back in plenty of time to catch the noon train to Caldwell.

Two blocks east and two blocks north. Simple enough, except for what awaited him at his destination. But he'd take whatever Blake's parents dealt. A guilty man must pay the price of his mistake, and once he'd been chastened by those he'd done wrong, perhaps the ghosts would let him rest. Then he could offer himself to Etta as a whole man.

Gabriel's stomach twisted as he searched for the right address. Accepting his punishment was the least he could do, but he dreaded it nonetheless. He finally stopped outside a brown brick, side-gabled bungalow and checked the address. Orange and yellow flowers edged both sides of a central walkway leading to the cement porch where a glider swing moved slowly in the spring breeze. He could imagine Blake growing up on this tree-shaded street, playing with the neighbor kids and walking to nearby schools. It must have been a pleasant childhood, free from want or danger. Gabriel took a deep breath, fighting the guilt that threatened to swallow him whole, and knocked determinedly on the front door.

The muffled voice of a young boy sounded from inside. "I'll get it, Dad."

Gabriel removed his hat and locked his knees as the door swung open.

Anthony Blake smiled at him with the open earnestness of youth.

Gabriel's voice recoiled as his throat tightened in shock. He'd seen Anthony's dead body, had visited the younger man's grave before leaving France. How could he be here?

"May I help you?" the young man asked.

Gabriel backed away. What miracle had resurrected Anthony and returned him to his family?

A woman's voice called from somewhere in the house. "Who is it, Robert?"

Robert. Anthony Blake's younger brother. Not Anthony. Robert.

A middle-aged woman with blonde hair and a flowered apron joined Robert at the door. The two of them turned curious gazes on Gabriel.

"Good morning," he said, but his voice came out as a hoarse whisper. He cleared his throat and tried again. "Good morning. I'm Gabriel Benson. I knew Anthony in the Army and—"

The woman gasped and her hand went to her throat. "Gabriel Benson? Lieutenant Benson?" She stepped onto the porch. "Oh...oh…" She touched her lips with her fingers and her eyes filled with tears.

Gabriel's chest tightened at the woman's show of emotion. This was just the beginning. There were many more recriminations to come.

The woman stepped closer and wrapped her arms around his shoulders. "Oh, Lieutenant Benson. Thank you so much for coming."

Gabriel wouldn't have been surprised if she'd slapped him, but an embrace and a warm welcome stunned him.

She stepped back and took his hand. "I'm Celia Blake, Anthony's mother. Please come in. I just put on a fresh pot of coffee."

The boy who'd answered the door shook his hand vigorously. "Hi, Lieutenant Benson. I'm Anthony's brother."

"Nice to meet you," Gabriel mumbled as he followed Anthony's mother into the house.

"Vernon?" Mrs. Blake called. "Vernon, one of Anthony's officers has come to call."

A slender man wearing slacks and a white shirt with suspenders walked into the parlor. A newspaper dangled from his fingers. "Morning," he said. "Nice to meet you."

Gabriel shook Mr. Blake's hand while Mrs. Blake pulled out a chair at a linen-draped table. "Have you had your breakfast?" she asked.

"Yes, ma'am. Thank you."

Robert stood at Gabriel's side. "Dad, this is Gabriel Benson, Anthony's lieutenant."

Vernon's eyes rounded. "Oh, Lieutenant Benson. So nice of you to pay us a visit. Please…" He pointed to a chair. "Please sit down."

Gabriel waited for Mrs. Benson to take a seat, but she declined the gesture. "I'll get us some fresh coffee. You go ahead and make yourself comfortable. Robert, would you give me a hand?"

"Sure, Mom." The boy followed his mother out of the room.

Other than the noises from the nearby kitchen, the Blakes' house was silent.

Mr. Blake lit a pipe and puffed fragrant smoke toward Gabriel while examining him with narrowed eyes.

How did one begin the type of confession Gabriel had to reveal?

"Where are you from, Lieutenant?" Mr. Blake asked around the pipe clenched in his teeth.

"Burnet."

"Oh, sure," Mr. Blake said around puffs. "I know where that is. Northwest of the capital, isn't it?"

"That's right."

"The train from Austin comes in at eight o'clock. When it's on time. Did you arrive last night?"

"No, sir. I came from Forth Worth."

"Fort Worth? Then you came in on the seven-thirty."

"Sounds as though you've got the railroad schedule committed to memory."

"Just the Waco arrivals. I travel all over this part of the state on sales trips. Did Anthony tell you I'm a cotton buyer?"

"Not that I remember."

"I travel all over the Brazos Valley, buying cotton for a consortium of mills around here. In fact, I'm leaving tomorrow morning on another trip."

Mrs. Blake returned with a tray of cups and saucers. Robert followed her with a white enamel coffeepot. "Here we are," she said. "Cream and sugar are already on the table."

Gabriel drank the hot black coffee and tried to remember if Anthony had taken any of Nichols's sugar. He could remember precious little about the young soldier, only that he'd been green, trusting, and eager to see battle.

"Anthony wrote us every week," Mrs. Blake said, "and he always had some funny story about his platoon."

"He sure did," Robert said. "Remember when he wrote about the most important rule he learned?"

Mr. and Mrs. Blake chuckled.

"Do you know the Army's most important rule?" Mr. Blake asked Gabriel.

Several answers flitted through Gabriel's mind, jokes the men had told among themselves, not all of them suitable for ladies. "What did Anthony think it was?"

"Never tell a sergeant you have nothing to do," Robert answered.

"That's a good one, all right," Gabriel said.

"Anthony also wrote about you," Mrs. Blake said. "He was glad you were the platoon leader."

"Anthony was a fine boy. He made us all proud to know him."

Mrs. Blake's voice dropped to a near whisper.

"The letter from Captain Brooks said that Anthony was killed in action during the siege at St. Etienne. Can you tell us more? Were you with him when he died?"

Gabriel swallowed hard and sat back in his chair. This was why he'd come. May as well get it over with. "Did you read about the battle at St. Etienne?"

"Yes," Mr. Blake answered. "I read a rather detailed account in the *Dallas Morning News.* I don't know how our boys got through the German lines."

By the time Gabriel had made it back to the American camp, the battle had been over. But the dead lay where they had fallen, their twisted bodies betraying the final peace that death was supposed to give. "To tell you the truth, I don't know how they did it, either." He continued his story, recounting how he'd led the squad along the eastern flank of the battlefield. "Anthony never faltered once. The men in the squad took turns at point, but I hesitated when it was Anthony's turn. He was the youngest, and I hated putting him in more danger. Nevertheless, he took his place at point before I could decide one way or the other. No one in the platoon ever had reason to doubt him."

The Blakes looked at Gabriel as though they were enthralled with his story. But he couldn't continue to hold their gazes. He stared into his coffee as he related the most difficult part of his narrative. "We took a direct hit from an artillery shell. It knocked me out and killed everyone else in the squad."

Robert stood and walked to the window.

Mrs. Blake cried quietly.

Mr. Blake poured more coffee into Gabriel's cup.

"There's more you need to know," Gabriel continued. "Anthony's death was my fault. I got lost in all that smoke. I should have turned back, retraced our path…but I didn't."

A minute of silence ticked by.

Mrs. Blake sniffed quietly, and Robert continued to stare through the window.

Mr. Blake left the table.

Gabriel's throat ached with unspoken emotions. If only he could return to France and change his decision. If only he'd sent Anthony back to camp to retrieve something. But such wishes were futile. He could no more change the past than he could walk on air.

Mr. Blake returned with a stack of mail. "These are Anthony's letters. There's one I'd like to read to you."

Gabriel nodded. Listening to Anthony's words was minor penance.

Anthony's father slipped the letter out of the envelope and unfolded it. "Dear Mom, Dad, and Rob." He glanced at his wife as though seeking permission and then returned to the letter. "I hope you're not worrying about me. Life in the Army isn't as bad as people say. I've fallen in with a good group of guys. Nichols is the clown of our group. Even his complaints are funny. We call Sgt. Schmidt the 'old man' because he's over thirty. The sarge acts like a scrappy dog that's been left out in the rain too long, but he takes care of us in his own gruff way. Our lieutenant is Gabriel Benson. He's tough but fair, and that's all a soldier needs. One day, back in basic, Lieutenant Benson saw Sgt. Schmidt chewing me out. Benson must have felt sorry for me, because he talked to Sarge. Next thing I knew, I was assigned to the lieutenant for the rest of the week. All I had to do was carry messages, but it got me out of Sgt. Schmidt's line of fire for a while. So you see, as long as I've got good officers looking out for me, I'll be fine."

Mr. Blake laid the letter on the table. "Almost all of Anthony's letters have something good to say about you."

Gabriel closed his eyes and let out a long, quiet breath. He'd come to confess and accept his punishment, but the Blakes were trying to console him instead. When he opened his eyes, Mr. Blake was leaning forward, resting his elbows on his knees.

"When Anthony told me he'd volunteered," Mr. Blake said, "I thought immediately of my own father. He'd been a Confederate soldier with Hood's Brigade, and he had one unbreakable rule. None of his sons would ever be allowed to join the military. My father didn't talk much about his war, but he did tell me about the chaos of battle. So, although I don't know firsthand what you and my son faced that day at St. Etienne, I do know it's not your fault. It's not your fault Anthony signed up. It's not your fault he was sent to France, and it's not your fault he got caught in German artillery fire."

Mrs. Blake stood and walked slowly to Gabriel's side. "I can't tell you how much it means for you to take the trouble to visit us, Lieutenant Benson. Knowing what happened, knowing that my son didn't suffer…it's everything."

"We'll never forget our son," Mr. Blake added, "but now we're no longer haunted by the question of how he died."

How could Anthony's family be so kind? Didn't they understand Gabriel was accountable for their son's death? Didn't they realize he was to blame? Should he explain his culpability again? No. He'd told his story and repeating it would only be salt in the wound. Gabriel stood. "I should be going. Thank you for the coffee."

Mr. Blake and Robert shook Gabriel's hand. Mrs. Blake embraced him. After more thanks and their wishes for a good trip home, Gabriel left, forcing himself to walk at a normal pace until he was out of sight.

Gabriel's nerves skittered under his skin like angry ants. He'd come to confess and to receive his just punishment. Where was the righteous anger he deserved? Didn't the Blakes realize that his actions had led to Anthony's death?

There was no way he could sit in the railroad station for two hours. With a clenched jaw and hunched shoulders, he turned toward the center of town for another long walk.

৯৩৯

"You've definitely got a thief working for you."

Etta shut her eyes, trying to banish the ledgers on her desk and the evidence George Owens had found. But when she opened her eyes, he was still leaning over her, the overpowering scent of his aftershave lotion causing her nose to tingle.

"The embezzler has been intercepting loan payments for five months. I'd say your chief suspect is Arthur Lewis since he manages loans, but he's only been here two months."

"If you found evidence of the theft going back that far, why did we just notice it?"

"Two reasons." George ticked off the findings on his fingers. "First, you regularly have your accounts audited once a year. The embezzler knew that and started falsifying the ledgers just after the last audit.

Second, there have been some changes to your normal routines in the past few months. Arthur Lewis taking over the loan department and your father's recent absence may have forced the thief to change his tactics."

A sharp pain shot through Etta's head. This was too much. Too much to think about, too much to deal with, too much for her to tackle alone.

George perched on the corner of Etta's desk. "Now that you know how the money is being siphoned off, what are you going to do next?"

Etta leaned back in her chair and rubbed her forehead. "I don't know yet. Your audit shows where the problem is but doesn't pinpoint any one person. I'm going to need more evidence."

"I agree. I'll probably be called to testify if this ever goes to trial, but for the time being, my work here is finished." He closed the ledger books and stacked them on the edge of Etta's desk. "Doesn't your Board of Directors meet next week?"

"Yes. I'll have to tell them about your findings."

"I think you should wait. Fraud almost always happens in three steps. The theft itself, concealment of the theft, and conversion of the money. The thief rarely squirrels away the money for his old age. It's more likely he'll spend it on high priced items like luxury automobiles or real estate. A person who's living beyond his means is usually the first person to investigate. Does that sound like any of your employees?"

It sounded like Uncle Carl, but Etta balked at sharing her thoughts. It could be someone else, someone she hadn't considered. "I don't feel right keeping my discovery from the board, but I'll also explain that the matter is under investigation. My father always preached the benefits of full disclosure, and I'm not about to go against his philosophy now."

"My firm could put you in touch with one of the detectives we use," George continued. "A lovely young woman like you has no business delving into the dirty world of thieves and liars."

How would she even begin to follow the embezzler's trail? "Perhaps you're right. Give me a few days to think about it."

George put one hand on the back of Etta's chair and leaned in. "I'm so glad you called me to look into this problem. I'd planned to speak to your father about this but, given his recent illness, I see no reason not to speak to you directly."

Etta pushed against the chair's rigid back. "Did you find some other irregularities in the bank's ledgers?"

George smiled at her the way one would smile at a child. "No, Henrietta. What I want to ask is permission to call on you. I've always thought you'd make someone a fine wife, and if I don't act soon, someone else may snatch you up."

He spoke of her as though she were a prize-winning heifer. "Oh, Mr. Owens...I don't know how to respond...I...uh..."

He chuckled softly. "That's why it's best for a man of good intentions to speak to the girl's father first." George covered her hand with his.

How could she get out of this? If she declined, she'd risk ruining the working relationship she had with him. If she accepted, she'd give him reason to think there was a chance for more than a business partnership. She withdrew her hand from his grasp and stood. "I can't tell you how flattered I am by your offer, Mr. Owens, but I simply can't give you an answer now. Between my father's illness and my responsibilities at the bank, I'm unable to think about the future."

George's disappointment was evident in the tight line of his mouth. "Of course, Henrietta. But there's no reason we can't get to know each other better. How about dinner and the pictures next Saturday? Shall I pick you up at seven?"

Her breath fluttered in her chest like a wild bird hurling itself against the bars of a cage. Perhaps she could postpone his more serious intentions if she accepted his invitation to dinner. "I'll be visiting my cousin in Austin next weekend. That would save you the trouble of driving all the way to Burnet."

"Wonderful. Will you give me the address?"

She'd do that as soon as she asked Nora for permission to spend the weekend and begged her to act as chaperone. "May I send you a note after I've finalized my plans with my cousin?"

"Of course. I'm so happy this is all working out so well. You'll see, Henrietta. We'll fit together like a hand and glove."

More like a pebble in the toe of a shoe. Etta forced herself to smile.

8

From what Gabriel knew of Kenneth Scott, he'd been a farm boy, lured away from Caldwell by his sense of duty and a desire to get away from small town life. Kenneth had been older than the other men and had rarely spoken about his home. Much to his surprise, Gabriel had discovered a wife registered as Kenneth's next-of-kin.

As he walked down a dusty road that wound through fields of corn, Gabriel tried to recall anecdotes about Kenneth to share with the Scott family. But what he remembered most was how unhappy the man had been. Kenneth had been a drinker, the only man in the squad who spent off-duty hours in the nearest tavern. Alcohol changed him from laconic to surly, and Gabriel had been forced to discipline the private more than once. At least Kenneth had held his own when the company saw action. He'd followed orders quickly and accurately, never argued or shirked his duty.

At last, Gabriel arrived at the orchard the town's postmaster had indicated. Hand-painted letters on a wooden sign announced "Scott Family Pecans," and beyond that stood a small frame house with peeling white paint. A young, thin woman wearing a flowered house dress and a faded apron swept the front porch with a worn broom. She shielded her eyes with one hand and watched Gabriel approach the house.

"Good afternoon," he said.

The woman wore her light brown hair in a tight bun at the nape of her neck. Her dark gaze watched Gabriel with the wariness of a coyote protecting its den.

"My name is Gabriel Benson. I served with Kenneth Scott in the 36th Division out of Fort Bowie. I'm looking for his widow, Lorena Scott."

The woman dropped her hand but didn't smile. "I'm Lorena Scott," she said curtly. "I heard your name before. Kenneth didn't write home much, but he mentioned you. I guess you want to talk to his family." The woman's ruddy skin was stretched tautly over her face and deep-set wrinkles marred her forehead.

"If it's no trouble."

"No trouble. I'll call Kenneth's brother. He'll want to meet you." She perched her hands on bony hips and walked to the edge of the porch where she pulled the rope attached to a black cast iron bell. After several loud rings, she opened the worn screen door and motioned for Gabriel to enter.

Gabriel removed his hat. Once inside, he realized the house was one large room. A rocking chair sat near a blackened fireplace and a small table with two benches served for a dining room. A metal bed frame with a thin mattress took up one corner of the bare, but clean, room.

"Go on and sit down," Lorena said. "Donald will be here soon. You want some water?"

"Yes, thank you."

She went to the far corner where a metal sink with a hand pump sat beside a rusted cast iron stove. "We've got the best well water in twenty miles." Lorena took a canning jar from a wooden shelf, dipped it into a metal bucket, and set the jar on the scarred table. Gabriel sat on the crudely made bench and drank the cool, sweet water. "That's really good," he said, wiping his mouth on the back of his hand.

"Told you so."

A dog barked from outside and a tall man wearing faded overalls and a stained shirt stepped through the back door. A young boy dressed in clothes too small for him tagged behind.

The man was brawny and smelled of sweat. He folded his arms across his chest and glared at Gabriel, who stood.

"This here is one of Kenneth's Army friends," Lorena said.

Gabriel straightened to his full height. "Gabriel Benson. I served with Kenneth in France."

The other man uncrossed his arms. "I'm Donald Scott, Kenneth's big brother."

Gabriel shook Donald's heavily calloused hand. "Nice to meet you." Gabriel smiled at the boy who peeked from behind Donald's leg. "Is this your son?"

Lorena bent down to the boy's level. "This here is Kenneth Jr. He's mine." She swung the boy up and perched him on her hip. "You been helping Uncle Donald?"

The boy nodded and laid his head on his mother's shoulder.

"This here is Lieutenant Benson. Can you say hello?"

The boy turned chocolate-brown eyes toward Gabriel and shook his head.

Lorena smiled for the first time, showing several gaps where teeth should have been. "Can you tell him how old you are?"

The boy concentrated on his hand, finally

managing to hold up four fingers.

"Four years old," said Gabriel. "And here I was thinking you were at least eight. You're such a big boy."

"I help Uncle Donald with the milk cows," the boy said, "and I can get the eggs all by myself."

A new pang of guilt set up camp in Gabriel's heart. Because of Gabriel's bad decision, the boy would never know his father. "I can see you're a great helper."

"You want some water, baby?" Lorena asked.

The boy nodded, and Lorena carried him to the kitchen corner. Donald gestured to the table as a way of asking Gabriel to take a seat. "Weren't you the officer in charge of Kenneth's platoon?"

Gabriel slid onto the bench. "That's right."

"Kenneth didn't send more than three letters home the whole time he was gone. We don't know much about his life in the Army, but I guess he was happy there. He sure was miserable here." Donald Scott scratched one of his muscular forearms with dirty fingernails. "Our Pa used to say Kenneth was born hating the farm. We all expected him to move away, but fatherhood caught up to him."

Gabriel glanced at the boy who was drinking from a stoneware cup missing its handle. He handed the empty cup to his mother, and Lorena carried her son outside, the screen door slamming behind her.

Donald leaned over the small table. "Do you know what I mean by that, Lieutenant?"

Gabriel had an idea what Donald meant, but he'd learned long ago that jumping to conclusions usually landed him in hot water. "Kenneth's wife seems like a nice girl."

Donald's upper lip curled into an ugly sneer. "She comes from nowhere. Raised in an orphanage in Harris County. Kenneth was working construction around Houston when he met Lorena. Next thing you know, she was in the family way. He brought her back home and then joined the Army first chance he got."

Gabriel didn't know why he felt the need to defend Lorena. Perhaps it was because she had no one to speak up for her. "She appears to be a good mother."

Donald pushed out his bottom lip while he considered Gabriel's words. "Yeah, I'll give her that much. And she's a hard worker. She keeps this house spotless, and her garden produces enough vegetables for all of us."

"How many of you are there?"

"Six. My wife and I have two girls. We live down the road a bit."

A more complete picture of who Kenneth Scott had been formed in Gabriel's mind. Kenneth hadn't wanted to be tied to the farm or to his accidental family. The Army had provided an escape.

Gabriel finished his water and sat quietly at the small table. Through the screen door, he saw the boy playing with a brown and white dog while Lorena cheered him on.

Donald ended the lull in their conversation. "We got a letter from Captain Brooks telling us what a fine soldier Kenneth was. Were you with my brother when he died?"

Gabriel took a deep breath. It was time to get to the point. "Yes, I was. We were at St. Etienne. Did you read about that battle in the newspaper?"

"We don't get much news out here."

"It was the only time Kenneth's platoon saw action." Gabriel described the battlefield and his squad's mission.

Donald listened intently, his gaze never wavering from Gabriel's face, his expression never changing until Gabriel described the artillery hit that had widowed Lorena and taken away Donald's brother. Donald closed his eyes and rested his forehead on his fists. After several long seconds, he looked at Gabriel. "It sounds like hell on earth. I can't imagine how my brother must've felt being in the middle of all that."

"Private Scott was a quiet man. I don't think he ever talked unless someone spoke to him first."

Donald shook his head once. "That doesn't sound like my little brother."

"Private Scott never challenged a superior's orders and always did his duty."

"Are you sure we're talking about the same person? Thirty years old, six foot tall, kind of reddish hair?"

"That's him. He had a scar right here." Gabriel pointed to the center of his chin.

"That's Kenneth all right. He got that scar choppin' kindling. A piece of wood flew off and cut him there." Donald rubbed his own chin as though he'd been the wounded one. "I guess the Army taught him that griping wouldn't get him what he wanted. Our Pa had to take him to the wood pile more than once for smartin' off. And when Kenneth came back home with a pregnant bride, he grumbled like an Israelite in the desert. My brother jumped at the first chance to leave his wife and child."

It was easy to understand why there might have been bad feelings between the Scott brothers, but it was none of Gabriel's business. "Mr. Scott, there's more I need to tell you about the day your brother died."

Donald settled back in his seat, as though steeling himself for bad news. "Did Kenneth hurt someone? Or turn coward?"

"No. Nothing like that."

"Did he do anything that would bring shame to our family?"

"No."

"Then I don't need to know. I'd rather think of my little brother as dying in the service of his country. There's something noble about that. I know I shouldn't say this, but I don't believe Kenneth would've ever come back here. And despite what I said earlier, my wife and me don't really mind having Lorena and her boy. We both wanted a son, but my wife can't have more children. Plus, Lorena helps out quite a bit. She even gives us part of the government benefits she receives for being a widow."

Gabriel wasn't going to get the recriminations he deserved. He could force Donald to listen to the rest of his story, but that would be pure selfishness. Wasn't there a Proverb about fools venting their spirits, but wise men holding back?

Gabriel stood and carried his empty jar to the small kitchen. Through the window above the sink, he saw Kenneth Jr. and Lorena watering part of the vegetable garden. Was there anything he could do for Lorena and her son? Surely, he owed them something.

Donald stood. "Walk with me over to my place and I'll give you a ride into town. Want to stay for supper?"

"I'd appreciate a ride into Caldwell, but I think it'd be better if I'm on my own tonight."

"Something wrong?"

"To tell you the truth, you've given me a lot to think about. I do my best thinking when I'm on my own."

"I know what you mean. Around here, finding a quiet place to think is like finding the end of the rainbow. I don't know what's on your mind, Lieutenant, but whatever it is, I hope you get it settled."

Gabriel put on his hat and followed Donald into the spring twilight.

Kenneth Jr. emptied his watering can and smiled up at him, all earlier shyness forgotten.

Gabriel squatted to the boy's eye level. "I see you're good at keeping the garden, too."

"Sure I am. Momma teached me. We planted watermelons. Come see."

The boy ran to a sunny corner where green shoots promised an abundant crop. "I'm gonna grow the biggest watermelon in the whole world. It's gonna be as big as Momma's house."

Gabriel smiled at the boy's enthusiasm. How could Kenneth Scott have left such a precious son? Had Kenneth even known the boy?

"Come on, Ken Junior!" Lorena called. "Time to go see Aunt Betty."

The youngster scampered toward his mother and Gabriel followed.

Donald led them along a well-worn path to a two-story white farmhouse. The boy ran toward two girls who played on wooden swings, and Donald walked toward a stout woman who was hanging laundry from a clothesline.

Lorena turned and put her hand on Gabriel's arm

to stop him. "Thanks for coming, Lieutenant. I don't know what Donald told you, but I can imagine. Kenneth...well, he didn't much want to have a wife and a baby, but he did the right thing. Now I got me a home and a family, two things I always wanted, but never had. Want to eat with us? Betty there, she's a good cook."

Lorena was happy.

She didn't need anything from him, least of all a confession. "Thanks for the invitation, but I'd like to get back to town. I'm catching the morning train to Brenham."

"I see. Well...don't you worry anymore about Kenneth or his family. We'll be all right."

Donald waved at Gabriel and pointed at a banged up Model T. Gabriel's ride was leaving. "It was nice to meet you, Mrs. Scott."

Lorena blushed. "Oh, nobody around here calls me that. It's either Lorena or Mommy. You have a safe trip, Lieutenant." She ducked her head and walked toward the children who had begun to quarrel over who would vacate a swing so that Kenneth Jr. could have a turn.

Gabriel maneuvered his long legs into the passenger seat of the vehicle. Donald drove through the farmyard and turned onto the dirt road. Dust blew into Gabriel's eyes and mouth, causing him to clamp both tightly shut. He'd struck out twice, so far. Hopefully, he'd be able to explain the gravity of his mistake to the Patek family in Brenham.

❧❧

On the first Saturday in April, Sara Benson led Etta

into her front parlor. Etta's quilt top was affixed to a wooden frame in the center of the room. Sara placed a friendly arm around Etta's shoulders. "You did a fine job stitching the squares together."

Etta doubted the sincerity of Sara's praise, but appreciated it nonetheless. "It's kind of you to say so."

Sara moved two straight-backed chairs from her kitchen table to the quilt frame. "Sit by me and I'll show you the basic stitch. The women from the ladies' circle will be dropping by during the week. The quilting will go much faster with their help. You don't mind if we work on it without you, do you?"

"Heavens, no. If you waited until I had time, this quilt could take a decade to finish." Etta settled herself next to Sara. Why hadn't she ever taken the time to attend the quilting bees with her mother? A quiver of guilt passed through her heart as she realized the answer. Etta knew little about sewing because she'd always chosen her father's horses or working in the bank over spending time with the ladies. "Gabriel told me he used to hide whenever the ladies from church came to your house."

Sara laughed softly. "I know he did. Whenever he'd see me getting the house ready for a meeting of the Ladies' Circle, he'd suddenly remember a chore he had to do or someplace he had to go. His father isn't much better."

Etta watched Sara thread several needles. During Gabriel's absence, her brain had swarmed with thoughts of the bank and her father, but Gabriel was ever-present in her mind and in her prayers. She longed to hear his voice or to see him. As though it had a mind of its own, her skin recalled the feel of his hand in hers. His palm was calloused and the fingers strong, but he'd held her hand with the gentleness of a mare cleaning her foal.

"I don't know when Gabriel will make it back home," Sara said, "but I hope he gets whatever's bothering him out of his system. My son was the most even-tempered, agreeable baby ever born in Texas. But he came back from the Army as grouchy as a ninety-year-old man with rheumatism. Of course, one reason he's been so irritable is because he hardly sleeps at all. I hear him up and about almost every night."

How was it that mothers knew everything? Gabriel thought he'd kept his insomnia a secret, but even so, Sara worried about him.

"Now get a thimble," Sara instructed, "and I'll show you how to do a rocking stitch."

Etta slipped a thimble over the tip of her finger and watched Sara. Then she imitated the stitch.

"That's it," Sara said. "You'll get it in no time. Now, tell me how things are going at the bank."

Mothers might know everything, but Sara didn't know about the embezzler. Etta had been right to believe Gabriel would keep her secret, and since her mother had relied on Sara, Etta would as well. "Things at the bank aren't going so well. I recently discovered a discrepancy in the ledgers. Someone is stealing from us."

Sara gasped, her eyes wide with incredulity. "No! What are you going to do?"

Etta tucked the point of her needle in the fabric. She couldn't concentrate on the stitch while she talked about embezzlement. "I've already completed the first step. I called an outside auditor, and he found the problem. Someone's been intercepting loan payments."

Sara stopped stitching, as well. "Oh, this is awful.

You think it's someone who works at the bank?"

"It has to be. The books show the loan payments were received and credited, but the loan manager keeps a separate record, and he never received the payments."

"Have you told anyone about this? The county sheriff or William Clark? Since William's the county prosecutor, he might be able to help."

"For the time being, I need to keep this as quiet as possible. With my father away from the bank, the thief is growing bolder. He took money from the teller's cash drawers."

Sara sank back into her chair and shook her head slowly. "Oh, Etta. As if you needed another problem. Have you told Henry?"

"I can't burden my father with this. I have dinner with him almost every evening, and I can see he's improving, but he has far to go. His mood is all over the place. One night he'll be quiet and relaxed, the next he'll be as bad-tempered as a fussy two-year-old."

"What does Dr. Russell say?"

"I haven't spoken to the doctor. I'm afraid he'll just restate his advice about sending Papa to a convalescent home. But Mr. Simpson thinks Papa's moodiness is normal. He says people who've suffered injuries to their brains have a hard time managing their emotions."

"That makes sense." Sara returned to her stitching. "I like Charlie Simpson. He's a bit rough around the edges, but he's the most optimistic person I've ever met. Isn't it wonderful how the Lord sent the right person at the right time?"

"I thank God often for that blessing."

Sara sewed a few stitches then stopped and looked

at Etta. "What about this auditor you mentioned? Can he help you find the thief?"

Etta blew out a long breath. "That's another tricky situation."

Sara's eyebrows lifted. "Care to elaborate?"

"His name is George Owens. He works for a firm in Austin that's audited our books before."

"So, what's the problem?"

"He's interested in me."

Sara's face lit with excitement. "Really?" But her smile disappeared when she saw Etta's reaction. "Why is that a problem?"

Etta pushed her chair away from the quilt frame and crossed her arms over her chest. "Mr. Owens is a nice enough gentleman but..."

"But what?"

"I told him it's not appropriate for me to see him socially until this business at the bank is cleared up."

"Why not?"

"Because I've got to make sure no one suspects Mr. Owens of skewing his findings in one direction or another. If word gets out he's courting me, someone could accuse him of falsifying the evidence in order to help me."

"Courting you? Is he that serious?"

"He thinks I'd make a wonderful wife. Does that sound serious to you?"

"Boy howdy, it does. But why aren't you more enthusiastic about it?"

If Etta told the whole truth, she'd have to tell Sara she was falling in love with her son. But Etta wasn't ready to share every secret she had. "George Owens is what some girls call 'good husband material'. He's got steady employment, and he seems nice enough, but..."

Sara finished Etta's sentence. "But you don't like him."

"Is it that obvious?"

Sara removed several pins from her mouth and turned to look at Etta. "It used to be that a woman needed a man to take care of her, but that day has long past. You're an educated woman who holds her own in a man's world every day. You don't need a husband."

Etta understood Sara's meaning. The fight for women's suffrage had opened the door to all sorts of talk about independent women. But not needing a husband and not wanting one were different matters altogether. "A lot of people think I'm already a spinster, but to tell you the truth, I'd like to have a family. Someday."

"I'm not saying you shouldn't get married. I'm saying you don't *have* to get married. See the difference?"

Etta shrugged half-heartedly. "I guess so."

"And take it from me"—Sara continued—"You'll be spending the rest of your life with the man you marry, so for heaven's sake, you should at least like him." Sara kept stitching, her needles flashing in the afternoon sunlight, while Etta thought things over.

Etta didn't dislike George Owens, but the thought of his touch made her skin crawl. Gabriel on the other hand...

"What are you going to do about this auditor?" Sara asked.

"I agreed to go to the pictures and dinner with him next Saturday."

"What? If you don't like him, why in the world would you allow him to escort you to dinner?"

"He pressed me so much it was finally easier to

just accept his invitation. But," Etta held up one finger, "I'm going to persuade my cousin Nora to go with me."

"Isn't Nora expecting her third child?"

"That's right, but she's not too far along. I put a note in the mail this morning telling her about my plan."

"I imagine Nora will jump at the chance to leave her two youngsters at home with their father. And if this auditor is a good man, he'll understand why you've arranged for a chaperone on your first outing together."

Etta picked up her needle and returned to the quilt.

Benito was taking care of the horses and the flower garden, Charlie Simpson was taking care of Papa, and Rosa continued to take care of the house.

But there was no one to take care of the bank except her. How she wished she could talk to Gabriel about everything. What would he say about George Owens? Nothing good, she hoped.

9

The Union Depot in Brenham featured a large sign on its roof in the shape of the state capitol building.

Gabriel studied the structure for a few minutes, wondering who had come up with that idea. It set the building apart from all the other depots he'd seen, but to his eye it was merely false advertising. Anyone could visit the actual building in Austin free of charge.

After a prolonged conversation with the station master during which Gabriel learned much more than he'd ever wanted to know about the Czech immigrants who'd settled the area, Gabriel finally received directions to Private Josef Patek's family.

Brenham wasn't as big as Waco, but the place was livelier than Caldwell had been. At the center of town, the Italianate style red brick county courthouse was the hub of activity.

Men in business suits rushed in and out of the colonnaded doorway while workmen on ladders cleaned the rounded arch windows. A mix of automobiles and horse-drawn vehicles crowded the brick-paved streets that lined the perimeter of the square. Merchants sold everything from undergarments to furniture and farmers offered fresh-picked produce from the back of wagons. One enterprising middle-aged woman sold bouquets of flowers.

If Etta were with him, Gabriel would buy her a

bunch of pink roses. Did she like pink? Did she have a favorite flower? He had a lot to learn about the woman who occupied his thoughts both night and day. "Keep Etta safe, Lord," he said under his breath. He needed to be whole before he spoke to Etta about what was in his heart.

Gabriel shouldered his way along the crowded sidewalk until he turned east and walked through a quieter residential area.

The Patek house, an inviting gray shiplap with a hexagonal turret and a wraparound porch, was located on Pecan Street. Although it didn't come close to the grandeur of the Davis's country estate, it was a far cry from Lorena Scott's one-room cabin.

Joe Patek had often spoken with nostalgic ardor about his family home in Brenham, and looking around the well-groomed community, Gabriel could understand why. Everything about the street spoke of neighborhood baseball games on lazy Sunday afternoons and Christmas caroling on frigid December evenings.

On the left side of the house, a white-haired woman and an adolescent girl stood amid rose bushes. The woman dressed in the old style. A dark blue skirt covered her ankles and a long-sleeved lacy blouse covered her arms, but the girl's clothing was the latest fashion. Her white skirt stopped just south of her knees and a sleeveless pink top showed off slender pale arms.

The older woman noticed Gabriel first. "Hello, young man," she called in a strong voice. "May I help you?"

Gabriel removed his hat and slowly approached the pair. It would be impolite to come within reach of the ladies, and the last thing he wanted was to make them feel threatened. "Good afternoon. I'm looking for the family of Josef Patek."

"Then you are to be congratulated," the woman said in a formal tone, "for you have found his grandmother." Despite her formal manners, Joe's grandmother smiled as she answered, giving her an amiable demeanor.

"My name is Gabriel Benson. I served with Joe in France."

"Lieutenant Gabriel Benson of the Thirty-Sixth Division and before that, Burnet, Texas?" the older woman asked.

How did she know so much about him? "Yes, ma'am."

Joe's grandmother walked toward him, her progress slowed by the use of a silver-handled stick. "I am pleased to meet you, Lieutenant Benson. I am Honoria Hurta Patek. Allow me to introduce Josef's fiancée, Darina Batla."

Joe had talked about his girl, but Gabriel didn't know they'd been engaged.

Darina stepped beside Joe's grandmother, smiled broadly, and offered her hand. "How do you do, Lieutenant?" It wasn't much of a handshake. Darina's hand lay limp and cool next to Gabriel's palm. She tucked her chin and looked up at him through thick, dark lashes. Only actresses and women of ill-repute wore makeup, but Darina's cupid-bow red lips couldn't have been natural.

"It's a pleasure to meet you," Gabriel said automatically.

"Darina and I were just about to have tea," Mrs. Patek said. "You'll join us on the porch?"

It wasn't really a question. Joe's grandmother had issued an order with as much authority as any of his senior officers.

"Thank you, ma'am."

The older woman walked stiffly to a white wicker table and stood by a matching chair. Gabriel waited for her to be seated. Then he realized she expected him to pull out her chair. While he rushed to obey, Darina stepped into the house.

Mrs. Patek withdrew wire-rimmed spectacles from a leather case on the table. She slipped them on and lifted her chin. "Now I can see you better. Without my special lenses you were no more than a tall man with dark hair. Josef wrote about you quite frequently in his letters. I suppose you've come to tell us about him."

Gabriel placed his hat on an empty chair and sat down. "Yes ma'am, and to answer any questions I can."

"Did you know that the men of this family have served in our country's military forces for three generations?"

"No, ma'am."

"Oh yes. Josef's father fought in Cuba in '98 and my husband was a Confederate cavalry man. My own father was with Sam Houston at San Jacinto."

"That's quite a history."

"Indeed. We are all quite proud of Josef."

Darina returned with a tray of food.

Behind her, a dark-skinned woman wearing a maid's uniform carried another tray with a teapot and cups.

Gabriel stood and pulled out a chair for Darina.

"Thank you, Lieutenant," the girl said with another bright smile. "How nice to have a caller with such good manners."

Mrs. Patek poured tea into a flowered china cup with a matching saucer. "You'll find lemon, milk, and sugar on the table," she said as she passed the tea to Gabriel. "Help yourself to a cake."

Gabriel sipped the beverage and wished for coffee, but Mrs. Patek wasn't offering anything more than weak tea and small, square iced cakes. "Thank you, ma'am, but this is fine. I had lunch before I came."

Darina accepted her cup from Mrs. Patek and turned toward Gabriel. "Is this your first visit to Brenham, Lieutenant?"

"Yes, it is. I noticed the bluebonnets were budding. A few days more and the town will be full of them."

Darina placed her hand on his forearm and leaned closer. "You simply must come back and see our glorious bluebonnet fields. There's no place in Texas as beautiful as Brenham in April. Perhaps you'd like to bring your family."

"I'm not sure about that. My parents don't travel much."

"Is it just you and your parents? No wife or children?"

"No, ma'am."

Darina smiled again and twirled a strand of hair around her forefinger. "Isn't that nice."

Gabriel knew when a girl was flirting, but Darina's expertise made other girls' attempts pale in comparison. Perhaps it would be wise to change the subject. "Mrs. Patek, are Joe's parents in town?"

The older woman filled her cup. "I'm sorry to tell you this, young man, but my son and his wife died recently. Except for my two daughters and their families, I am Josef's only kin."

Darina leaned closer to Gabriel, giving him a whiff of floral perfume. "I visit Miss Honoria every day. Joe's aunts live in the country and don't get into town very often, but I keep an eye on her. It's the least I can do." Darina's smile looked as fake as her scarlet lips.

Gabriel turned his full attention toward Mrs. Patek and tried to disregard the coquette sitting next to him. "I only asked because I wanted to tell Joe's family about...well, about his final days."

Mrs. Patek folded the white linen napkin in her lap, giving undue concentration to evening the corners. "Yes, I assumed that was the purpose of your visit. Captain Brooks wrote a lovely sentiment about my grandson. He explained that Josef was part of a squad sent to scout a route of attack at St. Etienne. He also explained that Josef died as a result of an artillery bombardment." She stopped examining the napkin and raised her gaze to Gabriel. "Do you have anything to add to that?"

Gabriel's chest tightened as he reached the thorny part of his visit. He emptied his cup, licked his lips, and returned Mrs. Patek's forthright gaze. "You have the details correct, ma'am. The two pieces of information I can add are that I was the squad leader and that Josef died because of my mistake."

Darina's cup clattered against its saucer, and she coughed into her napkin.

Joe's grandmother, however, eyed Gabriel solemnly. "Perhaps you should explain yourself, Lieutenant."

Gabriel blew out a long breath, but the band of anxiety encircling his chest refused to ease. He rested his elbows on the arms of his chair and looked at the older woman's patient but uncompromising features.

"My squad got caught between American and German artillery fire. Some of my men wanted to turn back and retrace our steps until we reached our unit, but by that time, there was so much smoke and noise we were trapped. I hesitated, trying to decide what to do. The artillery shells were coming from both sides, exploding in front of and behind our position. My squad took a direct hit." Gabriel closed his eyes and waited for his heartbeat to return to normal. When at last he thought he could endure Joe's grandmother's inevitable reprisals, he opened his eyes and looked at her. "So you see, ma'am, if I'd chosen another way, Josef would still be alive."

Mrs. Patek gazed at him with dry eyes and a stern face. "Did you shoot my grandson, Lieutenant?"

Her question knocked Gabriel back into his chair. "What? No, ma'am." How could she imagine he'd done such a thing? "Of course I didn't shoot Joe."

"Then you're not at fault. Do you think my grandson did not know the risk he was taking when he signed up? Do you not think we all knew?"

Gabriel searched for a response, but Mrs. Patek answered her own question. "Of course, we knew. You are still a young man, Lieutenant, but I am seventy-eight years old. I have lost my parents, my brothers, my husband, my son, countless friends, and now my grandson. You are just beginning to learn what I have known for many years. Losing those we love is the price of living a long life."

Josef and the other squad members would never have the opportunity to learn such a hard lesson. Was that a good thing?

Mrs. Patek fingered the silver head of her walking stick. "Have you traveled all the way to Brenham in hope I will chastise you?"

Gabriel's throat tightened as he fought back the surge of emotion threatening to embarrass him in front of Joe's grandmother. How had she seen so clearly into his troubled soul?

"If that is why you have come, you will receive nothing but disappointment," she continued. "I do not hold President Wilson responsible for Josef's death, nor do I blame the United States Army. A German artillery shell killed my grandson. Not you, Lieutenant."

Gabriel looked at the older woman with a mixture of astonishment and esteem. He deserved her scorn, but she'd been merciful. In one way or another, all of the families he'd visited had given him their grace. Anthony Blake's family grieved for their son but understood the innate peril of battle. Kenneth Scott had used the Army as a way to escape his responsibilities and his family had accepted his absence. Why was Gabriel traveling central Texas in search of forgiveness if no one held him accountable?

Mrs. Patek refilled his cup. "I am confident I will see those I've lost in heaven. That was our Lord's promise, and I've never had reason to doubt His word. Are you a believer, Lieutenant?"

Was he? Gabriel had always taken his religion for granted, just another part of the sweet life his parents had provided. But he prayed every day in one way or another—quick entreaties to keep Etta and his parents safe—and he'd definitely done his share of praying in the Army. "Yes, ma'am. I could probably do a better job of it, but I'm a believer."

"Faith is not an all or nothing proposition, young man. It is a journey. Each trial I have faced and each blessing I have received has strengthened my faith.

'When I was a child, I spake like a child, I understood as a child, I thought like a child.' Do you know that verse?"

Gabriel finished the quote. "'Now that I have become a man, I put away childish things'."

Mrs. Patek's smile indicated approval. "I use that passage to illustrate my point. When I was a child, I believed as a child. Now that I am near the end of my earthly journey, my faith is stronger. You are facing a trial now, Lieutenant. A very difficult trial. Have you asked the Lord for guidance?"

Gabriel thought back to the last time he'd seen Etta. She'd prayed for him that night by the creek and she'd received the Lord's answer. "I thought so, but nothing's working out the way I thought it would."

"From what you said earlier, I assume you search for forgiveness."

Gabriel looked at the amber liquid in his cup, unable to meet Mrs. Patek's incisive gaze. "I made a terrible mistake at St. Etienne."

Mrs. Patek gently touched Gabriel's wrist. Her spotted hand, made tender with age and kindness, send a current of warmth straight to his heart. "Our Lord has already forgiven you," she said, "and I do not hold you culpable. But I wonder if you have forgiven yourself."

Understanding spread through his chest like the light of a newborn star. He'd jumped to conclusions the last time he'd been with Etta, cutting off both her and the Lord from helping him to comprehend fully. It wasn't grief-stricken families from whom Gabriel should seek forgiveness. He needed to seek it for himself. He had to forgive himself for the mistakes he'd made. His throat tightened as tears filled his eyes.

Mrs. Patek squeezed his hand. "Forgiving ourselves is sometimes the hardest thing of all, but we are all human and, therefore, prone to mistakes."

Gabriel blinked back the tears and drained his cup. How could he ever forgive himself for leading ten men to their deaths? As hard as the memories had been, Gabriel suspected that absolving himself would be harder. "I'm not the kind of man who can quote the Bible, but I'm reminded of a Scripture my mother often used when I was growing up."

A twinkle lit the older woman's eyes as she released his hand. "I am not sure if that is a good thing or not. After all, the Good Book does say 'a wicked woman maketh a heavy countenance and a wounded heart.'"

Gabriel chuckled softly. "I don't even know that verse, ma'am, but when my mother felt as though I wasn't giving her enough respect, she'd say, 'Wisdom is with aged men, and with length of days, understanding.'"

The lines around Mrs. Patek's mouth deepened as she smiled.

For a moment, Gabriel could see the young girl she had been.

"Thank you, Lieutenant. That verse is indeed a compliment. Now, I have a favor to ask."

"Anything."

She laughed softly. "Oh, Lieutenant. You should never say that to a woman. You may be promising more than you bargained for."

Gabriel laughed with her. "Still, I would be happy to fulfill any request you made."

"Very well. What I would like is for you to escort Darina to her home. Her brother is quite tardy and, although she does not live very far away, I do not hold with young women walking the streets alone."

Gabriel glanced at the young girl, surprised to realize that in his determination to confess to Mrs. Patek, he'd forgotten Darina still sat silently at his side. "I'd be glad to see her home."

"Good. Now I am going to excuse myself. One of the few benefits of being old is that one need not be sociable when one is not up to it." Mrs. Patek rose slowly to her feet.

Gabriel stood and took her elbow to steady her.

"Thank you, Lieutenant. And thank you for taking the time to visit. I wish you a pleasant journey home and, if you are ever in Brenham again, I hope you will pay another call."

"It was a pleasure meeting you, Mrs. Patek. Thank you for the tea and…well, for everything."

She patted his arm and smiled.

Darina dashed to the door and opened it for the older lady. "I'll see you tomorrow, Miss Honoria, and I'll bring those cuttings I told you about."

Mrs. Patek touched Darina's cheek, smiled at Gabriel one last time, and entered her house.

Darina closed the door quietly and retrieved a wide-brimmed straw hat and a pocketbook from a nearby bench. "It's so gallant of you to see me home," she said with another beaming smile.

Gabriel slipped on his hat and followed Darina down the steps and onto the sidewalk. "It's nothing at all. As long as you can direct me from your house to the depot, I'll be fine."

Darina slipped her arm through Gabriel's and led him toward the corner. "Once you meet my family, they'll insist you have dinner with us. Please say you will. We get so little company these days."

"Sorry, but I have a ticket for the seven o'clock train to La Grange. I'll be glad to meet your family, but then I'll have to be off."

"Don't be silly. We'll just go to the depot right now and trade in that ticket for tomorrow." Darina tightened her grip on his arm. "I've just met you, Lieutenant. Please don't leave so soon." What was wrong with Darina's eyes? Was she batting her eyelashes at him? He'd read about such behavior in magazine stories, but he'd never seen someone do it.

"How old are you, Darina?"

"Seventeen. Why do you ask?"

"Just wondering." He removed her hand from his sleeve as gently as possible. "How far is your house?"

"Have you changed your mind about staying? We could take my daddy's car for a drive. Momma wouldn't mind if I went out with a fine gentleman such as yourself. There are so few real gentlemen around these days. What's a girl of marriageable age supposed to do?" Darina's intentions were as transparent as a soap bubble.

"I'm not staying, and if you don't tell me where your house is, I'll be forced to take you back to Joe's grandmother."

Darina's bottom lip began to quiver. "Please don't disappoint me. I've been so lonely since Joe went away, but now that you're here, we could have lots of fun."

Gabriel had never seen such an artful performance. "The last thing I want is to hurt your feelings, but I'm leaving Brenham on the seven o'clock train. Neither flirting nor pouting will change my mind."

Darina stepped away from him, a look of

indignation darkening her young face. "Pouting? Flirting? You think too much of yourself if you think I'm interested in an old man like you."

Her barb failed to wound. Even though he was not yet thirty, he recognized injured pride when he saw it. Gabriel removed his hat and held it over his heart. "If I've misunderstood, I apologize."

"Well, I would hope so." Darina bounded across the street and up the steps of a blue frame house. At the door, she turned to look at Gabriel, tilted her nose into the air, and sashayed into the house.

Gabriel turned his back so Darina couldn't see him laugh. She was young, pretty, and hunting a husband. She'd find one, probably sooner rather than later, but Gabriel was glad he was out of her sights.

৯৹৻ঔ

Etta awoke, remembered what day it was, and wished she could go back to sleep. At six o'clock that evening, she would meet with the bank's Board of Directors. How would they react when she told them about the embezzlement? Would they blame her for the theft or congratulate her for finding the problem?

She rolled over and pulled a pillow over her head. Why did she have to be in charge of this? She was merely her father's assistant. Investigating an embezzler was his job. It simply wasn't fair to expect her to fill his shoes.

A noise from outside her bedroom door let her know Charlie was on the job. His cajoling but no-nonsense tone was matched with angry grumblings from her father. Papa might not like Charlie's insistent commands, but there was no denying Papa was steadily improving. By the time Gabriel made it back, Papa might even be able to say a few words.

When would Gabriel return? Had he found the widows and grieving mothers? Had they understood that Gabriel was as much a casualty of war as their loved ones or had they assaulted him with accusations? When he returned, would his burden be lifted, or would it continue to torment his soul?

A band of longing tightened around Etta's heart. It didn't make sense to yearn for him to the point of heartache. They'd only shared a few hours together. But in that time, he'd touched her heart and left his fingerprints there. Her ears missed the sound of his voice, his gentle teasing, and his whispered confessions. Her gaze missed the sight of him, his confident walk and his heartwarming smile. If only she could sit by Gabriel's side, talking about everything that had happened or not talking at all. She longed to simply be near him. Breathing the same air would be enough. As long as he returned.

A shiver ran through her body as common sense whispered its chilly reality. Gabriel had made no promises. He hadn't spoken words of love or hinted at future plans. Etta had pinned her hopes on nothing more than her own fantasies. What was to keep him from turning his back on her and leaving again?

If only she could talk to her mother about everything that weighed on her heart. Her mother had always known how to advise her.

A light tap on her door was followed by Charlie Simpson's cheerful voice. "You awake, Miss Davis?"

Etta reached for her dressing gown. "Yes, Mr. Simpson. Do you need something?"

"I just wanted to make sure you came down for

breakfast. Rosa's making chilaquiles this mornin'."

How odd for Charlie to be concerned about Etta's breakfast plans. Besides, Rosa often scrambled eggs with green sauce, cheese, and corn tortilla strips. Maybe Charlie wanted to show off his burgeoning knowledge of Spanish. "I'll be down soon, Mr. Simpson."

"We'll be waitin'." He whistled softly as he made his way downstairs.

Etta scooted out of bed and chose her outfit for the day. The flowered skirt and matching blouse might be good for a spring outing, but she needed to appear businesslike, confident, and decisive. She settled for her gray gabardine suit. Nothing said "somber" like gray gabardine.

By the time she made it downstairs, Rosa was cleaning the breakfast dishes and Charlie was lingering over a cup of coffee. But as she stepped into the kitchen, she discovered why Charlie had been so insistent she join them. Sitting beside Charlie and dressed in a starched white shirt, navy stripe vest and matching trousers, was her father.

"Papa!" Etta's hands flew to her face.

Her father's crooked smile reminded her that the right side of his face hadn't yet recovered from its paralysis, but otherwise, he looked so normal!

Etta ran to his side. "Oh, Papa! You look wonderful!"

He nodded slowly. "an oo."

Speech still eluded him, but Etta gave thanks for the miracle that had brought him this far.

Rosa set a plate of food in front of an empty chair. "Sit down, mija, and let your father finish his breakfast. Señor Davis has come downstairs almost every morning this week."

Etta sank into a chair. Tears of joy blurred her vision. "That's amazing, Papa. You've come so far." She smiled at Charlie. "I prayed for Papa's recovery, but I never imagined he'd make such quick progress. Thank you, Mr. Simpson."

Charlie's cheeks turned pink. "Ah, don't going thankin' me, Miss Davis. Your papa may hate doing his exercises, but he does 'em. He'll be back at work before you can say how-dee-doo."

Her father moved his left arm toward her. "orse?"

"The horses are fine, Papa. Benito is still coming before and after school, and I check on them every day. They're getting a good rest, but it seems to me that you'll be riding again soon."

He raised his left shoulder in a careful shrug. "Ank?"

She'd never withheld information about the bank from her father, but now was not the time to trouble him. "The Board of Directors meets tonight. I've prepared all the usual reports, and Carolina Swanson will be taking the minutes in my place. We're showing steady growth in all the investments except agriculture, but that's to be expected since the War Department has decreased its demand. I moved more of our investment funds into manufacturing. People are buying automobiles like crazy. Perhaps we should consider putting more money into the petroleum corporations. I was thinking of increasing our investment by ten percent."

Her father nodded. "Eny."

Etta struggled to understand her father's garbled word. She looked at Charlie.

Charlie must have seen the confusion in her eyes,

because he jumped up, retrieved the pencil and pad Rosa used for her grocery list, and passed them to Henry.

Her father picked up the pencil with his left hand and painstakingly wrote on the pad.

Etta's heart tensed to see her father strain to do such a mundane task. He'd always been so capable and confident in everything he did, but now he labored to scratch out a few lines. At last, he dropped the pencil and pushed the paper toward her.

Etta studied the childlike scrawl. "Twenty," she said with a wide smile. "You think I should increase the petroleum investments by twenty percent."

"Hmph," he said with a confident nod. "Eny."

She sprang from her seat and kissed his freshly-shaved cheek. "Twenty. I'll do it today, Papa." She looked at Charlie and Rosa and held up the pad for them to see. "Twenty," she repeated.

"I told you so, Miss Davis," Charlie said with a chuckle. "Your papa's still in there, but his brain has to figure out new ways to operate."

"Now eat, mija," Rosa ordered with a stern expression on her face. "If you do your job and Señor Davis does his job, everybody will be back where they belong. Then I can do my job without this *hombre fastidioso.*" Although Rosa had described Charlie as annoying, she'd also given him a playful shove and a wink.

Maybe Charlie's romantic pursuits weren't in vain.

Etta squeezed her father's left hand and said a quick blessing over her breakfast. With such an auspicious beginning to her day, maybe this evening's meeting wouldn't be so dreadful after all.

ॐॐ

"Here's the lemonade," Carolina said as she set the glass pitcher into a large bowl of chipped ice. "I'll bring in another pitcher with water. Where are the sandwiches?"

"Here." Etta lifted the white linen napkins covering plates of finger sandwiches and an assortment of cookies from Hoffmann's Bakery. "I think we have everything."

Carolina straightened a stack of papers on the conference room table. "The board members will be here soon. I'd better get that water." She bustled out of the room.

Etta took one last inventory of the documents she'd prepared. All she had to do now was remember Gabriel's advice. What would a confident man do in this situation? Stand up, present the facts, and answer questions honestly and thoroughly. This was no time to shrink back into the quiet helper who'd sat at her father's elbow, ready to jump at his smallest request.

Judge Thompson, dressed in his usual dark suit and tie, was the first board member to enter the conference room. "Evening, Henrietta. Got everything ready I see."

"Good evening, Judge. Can I get you anything?"

He hung his hat on the rack near the door. "A nice, cool glass of that lemonade would hit the spot. How's your father?"

Etta filled a glass and handed it to him. "Better and better every day. Thank you for asking."

He settled himself into a chair at the head of the rectangular oak table. "I've got to get out to your place soon and let him know everything here is under control."

Etta bit her bottom lip.

Judge Thompson might change his mind after he learned the contents of her reports.

William Clark and Edgar Robinson strode into the room together. Both men hung their hats next to Judge Thompson's and draped their suit jackets around the backs of their chairs.

"Good evening, Miss Davis," Mayor Robinson said. "I trust the bank has had another good quarter."

"What can I get you?" Etta asked. "Would you like some sandwiches?"

"I'll have some," William Clark answered, "and a glass of that lemonade. You're looking well, Miss Davis."

"Thank you, Mr. Clark."

William was always so polite, and never failed to compliment Etta in some way. Her mother had often remarked on what a good son he'd been to his widowed mother, but he was at least ten years older than Etta. Most men his age were married.

"Did you see James on your way here?" Judge Thompson asked.

"No," Mayor Robinson answered as he helped himself to the food. "He's probably trying to get away from the store. If he's not here in the next ten minutes, I say we start without him."

"What's your hurry?" William asked. "Miss Davis has gone to a lot of trouble to provide these lovely refreshments. The least you can do is relax a few minutes and enjoy them."

"Will you give me one of those sandwiches, Etta?" Judge Thompson asked. "And two of those cookies, if you don't mind."

Etta set the plate of food in front of the judge and then refilled his glass. "I'm sure Mr. Moore will be here soon."

Carolina Swanson entered carrying a cloth-bound journal and a pitcher of ice water.

The men stood.

"Please keep your seats, gentlemen," she said. "I'm going to act as secretary tonight and take the minutes of the meeting."

"Can't start without me," James Moore said as he hurried into the room. "Sorry if I've kept you waiting."

"Not at all," Etta said. "What can I get you to eat, Mr. Moore?"

"Just some water." James fanned his face with his hat. "Mighty warm for April, don't you think?"

"It's good for the wildflowers," Judge Thompson answered. "We're going to have quite a show this year. Good rain and warm weather are all it takes."

"Mind if we get started?" Mayor Robinson asked.

"What's your hurry, Edgar?" asked James Moore. "Got a hot card game waiting for you?" Mr. Moore's comment seemed out of place.

In addition to being the mayor, Edgar was a long-serving deacon of the First Baptist Church.

But Mayor Robinson laughed it off. "Card games are for Methodists like you, James."

"No, no. You've got me confused with the Lutherans," Mr. Moore retorted.

Judge Thompson cleared his throat. "Well, as soon as you theologians quit arguing, I'll start this meeting."

The men chuckled good-naturedly, helped themselves to more refreshments, and finally took their seats.

"I hereby call this meeting of the Davis Bank and

Trust Board of Directors to order." Judge Thompson announced. "Are you ready, Mrs. Swanson?"

Carolina placed wire-rim spectacles on the bridge of her nose and nodded. "I'm ready, Judge."

"Very well." Judge Thompson took a long drink of lemonade, made eye contact with each person gathered around the table, and sat forward in his chair. "In Henry Davis's absence, let it be shown that Henrietta Davis will be presenting this quarter's information. Etta?"

Etta stood and gave each man a copy of her reports. "Thank you, Judge. I'd like to begin with the investment report. As you can see, the latest quarter shows steady growth in every sector except agricultural futures. This is concurrent with the end of the war, and I've listed my suggestions for reallocating our investment funds to reflect that change."

"Good thinking," William said. "I can see the bank's still in good hands."

From all accounts, William was a bulldog of a prosecutor, never letting go of a case until he was satisfied that justice had been served, but Etta had never seen that side of him. She smiled at him, grateful for his kind remarks. "The next report shows our various accounts, and as you can see from the profit-and-loss statement, we made a smaller profit than usual last quarter."

"Still, a profit is a profit," James Moore said. "My store operated at a loss when we first opened, and that's a hard row to hoe."

"Now that most people in town have automobiles, they'll be driving into Austin to shop," Mayor Robinson said. "Have you thought about how that's going to affect your business?"

"Gentlemen," Judge Thompson said gruffly, "need I remind you that we're here to discuss the bank and not Moore's Department Store?"

"Sorry, Judge," the mayor said. "Go ahead, Miss Davis."

Etta took a deep breath. Everything had gone well so far, but she was about to reveal the loss of thousands of dollars. She squared her shoulders and lowered her chin. As much as she dreaded the next part, this was her fight. "Next you'll see the loan reports. Business loans and real estate loans showed neither growth nor loss last quarter. My father's plan to create automobile loans shows the greatest increase in the number of people requesting the loan and in the total dollar amount collected."

"See what I'm saying?" Mayor Robinson interjected. "Our little town is going to lose business if we don't try to get ahead of this boom. Everybody and his uncle wants an automobile."

Judge Thompson rapped his knuckles on the table. "A good topic for the next town council meeting but not here and not now."

Mayor Robinson held up his palms in a conciliatory manner and relaxed in his chair. "Fine, fine," he muttered. "Sorry, Miss Davis."

"What's this in agricultural loans?" William asked. "There seems to be an error."

"Yes," Etta said, trying to keep the quiver out of her voice. "I'm aware of the discrepancy."

The other men shuffled their papers until they came to the correct one. "January looks all right to me," Mayor Robinson commented.

"But look at February and March," James Moore said. "Something's not matching up."

"Exactly." Etta drank a sip of water. The last thing she needed was a quiver in her voice. "When I found this problem, I called in an independent auditor. Do any of you know George Owens from the Worthington Accounting firm in Austin?"

"He was here last year, wasn't he?" Judge Thompson asked.

"Yes," Etta answered. "He conducted our annual audit. I called him as soon as this discrepancy was noted. It has become clear that someone has intercepted loan payments but marked them as paid."

William held up a sheet of paper. "The loan report shows only one loan seriously behind in payments."

"That's right. John Farrington's widow asked us to put his loan payments on hold until she could sell their ranch. She plans to move to San Antonio to be closer to her daughter."

"And you agreed to that?" James Moore asked.

"I knew her neighbor was interested in adding the Farrington acreage to his ranch. Simon Ward has already been in to talk us about the lien we hold on that land."

"I don't know," Mr. Moore said, "but it seems as though Eula Farrington could have made the payments. It's not good business to simply let money slip away."

"The bank's assets aren't about to be threatened by a few months of missed loan payments," William said. "There's no need to hound widows and orphans."

"But these missing funds are another matter," Mayor Robinson said with a frown. "If someone's putting loan payments into his own pocket, that's embezzlement."

All the men's gazes settled on Etta and her

stomach curled into a tight ball. Wasn't there someone else who could do this? Why did it have to be her? After a deep breath, she looked the mayor in the eye. "I'm aware of the problem, and I've taken the proper steps to discover who the thief is."

"Such as?" Mr. Moore challenged.

"First, I instigated an independent audit. The results showed me how the money was being taken. Once I find out who the thief is, I will require two signatures on each receipt for loan payments. Cash payments are now simply added to the tellers' drawers, but in the future they'll be kept in a separate till in the vault."

There was a moment of silence during which the men exchanged silent looks.

Etta didn't need a magical power to know what they were thinking. An embezzler was a serious matter, and the board members didn't think she'd done enough to catch him.

Mr. Moore spoke first. "Why haven't you already enacted the changes you described?"

Etta clasped her hands behind her back in an effort to hide her trembling. "As counter-intuitive as it sounds, I need the thief to keep stealing until I can pinpoint who it is."

"Oh no," Mr. Moore intoned, a dark scowl on his face. "That's bad business. No one in his right mind would sit by and knowingly let a thief rob him."

"I understand your logic," Etta replied, "but money can be tracked. If the embezzler spent the money, there will be a record of it somewhere. If he kept the cash, that too can be found."

"And if he saved the cash in a bank," Judge Thompson said, "there will be an account with his name on it."

"Or the name of someone whom he is using to help him hide the money," Etta agreed.

Mayor Robinson rubbed his balding head. "But if you let the thief continue, it may cost the bank thousands of dollars. Your father has always been an excellent steward, but it sounds as though you're going to let the bank's funds slip through your fingers."

William leaned forward in his chair. "You know, Miss Davis, this matter really should be handled by my office. As county prosecutor, I have the means to investigate this further."

Etta knees weakened and she sank into her chair. "I considered that, Mr. Clark, but if you step in now, the thief may stop."

"Isn't that what you want?" Mayor Robinson asked in an incredulous tone.

"Of course," Etta replied. "But I also want to identify the embezzler."

Judge Thompson nodded slowly. "It's a difficult call, but I think Henrietta is doing the right thing. Let's give her time to follow through with her plan."

"How much time?" Mayor Robinson wasn't ready to concede.

"I can't give you an exact timeline of how long it will take," Etta said. "Other than the members of the board, the only people who know about the embezzlement are myself and Arthur Lewis."

"Is Mr. Lewis one of your suspects?" William asked.

"Not really. He's the one who brought the matter to my attention."

Mayor Robinson stood and braced his hands on the table. "Miss Davis, you can't expect us to sit back and let you ruin the bank. If your father knew about this…"

Etta dropped her gaze. The mayor didn't have to finish his sentence. If her father had been the one to learn about the embezzlement, he would have taken immediate action.

Judge Thompson spoke up. "William, has your office tackled something like this before?"

William's pale eyebrows drew together in a thoughtful expression. "Not since I became county prosecutor, but I'm sure we could come up with something."

"I say we give Henrietta four weeks," Judge Thompson said. "If she hasn't discovered the thief's identity by then, we'll let William have a crack at it."

"Four weeks?" James Moore's doubt was evident. "I can't believe you're even suggesting it. If this happened in my store, I'd close the place, fire everyone, and start again."

"But unlike your department store, the bank can't simply close," Judge Thompson said. "Too many people depend on it."

Mr. Moore shook his head. "I still say four weeks is too long."

"Will you give me three?" Etta asked.

"No," Mr. Moore replied. "That's still too long."

"How much time will you allow?" Judge Thompson asked.

"Two weeks. That's all. But you mind me, Henrietta, I won't sit by and let you drive this bank into the ground."

Etta straightened her spine. What did Mr. Moore mean by that threat? Would he convince the other board members to relieve her from duty? Would he take over?

Judge Thompson gestured to Carolina. "Have you got all that, Mrs. Swanson?"

Carolina scribbled a few last lines and then looked up from her paper. "Yes, Judge."

"Then I say we adjourn for the evening," Judge Thompson suggested. "However, I'd like to reconvene two weeks from tonight. You can give us an update then, Henrietta."

There was a light rap at the closed door.

Carolina stood, but before she reached the entrance, the door swung open.

Carl greeted the group with a wide smile. "Good evening, everyone. Can you give me a few minutes? I have a matter to discuss with the board."

Etta grasped the arms of her chair in surprise.

Uncle Carl never came to the board meetings. Never.

James Moore pulled his pocket watch from his vest. "I can give you thirty minutes. Will it take longer than that?"

Carl stepped farther into the room and set his hat on the table. "I won't take any more of your valuable time than I have to. Mind if I help myself to the refreshments?"

Carolina popped up. "I'll get them for you, Mr. Stanley. Would you like lemonade or water?"

"Lemonade sounds lovely. Spring is in the air, gentlemen. Aren't we lucky to be living in this part of our great state?"

Judge Thompson didn't give anyone time to answer. "What's on your mind, Carl?"

Carl flicked his gaze to Etta and then returned it to Judge Thompson. "Would it be possible to excuse my niece from this meeting? I have some things to discuss which might distress a young girl."

What could Carl have to say that she couldn't hear? Beneath the table, Etta clutched the fabric of her skirt.

"If your concern is for the fairer sex, then we should also consider Mrs. Swanson," Mayor Robinson said.

Carl's smile never faltered, yet he managed to convey concern in his voice. "Perhaps that would be best."

"But Mrs. Swanson is taking the minutes," William reminded them. "Is someone else willing to take over for her?"

"If Carl's business is added to the minutes, which is the proper protocol to follow, then Henrietta and Carolina will know the content, anyway," Mr. Moore said.

"Good point," Judge Thompson allowed. "Carl, I believe Henrietta and Carolina may as well stay where they are. Now what's on your mind?"

Carl settled into a chair and folded his hands on top of the table. "First, I want to say how good a job I believe Henrietta's done in her father's absence. We all wish Henry a speedy recovery, but from what Dr. Russell has told me, it doesn't sound as though Henry will be back for a long time."

"How is your father, Miss Davis?" William asked. "My mother wants to pay a visit, but I told her we'd best wait."

"He's made remarkable progress," Etta answered, "but your instincts were right about visiting. I'll be sure to tell my father that you and your mother were asking about him."

As though he resented having the spotlight removed from him, Carl drummed his fingers on the table. "However," he said in a loud voice, "I'm sure we all agree that the responsibility of running the bank shouldn't be left to a girl. Besides, Etta should be home helping her father."

What was Carl up to? Who did he think would run the bank if she stayed home?

"I suppose you're volunteering to step into Henry's shoes," Judge Thompson said.

Carl ducked his head. "Well, I…"

"Carl is familiar with the day-to-day procedures," James Moore said.

"And he's a member of the family," Mayor Robinson added.

An icy hand grasped Etta's heart as she realized what was behind Carl's unexpected visit to the meeting. He wanted control. She truly hoped she was wrong, but if her uncle was the embezzler, putting him in charge would ruin the bank and all of its depositors.

She couldn't let this happen.

William stood. "I'm not in favor of Carl taking over. Miss Davis has done a good job despite difficult circumstances, and there's no reason not to continue to trust her."

Mayor Robinson rubbed his chin. "It is an awful lot for a lady to take on. I'm not saying Henrietta hasn't done her best, but…"

The young prosecutor turned toward the head of the table. "What do you say, Judge?"

Judge Thompson's white eyebrows framed serious eyes. "I say we think about it. We're going to reconvene in two weeks in order to get an update on that other matter and we can discuss Carl's offer, then."

"What other matter?" Carl asked.

No one answered. Board members had a pact that bank business would only be discussed behind closed doors when everyone was present.

"If there's no other business," Judge Thompson said, "I'm ready to adjourn this meeting."

Carl's voice took on a tone of urgency. "Surely you gentlemen don't expect to leave little Etta in charge of this bank for two more weeks. It's simply too much for her to take on. At least let me supervise her."

Carl's insistence that he be allowed more access to the bank was raising Etta's suspicions as surely as the hair on the back of her neck.

James Moore checked his pocket watch again. "You may as well let it go, Carl. One thing about this board, we don't do anything quickly. We'll meet in two weeks and make a decision then."

Carl threw up his hands as if conceding the fight. "Fine. But don't say I didn't warn you when this bank has to close because the funds have been mismanaged." He snatched his hat from the table, flung open the door, and strode into the hallway.

The door banged shut behind him. "What in the world was that all about?" Mayor Robinson asked. "Carl couldn't know about the missing funds, could he?"

Not unless he was the one taking them. But Etta refrained from voicing her opinion.

"I don't see how anyone other than the six of us could know," Judge Thompson said, "and we've never had a problem maintaining confidentiality before. Despite Carl Stanley's dire prediction, I'm convinced the bank won't fold in two weeks. Now, if there's no other business, I'm going to adjourn the meeting." He turned his sharp gaze to each person gathered around the table and hearing no other issues, said, "This meeting is adjourned."

Judge Thompson, James Moore, and Mayor Robinson stood, gathered their hats and jackets, and departed with noisy but genial farewells.

Carolina reached across the table and squeezed Etta's arm. "It's going to be all right."

Etta rested her head in her hand. Now that the meeting was over, her shoulders ached and her stomach felt empty. Had she eaten anything since breakfast?

Carolina gathered her notebook and fountain pen. "I'll type up these notes and file them for our next meeting. Now stop worrying, Etta. You're every bit as good at this job as your father. I'd even say you were better. After all, you're the one who uncovered the problem."

William Clark opened the door for the older lady. "Goodnight, Mrs. Swanson."

Carolina beamed at the young man. "Goodnight, William. Please give your mother my best."

"I'll do that." William closed the door quietly and sat next to Etta. "Well, now. That certainly wasn't like our usual quarterly meetings. A thief, a blustering uncle, and Henrietta Davis taking them on like Joan of Arc at the siege of Orleans."

Etta bowed her head and laughed, all the tension of the day flowing out of her body like air from a bellows. "Oh, Mr. Clark. I haven't laughed in a long time. Thank you."

"I like to see you laugh. You should do it more often."

"I agree. But lately...well, there hasn't been much to laugh about."

William's voice took on a sympathetic tone. "I know. I'm sorry you're having such of tough time. But remember, you're not alone in this fight."

"You're right. Sometimes it feels like everything depends on me, but I do have friends I can call on for help."

William leaned closer. "I hope you consider me one of those friends."

"Of course. You've always been so thoughtful to both my family and me. And I won't forget to contact you if my investigation leads to something the prosecutor's office should know."

William reached for her hand. "I'd like to be more than a friend, Henrietta. If you're amenable to the idea."

Etta leaned away from William as the meaning behind his words became clear. "Oh. I didn't realize. I mean..." Etta's face and throat grew warm. "You're very kind to think of me that way, Mr. Clark."

"I think it's time you called me William, don't you? May I call you Henrietta?"

"Oh...of course...if you'd like."

William smiled and rubbed his thumb over the back of her hand. "May I call on you soon? When your father is up to it, I'd like to have a talk with him."

Years of nothing and now both George and William were interested in her? What was happening?

"My father has begun having breakfast at the table, but I don't know how much longer it will be before he's up to guests."

William eased closer. "Perhaps you'll join me for lunch one day, or we could motor into Austin for a nice evening out."

"Lunch!" She squeezed her eyes shut upon realizing she'd shouted the word. But she was already making a trip to Austin to see George Owens. Cousin Nora would surely tease her about her sudden popularity. "I'd prefer to stay in town."

"Of course. I should have realized you wouldn't want to be too far from your father at a time like this."

Etta swallowed the spurt of guilt she felt at hiding one suitor from the other. How did other women handle things like this?

"I'd best say goodnight. Mother never eats dinner until I get home, and I shouldn't keep her waiting. Let me know if there's anything I or anyone in my office can do to help you."

Etta's mouth was suddenly dry. She drank deeply from her glass of water. "I will. Thank you."

William squeezed her hand and stood. After putting on his hat and giving her one last smile, he left the conference room whistling a happy tune.

Etta blew out a long breath and slumped in her chair. Was this the way the ugly duckling felt when it learned its true identity? Etta's life in Burnet had always been supervised by at least one of her parents. She'd attended every tea and church social at her mother's side, and since graduating from college, she'd been her father's assistant. Whether he wanted an errand run or a report updated, she was there, silently standing by to do his bidding.

But without her mother to lead the way or her father to issue commands, Etta had been forced to make her own way. She'd gladly return to the life of the quiet accessory rather than face the next two weeks. That's all the time she had to find the thief and figure out a way to stop him. What would Gabriel think about all this? It would be easier if she could talk to him, but there was no telling how much longer it would take him to complete his journey. If only she could talk with him beneath the stars again. She'd sit by his side, maybe even nestle her head on his shoulder, and listen as he told her everything that had happened while he'd been gone.

But instead of Gabriel, she had George Owens and William Clark. Not that there was anything wrong with those gentlemen. Any woman would be excited at the prospect of being courted by either one of them. She'd known George for several years, and William had grown up in Burnet. But did the amount of time spent with someone equal depth of feeling?

George Owens had always been a business acquaintance, one of many suited men who came and went in her father's sphere, and William Clark had always been a family friend who'd gone to law school, and then been appointed to the prosecutor's position.

If she had to choose between the two, William was the more attractive choice.

If only Gabriel would come home and make his intentions known. Etta imagined him striding into her father's study. He'd scowl at her other suitors and send them running, take her hand, and then lead her out of her father's house and into the future.

Such fanciful thinking! No one would ever suspect quiet, obedient Henrietta Davis of having such far-fetched dreams. It would be best if she kept her head out of the clouds and her imagination tightly reined.

After all, George and William were fine gentlemen with immaculate manners. They'd done the right thing, first talking to her and planning on speaking to her father. But what had Gabriel done? Nothing. If she waited for something that never came, she'd sacrifice a home and family of her own.

"Oh, Gabriel," Etta whispered to the empty conference room. "Come home and stake your claim on my heart. Otherwise, I'll be tempted to settle for second best. Come home, Gabriel. Come home."

10

Gabriel paced the wooden platform of the Brenham depot, waiting to board the train to LaGrange. His bag rested at this feet and his ticket sat securely in his jacket's breast pocket. Everything was ready for the trip. Everything except him.

Pain throbbed through his neck and shoulders as though he'd been carrying a heavy weight for too long and his queasy stomach rejected all thoughts of food. Ever since he'd walked back to the Brenham train station, his midsection had jumped like basket full of nervous crickets.

What was wrong with him? He'd almost grown accustomed to insomnia and the constant irritation that burrowed beneath his skin, but this sensation was different. He wasn't ill; every other part of his body felt normal. But either a small animal was fighting to free itself from his belly, or something was wrong.

Could he be homesick? He hadn't longed for home since his first weeks away at college. Even Army life hadn't engendered more than a passing yearning to see his parents. But he was sick of grimy depots and crowded trains. The thought of another trip with nothing to do except read outdated copies of magazines or relive his disastrous battle experiences held no attraction. A few of his mother's home-cooked meals would go a long way. Not to mention he could drop in on Etta.

Would Etta's face light up when she saw him, or would his unexpected arrival be just another event in her busy day? He could always use her father's horses as an excuse to visit, but did he need an excuse? Before he'd left, they were becoming good friends, and if he ever managed to restore his battered soul, he'd like to make her more than a friend.

Serenity and joy lived side-by-side in Etta's soul. Although he'd known her all his life, he'd only recently discovered how amazing she was. When she'd prayed for him, his heart had lifted, as if sensing hope for the first time, and when he'd cried, she'd kissed his tears away. What would it take to win her love?

He'd been so sure about visiting the families of the men in his squad. He'd been wrong about that, too. But how could he forgive himself?

Gabriel made his way back to the ticket office. He'd have to wait until the next morning for a train to Burnet, but he didn't mind. He had some powerful thinking and praying to do before he headed back to Etta.

⚘

Nora squealed with delight and drew Etta into a warm embrace. "I'm so glad you've come for a visit! It's been much too long."

Etta's blonde, blue-eyed cousin smelled of bacon and baby powder. The bun on the back of her head was askew and several stray curls floated about her flushed face. The flowered apron tied around her tan housedress did little to hide the evidence of her pregnancy.

As a girl, Etta had often confessed the sin of envy

during her daily prayers. Although she'd never meant her cousin any harm, Nora's popularity had left Etta feeling as unwanted as an old shoe. Nora had been blessed with good looks and a naturally happy disposition, a combination that drew admirers and suitors. At parties, it had always been Nora in the center of the crowd while Etta sat quietly on the sidelines. Now in her mid-thirties, Nora's beauty had softened, but her innate cheerfulness radiated like fireflies on a summer evening.

A small hand pushed against Etta's thigh and a child's body squeezed between her and Nora. "Momma!"

Nora laughed softly and squatted to speak to her son. "What is it, Nate?"

"Nen wants you."

"She does? Did she tell you that?"

The three-year-old nodded solemnly and then looked up at Etta with wide blue eyes.

"Do you remember Cousin Etta?" Nora asked.

The boy shook his head and stepped behind his mother's skirts.

Nora stood and winked at Etta. "It seems as though Nathan Jr. has developed a sudden case of shyness."

Etta's heart softened in sympathy. She knew quite a bit about the price of shyness. "That's perfectly all right. But when he's up to it, I have a toy for him."

One blue eye peeked out from behind Nora. "Nen's just a baby. She doesn't play with toys."

Etta withdrew a tin truck from her bag and held it out to Nathan. "Oh, this toy isn't for a baby like Ellen. It's for a big boy like you."

Nora touched her son's head. "What do you say,

Nate?"

The boy snatched the toy from Etta's hand and ran up the stairs. "Thank you," he shouted across his shoulder.

Nora laughed and stretched her arm across Etta's shoulders. "It was kind of you to bring him something, Etta, but it wasn't necessary. I love it when you visit."

Etta stepped over building blocks and tin soldiers as she followed her cousin through the parlor and toward the kitchen. "What's the fun of visiting if I'm not allowed to spoil your children?"

"Spoil them too much and I'll send them to live with you. Then you'll be sorry." Nora walked into the kitchen and went straight to her daughter. Ellen had slid into a near supine position in her high chair but that hadn't stopped her from munching contentedly on a small slice of toast. "What happened, baby girl? Too much butter?"

The kitchen table was crowded with newspapers and dirty dishes. Etta sat in an empty chair next to the child and removed the beribboned straw boater that matched her green serge skirt. "How old is Ellen now?"

"Almost two," Nora answered as she righted the baby. "Her birthday is in a few months."

A wave of longing surged through Etta's heart as she stroked the little girl's downy head. If she allowed George's or William's pursuit to reach its logical conclusion, she could have her own child someday. "And the new one? Any idea when I'll have a new baby cousin to spoil?"

"Not until August, thank you very much. I'm doing my best to get Ellen out of diapers before the new one arrives, but so far I'm not having much luck."

Nora poured coffee into two cups and set them on the table. "Now," she said as she took her seat, "tell me how Uncle Henry's doing."

"Better," Etta said as she stirred sugar into her coffee. "He's taking his meals at the table, and he's able to walk short distances with a cane. But he's still having a hard time speaking, and he has limited movement in one arm."

"I'm so glad he's feeling better," Nora said. "I should have come to help you, but..." Nora's hand went to her abdomen and her gaze landed on the baby.

Etta rushed to reassure her. "It's all right. You've got more than enough to keep you busy here. Besides, you'll make it up to me when you act as my chaperone tonight."

Nora's mouth curved into a sly grin. "Tell me everything! Why don't you want to be alone with this gentleman? What's his name again?"

"George Owens. He's an accountant with the Worthington Firm here in Austin."

"What's wrong with him?"

"Nothing," Etta answered quickly in a high-pitched voice. But upon seeing Nora's look of incredulity, her shoulders sagged and her voice took on a despondent tone. "Everything."

Nora rested her cheek in the palm of her hand. "Oh, my! Now you really do have to tell me everything."

Etta took a long drink of coffee in order to delay her response. "Have you ever met someone who made your skin crawl?"

Nora rolled her eyes. "No wonder you don't like him."

"But I can't explain why. He's not bad looking,

he's got a good job. He's never stepped over the lines of propriety…"

"But you don't like him."

Etta sank back into her chair. "It's no wonder I'm an old maid. A perfectly fine gentleman shows an interest in me, and I turn up my nose."

"You're far from being an old maid, Etta. This is a new century and women are no longer required to be married. Everyone says we'll have the vote next year. Don't tell me times aren't changing."

"Maybe but I'm not changing with them. Ever since Papa's illness, I've been taking over his duties at the bank. I may know a lot about banking, but I wasn't raised to fight in a man's world."

Nora frowned over her cup. "Who have you been fighting?"

Etta tilted her head from one side to the other. "Not fighting exactly. It's more like…like standing up for myself."

"Sounds to me as if you've been busy. Who's been challenging you?"

"Carl."

"Aunt Catherine's brother?" Nora's shock was obvious. "I've only met him a few times, but he seemed harmless."

Etta raised one shoulder in a half-hearted shrug. "Uncle Carl doesn't think I should be doing Papa's work."

"Don't tell me *he* wants the job."

Etta nodded. "Sometimes I think I should just give in and stay home with Papa. I couldn't even refuse George Owens's invitation to the pictures."

"Some men can be mighty persuasive, but you'll have to learn to say no if you don't want his attentions."

"But how does one say no without being cruel? I don't want to hurt him."

"Let's practice." Nora pulled a strand of loose hair across her upper lip and deepened her voice. "Etta, my dear, would you like to spend the evening with me?"

This was why Nora had always been so popular. She could cheer up Medusa. "Who are you supposed to be?" Etta asked with a grin.

"Mr. Not-right-for-you. Now, as I was saying, would you like to spend the evening with me?"

"No, thank you."

Nora perched her fist on her hip and leaned back in feigned shock. "How can you turn me down? I make a thousand dollars a year!"

"I'm sure there's another woman who would make a better match for you than I."

"But none as lovely as you!" Nora patted Etta's hand the way one would pat a child's head. "Come now, my dear, you simply must allow me to escort you to the dance."

"No, thank you."

"What? Why, any woman in her right mind would jump at the chance to be seen on my arm. I'll call for you at seven."

"I don't wish to go with you, Mr. Not-right-for-me."

Nora harrumphed with indignation. "Well, I never!"

Etta dissolved into laughter, and Nora brushed her hair away from her face. "You didn't seem to have a problem saying no that time," she said in her normal voice.

"Maybe you can help me practice tonight."

"Fine with me." Nora stood, removed Ellen from the high chair, and perched the baby on her hip. "I hope your gentleman takes us to see the new Harold Lloyd picture. I think he's funnier than Chaplin."

If Etta had her way, George would cancel his plans, and she and Nora would go to the pictures alone. "Is your mother coming to sit with the children while we go out?"

"No. She and Dad went to Oklahoma City to see his sister. Nathan will watch them."

Etta didn't know Nora's husband well, but caring for small children was women's work. "Are you sure your husband won't mind?"

Nora cleaned her daughter's face with a damp cloth. "They're his children, too, Etta. He's capable of feeding them, cleaning them, and putting them to bed. Just because the railroad keeps him busy six days a week doesn't mean it's all fun and games around here. It will do him good to be reminded of just how much work I do."

Etta bit her bottom lip. She hadn't meant to kick the hornet's nest hidden in Nora's marriage.

The baby let out a squeal of laughter. Nora wiped the child's hands. "Do you want to go to the moving pictures, baby girl? Someday I'll take you and your brother."

Etta breathed a sigh of relief.

Nora's pique had evaporated as soon as she'd spoken to the baby. Nora stroked her daughter's blonde ringlets and kissed her. "Now let's go upstairs and see what Nate's up to. Then you can show me what you're planning to wear tonight."

Etta glanced at the dirty pots and pans piled on the counters. Was Nora going to simply leave the greasy mess? "You go on and I'll…"

Nora stopped in the doorway and glanced over her shoulder. "You'll what?"

Time spent with children was obviously more important to Nora than a spotless kitchen. "Oh, never mind." Etta carried her cup to the sink. When Nora got around to cleaning, then Etta would lend a hand. "I brought a new dress for Ellen. I hope you like it."

"There you go again," Nora said as she carried the baby up the stairs. "Spoiling must come second-nature to you."

❧

It was neither Buster Keaton nor Charlie Chaplin showing at The Majestic Theater that night. Instead, Etta sat between Nora and George and watched a melodramatic retelling of a young girl who pined for the man who'd gone off to fight in the Great War.

Nora was thoroughly entranced by the moving picture, never once moving her gaze from the screen even when Etta nudged her foot to get her attention. Nora was supposed to be acting as chaperone, and no chaperone worth her salt would allow George to put his arm around Etta's shoulders and pull her close.

To his credit, George didn't objected to Etta's cousin accompanying them. He played the role of a gentleman until the theater lights dimmed. Then, when Nora no longer kept her gaze on him, he kissed Etta's cheek and whispered, "I can't wait until your family trusts me enough to let you out without a chaperone."

Etta successfully fought the urge to wipe her cheek but succumbed to an uncontrollable sneezing fit brought about by George's cologne. After three sneezes in a row, she pushed him back and wiped her nose with the linen handkerchief she always carried. "Thank you for understanding about Nora. I suppose it seems a bit old-fashioned."

"Can't blame your father for wanting to protect his daughter. Besides, I'm a patient man. I'll earn your father's confidence soon enough."

The piano player sounded an attention-getting flourish, and the picture began.

George slid his right arm across her shoulders, pulled her close, and joined his hand with hers.

Etta kept the handkerchief close at hand but was spared any further sneezing. She worked her way out of George's proprietary hold and tried to focus on the screen.

An overly expressive young actress with impractical long, dark hair yearned for the man who'd gone to war. Despite the star's exaggerated portrayal, Etta understood the emotions. She may not have pined for Gabriel while he'd been in the Army, but now her heart ached for him. How much longer until he came home? Would he be glad to see her, or would they be strangers? So much had been left unsaid.

If Etta's secret dreams came true, Gabriel would return fully healed and happy. He'd pull her into his arms, confess his undying love, and they'd walk hand in hand toward their future. Etta tingled from want of her first kiss. So many times she'd secretly watched Gabriel as he talked or cared for the horses. His mouth was full and strong, and the thought of his lips on hers filled her stomach with butterflies.

Etta shook her head to erase the images. She was a practical-headed businesswoman with an embezzler to find. Girlish dreams of love and happily ever after had no place in her world.

Nora sniffled and reached for Etta's handkerchief. "These sad stories do it to me every time," she whispered, wiping away her tears.

Etta shifted her concentration to the story unfolding on the screen. One of the young men had died in battle. His sweetheart collapsed when she heard the news. Did Gabriel have to deal with those kinds of reactions when he visited the families of his fallen comrades?

For the hundredth time, Etta wished she'd asked Gabriel to write or telephone before he'd left. If only she could be sure he was all right. If only...

With a sigh of resignation, Etta's shoulders slumped along with her mood. The reality of Gabriel returning to Burnet with the intention of marrying her was unlikely. She'd be better off if she simply allowed one of her new suitors to court her. She could probably persuade George to lessen his cologne usage, and given enough time, she might even be able to overcome her resistance to him.

And there was always William Clark. His family had been friends with hers for many years, and his devotion to his mother proved what a good and loyal person he was. William never attended a social function without his mother. Mrs. Clark would probably even accompany them on their honeymoon.

Etta stifled a laugh as she visualized her wedding photograph. She'd stand on one side of William and his mother would stand on the other.

George must have mistaken her reaction for tears because he patted her hand and murmured, "There, there. It's almost over, and I'm betting there will be a happy ending."

Etta turned her face away from his. How long until this evening was over? George had already mentioned a visit to the ice cream parlor after the picture. Then there'd be the ride home and the awkward goodnights.

At last the on-screen sweethearts were reunited and the houselights came on.

Nora exhaled noisily and dabbed her moist eyes. "Wasn't that wonderful? Oh, Mr. Owens, I can't thank you enough for this wonderful treat. I do so love the pictures. Wasn't it a lovely, touching story, Etta?"

Since she couldn't have summarized the plot if her life depended on it, Etta evaded the question. "I'm glad you enjoyed it. The actress was beautiful."

"She can't hold a candle to you," George said with a wink, "nor to your cousin."

Nora reached across Etta and playfully slapped George's forearm. "How you go on. Will you two please excuse me? I must visit the powder room."

George answered before Etta could voice her desire to accompany Nora. "You go right ahead. Henrietta and I will get the automobile and pick you up at the front entrance."

With a nod of agreement, Nora scurried up the aisle and disappeared into the noisy crowd.

"Now then," George said as he offered his hand to Etta, "are you ready for a cold, refreshing treat?"

Etta laid her palm in his and stood but dropped his hand as she smoothed her skirt and tucked her handbag beneath her arm. "If you don't mind, George, I think it would be best if Nora and I went home."

"Is your cousin unwell? Perhaps we could take her home, and then you and I could spend some time alone."

Etta tucked a strand of hair behind her ear, then realized her trembling hands were giving away her uneasiness. "No, it's not that, it's just...well..."

George slipped his arm through hers and led her up the aisle toward the exit. "Leave it to me, Henrietta. I know a thing or two about getting around chaperones." He led her into the cool night air and helped her into the front seat of his sedan. When they arrived at the theater's entrance, he sprang from his seat and hurried to open the rear door. As Nora approached, George smiled disarmingly. "Henrietta and I have a special favor to ask."

Nora's gaze moved to Etta. "What's on your mind?"

Etta slid from her seat and moved toward her cousin. "I told George it would be best if he took us home now."

"But," George interjected, "we thought perhaps you'd allow Henrietta to accompany me to the ice cream parlor alone."

Nora's eyebrows raised in question, but the look she gave Etta made it clear she was waiting for Etta to speak up.

Etta swallowed hard and turned toward George. "I'd like to thank you for taking Nora and me to the picture show. It was most kind of you. But now, I'd like to go home."

George narrowed his eyes. "Are you sure, Henrietta?"

"Yes, thank you."

He continued to study her as though waiting for her to change her mind.

Impatient drivers honked their horns and people waiting to buy tickets jostled both her and Nora.

Wouldn't it be easier if she just acquiesced to George's wishes? Perhaps Austin's Congress Avenue on Saturday evening wasn't the time or place to make one's stand.

"Then home it is," George answered.

Etta let out a huge breath as she squeezed into the back seat with Nora.

George resumed his seat behind the steering wheel.

Nora nudged Etta in the ribs. "Round one, Henrietta Davis," she whispered.

Etta clutched her pocketbook tightly in her lap. Round one was only the beginning of the fight.

Upon arrival at Nora's house, George's gentlemanly manners were still on display. He helped Nora and Etta alight from the car and escorted the ladies to the front door. "Thank you, again, Mr. Owens," Nora said, shaking George's hand.

"The pleasure was all mine," he replied.

Nora looked pointedly at Etta. "Ten minutes," she said in her most authoritative tone. "After that, my husband will be out to check on you."

"No need to worry," George said. "Miss Davis will be as safe as a baby in her mother's lap."

Etta's jaws clenched as she imagined herself sitting in George's lap. With one last meaningful glance over her shoulder, Nora entered her house.

George withdrew a watch from his vest pocket. "Ten minutes, eh? Not much time to say goodnight." He placed his hands on Etta's arms. "Would you like to go for a drive in the country tomorrow afternoon?"

"George, I…"

"Yes, Henrietta? What is it?"

"I…uh…" She took a fortifying breath. "George, I

think it would be better if I...if we..."

George chuckled softly and stepped closer. "My, oh my. I'm not sure what you've got on your mind, but it certainly is making you nervous. Don't worry. Your nerves will go away after we've spent more time together."

"No. I...I don't think that would be a good idea."

"Don't be silly, Henrietta. How else will you ever get to know me? Unless, of course, you think you know me well enough already. Is your father able to receive visitors yet? I can come to Burnet later this week."

"No. Oh, George. What I'm trying to say is—"

"You'll need to meet my family, of course. Mother will take to you right away. She's been hinting that it's time for me to settle down and give her some grandchildren."

One evening together and George was already planning a family?

Etta had to put a stop to this before her reticence led straight to the altar.

George removed his hat and brushed her cheek with his lips. "Goodnight, Henrietta. I'll call on you tomorrow after church."

He opened the front door and waited for Etta to enter.

If she went inside now, she'd have to admit her failure to Nora. Worse than that, she'd have to live with her inability to stand up for herself. Etta closed the door, took another deep breath, and faced George. "Your attentions are most flattering, Mr. Owens, but they are misdirected. I do not feel the same way about you as you feel about me."

George smiled at her as though he were dealing

with a quarrelsome child. "Nonsense, Henrietta. You and I will make a powerful couple in the world of finance. Someday, you'll inherit Davis Bank and Trust, and I'll be at your side. I know your family's bank is small now, but together we could make it one of the leading financial institutions in the state." George had it all worked out. As the bank's auditor, he knew everything about the bank's assets.

"I didn't want to bring this up in front of your cousin," George continued, "but I wanted to ask where the embezzlement case stands. You need someone to advise you, Henrietta. Since your father's not able to look after your best interests, I'd be the best man for the job."

But ethics dictated that he recuse himself from the investigation. If Etta allowed him to wade deeper into the matter, she may find that she was the one in over her head.

George placed two fingers under her chin and tipped her head up. "Besides, my dear, we're going to spend the rest of our lives together. As your husband, I'll be able to control the bank's day-to-day business as well as lead it into the twentieth century." He stepped so close, she could feel his breath on her cheek. "Women have no place in the world of high finance."

Indignation fused steel into Etta's spine. She placed her palms on George's chest and pushed him back a step. "No, George. No, no, no. I'm not interested in the future you just described, and I'm not interested in you. I don't want to go for a ride in the country tomorrow afternoon, and I don't want to meet your mother. Thank you for the evening out, but this is the end to anything other than our business relationship." Etta opened Nora's front door, stepped over the threshold, and turned back toward George.

His mouth hung open in obvious astonishment.

"Goodnight, Mr. Owens," she said before closing the door.

No sooner had the door clicked shut than Nora grabbed Etta around the waist and pulled her toward the parlor. "Oh my goodness! I could hardly believe my ears. You told him!"

Etta covered her mouth with her hand. "I was unforgivably rude, wasn't I?"

"Are you joking? If you ask me, George Owens needed a swift kick in the pants!"

"You don't think I injured his pride?"

"What if you did? Isn't it obvious that George is more interested in the bank than in you?"

Etta rubbed her forehead. "I didn't realize that before tonight."

"Uh-huh. He showed his cards too early, but thank goodness, he did. No wonder he made your skin crawl. I think your guardian angel was trying to warn you."

Etta's hands trembled as she removed her hat and set it and her handbag on the divan. "I suppose my guardian angel can take a break now. Surely George got the message."

Nora slipped her arm through Etta's and escorted her upstairs. "Western Union couldn't have been clearer."

11

Ethan Benson opened the screen door at the back of his house and called, "Sara! Come and see what I found in town."

Sara didn't move from the kitchen counter. "I'm elbow-deep in flour. What is it?"

"It's not a what, it's a who."

Sara turned her head and let out a squeal of delight. "Gabriel!" She held out her arms, and Gabriel stepped into her embrace. "'Bout time you came back!"

Gabriel buried his nose in her hair. "You smell like cinnamon."

"I'm making apple crumble for tonight's prayer meeting."

"Do I have to wait until tonight to get a bite?"

Sara laid her hands alongside her son's face. "Of course not. I just finished baking an extra one for us. Now sit down and visit while I get this one in the oven."

"Don't forget about me," his father said. "Gabriel's not the only one around here who appreciates your cooking."

Sara kissed her husband's cheek. "Nothing I like better than having my two men at the kitchen table. The Nielsen boy brought fresh milk this morning. Will you pour us a glass?"

"Now you're talking," Gabriel's father said, moving toward the ice box.

After sliding the dish into the gas oven, Sara cleaned her hands and touched Gabriel's chin. "I got some flour on you. Hold still while I clean you off."

While she brushed his bristled cheeks with a dish towel, Gabriel looked into her kind eyes. His heart shuddered at the realization that he'd someday lose her just as Etta had lost her mother. Like everything in his life, he'd taken his mother's steadfast presence for granted.

Sara pulled his head down so she could kiss his forehead. "How are you, son?"

"Fine, Mom. I'm awfully tired of trains, but other than that...catch me up on what's been happening around here."

Sara narrowed her eyes and studied him. "Sounds to me like maybe you've found a cure for your itchy feet. Think you'll stay home for a while?"

Gabriel's desire for adventure had led to disaster. Besides, everyone he cared for was less than a mile away from his mother's kitchen table. "No more itchy feet, Mom. If I can find a job, I'll be thankful to stay right here for the rest of my life."

"You ought to check out the new highway department in Austin," His father said. "I read in the paper they're handing out contracts left and right for updated roads and bridges and tunnels and who knows what else. Seems to me they could use a few engineers."

"You're the first person in the family to get a college education," Sara said with an affectionate squeeze to his shoulder. "It'd be a shame to let it go to waste."

Gabriel joined his father at the kitchen table. "Think the Highway Department would hire someone with no experience?"

His father poured cool milk into a tall glass and passed it to him. "You're a veteran. Your Army experience plus your degree should count for something."

"I hope you're right." Gabriel stretched out his long legs and leaned back in the chair. "I want to check on Mr. Davis's horses and take care of a few more things around here. Then I'll go to Austin and see what's what. How's Etta's father doing?"

Sara placed three bowls of the apple treat on the table and sat across from Gabriel. "Henry's made remarkable progress. I went by the house yesterday to deliver eggs, and there he was, sitting in the courtyard as though nothing had ever happened."

"But he still can't talk," Gabriel's father said. "Whenever he tries, it just sounds like gibberish."

From what Gabriel had seen in the aid stations and hospital in France, Henry Davis was one of the lucky ones. "Is Etta still working at the bank?"

"Sure," his mother said. "Despite what some people say, there's no one better for the job than she."

Had Etta's problems at the bank worsened in the time he'd been gone? "What does that mean? What are people saying?"

"Do you remember her uncle?"

Gabriel nodded.

"Etta told me Carl is trying to convince the Board of Directors to name him as the bank president."

The dessert Gabriel had been enjoying suddenly felt like a lump of clay in his throat. "He'd push Etta out?"

"In a second." Sara snapped her fingers to emphasize the point. "I've been saying some mighty fervent prayers for Etta lately. She's got quite a fight on her hands."

Etta was probably overwhelmed by all she had to deal with. "I think I'll go over to the Davis place after I shave and get cleaned up."

"That's a good idea," his mother said, "but Etta went to Austin to visit her cousin. I'm not sure when she's due back."

Gabriel carried his empty bowl and spoon to the sink. If he went to the Davis house on the pretext of checking on the Arabians, he might be able to find out when Etta would return. Every cell in his body yearned to be with her. Without Etta by his side, he felt like a ghost ship, floating without direction from one vague compass point to another.

❧

Etta did her best to avoid the numerous holes on the two-lane road from Austin to Burnet. She enjoyed driving her father's car and was glad her mother had insisted she learn, although a woman driving alone was frowned upon by polite society. There was talk about requiring motorists to receive some type of mandatory license as they had in other states, but the general consensus in Texas was that there was still more open space than drivers.

Spring had arrived in all its bounty. The fields burgeoned with pink evening primrose and orange Indian paintbrush. And the bluebonnets, of course. Like a child counting the days until Christmas, her mother had eagerly watched for the bluebonnets each spring.

"More beautiful than Solomon is all his glory," her

mother had often remarked. Etta smiled at the memory. Every day brought some new reminder of her mother, but the sharp pain of loss had eased. She'd been blessed with a loving mother, and staggering under the weight of grief would dishonor that love. Her mother had raised her to be both strong and tender. Etta could do that. She could find the strength to discover who was embezzling funds from the bank.

She still held a slim hope that Carl wasn't stealing from the bank, but if the evidence pointed to him, she'd follow through.

Catherine Davis would have been ashamed to know her brother had committed such an insidious crime, but even she would have done whatever was necessary to stop him.

Starting tomorrow, Etta would drive out to the farms and ranches of clients whose accounts showed a discrepancy. If she spoke with candor and assured the borrowers that their loans were not in arrears, perhaps they could tell her who had intercepted their payments.

Just a few months ago, Etta would never have undertaken such an investigation. She would have gladly waited on the sidelines while her father or William Clark looked into the problem. But now it was up to her to take care of business. She hadn't let George Owens coerce her into marriage, and she wouldn't let anyone exploit her inexperience.

Now that George understood Etta wasn't interested in marriage, or in letting him take over the bank, the question of William Clark loomed on the horizon. William was pleasant looking, an upright citizen, and well-employed. There'd been some talk during previous board meetings about William running for political office in the future, and he'd undoubtedly be good in that type of work. But did Etta really want to marry William? Did she want to have a family with him?

Etta shook her head as her heart told her the answer. If she'd never known Gabriel, she probably would have accepted William's proposal with gratitude. But she'd come to care for Gabriel in a way that surpassed mere friendship.

Etta had tried in vain to curb dreams of Gabriel's lips on hers and of his arms pulling her tightly against him. How impractical love was. William had made his intentions clear, but Etta couldn't pledge herself to him. Gabriel, on the other hand, hadn't made any promises, but she was ready to abandon caution and follow him into the future.

But if she didn't accept William's offer and Gabriel didn't return her affection, would she be sentencing herself to spinsterhood? There were worse things. Very few married women worked. Even Carolina Swanson, who was very good at her job and one of their most reliable employees, had looked for work only after becoming a widow.

Etta's work at the bank was interesting and important, and she wouldn't want to sacrifice it for a husband and children. But, as everyone said these days, times were changing. With women's suffrage and prohibition on the horizon, families were bound to change. Maybe a working wife and mother wouldn't be the outrage it had once been.

As Etta turned onto the road that led to her home, one of her mother's oft-quoted Bible verses came to mind. "Don't worry about tomorrow, for tomorrow will worry about its own things." The words hadn't made sense before, but now she understood their meaning. First, she needed to solve the bank's problem. Her future would unfold the way it should, whether she worried about it or not.

༜

Prayer meetings at Gabriel's church were held once a month, and in addition to the benefits of quiet meditation and shared concerns, the fellowship following the service offered congregants a sense of community and shared burdens. Gabriel sat with a group of men, listening with only one ear and thinking about Etta.

"Did you read about Zapata?" Homer Chapman, a short, heavyset man near his father's age, asked.

"'Bout time somebody shot that son of a gun," Abe Schultz replied.

Gabriel's tepid coffee turned bitter in his mouth. Men who had never seen battle talked so casually of death. Emiliano Zapata had fought for the rights of the poor, but taking up arms had ultimately led to his own demise. Perhaps violence could be justified in some instances, but Gabriel would be happy to never fire a gun again.

He ambled to the nearby group where his mother and other ladies of the church stood in a tight circle. His earlier trip to the Davis's house had yielded few results. The housekeeper had told him Etta was expected back later that day, but she didn't know a time. Mr. Davis had waved to him from a shaded chair in the courtyard, but remembering his father's earlier assessment of Mr. Davis's speaking ability, Gabriel hadn't tried to engage him in conversation.

Normally, Gabriel would have avoided the cluster of women, but he knew they had an inclination to harmless gossip. If anyone knew the latest rumors about Etta, it would be one of his mother's acquaintances.

Mrs. Franklin held a sleeping toddler in her arms. "When are you moving to San Antonio, Eula?"

The recently widowed Mrs. Farrington answered. "As soon as the papers are signed and the bank business is finished."

"We're going to miss you," Mrs. Henderson said, "but I understand why you'd want to be closer to your daughter and grandchildren."

"Is Simon Ward still buying your land?" asked Mrs. Hoffman.

"That's right. If I don't take a cruise around the world, it should be enough to last me."

The women laughed softly at Mrs. Farrington's comment. Weren't these women ever going to say anything about Etta?

Mrs. Stoutman spoke next. "How many grandchildren do you have now, Eula?"

Oh, brother. Gabriel felt a familiar irritation burrowing under the skin at the back of his neck. He'd blow his top if he didn't get away from these ladies soon.

Mrs. Farrington's eyes lit up as she smiled. "Two girls and one boy. I've been sewing lots of new dresses. I can hardly wait to try them on the girls."

Sewing? If Gabriel didn't get their conversation on the right track, the ladies would be talking about recipes next. He leaned down and whispered into his mother's ear. She glanced at him with a puzzled gaze but nodded.

"Has anyone heard the latest about Henry and Etta?" Sara Benson asked.

Mrs. Farrington veered away from the subject of her grandchildren. "I have an appointment at the bank in two days. Simon Ward is going to take over the loan payments as part of the land deal. We have to sign some papers."

"You were lucky your neighbor wanted to buy your place," Mrs. Stoutman said. "Otherwise, you might have taken years to sell it. You know the Hoffpauir place was on the market..."

Gabriel clenched his teeth. He couldn't stand their chatter much longer.

His mother must have sensed something, because she guided the conversation back to where he wanted it. "Etta has done a fine job taking over for her father."

"To tell you the truth," Mrs. Henderson said, "I didn't think little Etta had it in her. Who knew that fancy college education of hers would prepare her to be a banker?"

"I'm not the least bit surprised," Sara said. "I'm sorry Henry is ill, but it did give Etta an opportunity to show everyone what she's made of."

Ida Clark sniffed and spoke for the first time. "I'd be happier if Etta had stayed in her father's shadow."

Sara frowned at the older lady. "Why, Ida. What does that mean?"

Mrs. Clark blushed and cast her gaze to the floor. "I don't mean to be unkind. I know Etta has always been a good girl, and we all simply adored Catherine." The women nodded in assent. "But you all know how I rely upon William."

What did William Clark have to do with Etta? Gabriel nudged his mother's shoulder.

"Your son is devoted to you," Sara said. "What concerns you?"

"Well…" Mrs. Clark glanced around the circle of women as though checking for spies. "…William told me he'd spoken to Etta about marriage."

The women gasped in unison.

Gabriel's heart skipped several beats.

Mrs. Henrichson was the first person to find her voice. "You don't say!"

Mrs. Clark touched the corner of her eye with a lacy white handkerchief. "I'm afraid so."

Mrs. Franklin patted the back of her sleeping child. "Etta will make William a fine wife. After all, she comes from one of the best families in the county."

"Surely you must have been expecting this," said Mrs. Henderson. "You didn't expect your son to stay single for his whole life, did you?"

Mrs. Clark sniffed into her handkerchief. "Ever since my husband died when William was a boy, my son has been devoted to me. But a wife can have a mighty strong influence on a man. Without my boy to take care of me, what will happen to me?"

Mrs. Henrichson clucked her tongue. "You're worrying about something that might not even happen. Henrietta has done right by her father, hasn't she? If the time comes, I'm sure she'll do right by you, too."

Ida Clark flattened her lips into a rigid line. "William plans to speak to Henry Davis just as soon as he's able to receive visitors. Once my son makes up his mind about something, there's little chance of dissuading him."

Gabriel couldn't listen to one more word. He turned away from the women and strode out of the building. Of all the betrayals! He'd shared things with Etta that he'd told no one else. Surely, she knew what she meant to him. Why hadn't she honored their understanding?

He kicked the hard ground and fisted his hands. If Etta wanted William Clark, she was welcome to him. Gabriel's stomach roiled at the thought of William touching her. Who was he kidding? He loved Etta. He'd been fighting to repair his broken parts so that he could propose marriage. But William Clark had beaten him to it.

William Clark, Attorney-at-Law. Who never went to war. Who had a nice, cushy office job. Of course, Etta would prefer William over him.

Gabriel cursed under his breath and stomped away from the church. The night sky stretched above him just as it did every night, but this time Gabriel could have sworn the stars were laughing at him.

12

The next morning, Etta refilled her father's cup with black coffee but refrained from doing more for him. Charlie Simpson had cautioned that her eagerness to help her father would only inhibit his progress toward independence. She averted her gaze as her father labored to spoon sugar into his cup without spilling it on the table.

Rosa set another biscuit on Charlie's plate. Although she couldn't be sure, Etta thought she detected a special warmness in the smile Rosa gave him.

"Did Benito talk to you this morning?" Rosa asked as she passed behind Etta's chair.

"Yes. He left Mira in the stable because he wants me to look at her hoof." Noting the concerned expression on her father's face, Etta hurried to explain. "Benito thinks an abscess might be forming. Don't worry. I'll take care of it."

Henry nodded and slowly raised the cup to his mouth. His hand still trembled, but the coffee stayed in the cup.

"In fact," Etta said as she ate the last bite of eggs, "I think I'll do that right now. I have some clients to call on this morning before I go in to the bank, and I'll stop by the vet's office while I'm out."

Etta kissed her father's freshly-shaven cheek and carried her dish to the sink. The early morning sun glistened on dew-covered wildflowers as she walked from the house to the stables. She stopped to take a deep breath of spring air and to thank the Lord for her father's recovery. If her father kept improving at this rate, she'd soon see him riding. That would be a day to rejoice. Nothing buoyed her father's spirits as much as working with his horses.

Cats danced around Etta's feet as she neared the stable. "Nothing today," she said, squatting to pet the playful animals. "I'll bring you something later." She'd have some explaining to do when her father returned to the stable. He wouldn't like it that she'd been coddling the kittens.

Antares and three mares browsed placidly in the pasture as she entered the stable. Upon hearing her footsteps, Mira nickered a greeting from her stall.

"Good morning to you, too," Etta said. "I hear you may have a sore foot."

She hastened to the stall with light steps. But her heart stopped as quickly as her feet when she saw Gabriel standing next to Mira.

"Gabriel!" She rushed toward him, delight coursing through her veins at the sight of him. "When did you get back?"

Gabriel turned his back to her and stepped behind the mare. "Good morning, Etta. How are you?"

Etta's excitement froze in her throat. "What?"

"I thought I'd come by and check on your horses. It looks as though Benito's been doing a fine job." Gabriel squatted and lifted Mira's hind leg. "I agree with him about the hoof. Would you like me to call the vet?"

Etta's throat ached from the emotion she fought to keep at bay. She'd dreamed of running into Gabriel's arms, but he obviously wasn't as glad to see her as she was to see him. "Is something wrong? Why didn't you let me know you were back?"

"Everything's fine, Etta. Except Mira's hoof. I'll call Doc Scott and see when he can get by here."

Why was Gabriel being so cold? What had happened to change him?

Etta searched his face for the man she'd fallen in love with. The same light blue eyes glanced at her, but now they were shuttered. He appeared to be freshly-shaven, so it wasn't stubble that darkened his expression. Etta clasped her hands behind her back and stood near the stall door.

Gabriel remained in the corner of the stall, as though using the horse's body as a shield.

Mira flicked her ears and shifted her weight from one side to another, perhaps sensing the uneasiness between the two humans she normally trusted.

Etta blinked away traitorous tears. "Is that all you have to say to me, Gabriel?"

He rested his hands on Mira's back and glared at Etta. "What else is there to say?"

Etta turned her face away and gazed at the open stable door. Why was she subjecting herself to such treatment? She'd done nothing except pine for Gabriel the whole time he'd been gone. How silly she'd been to dream about his return.

"I'm glad you're home." Etta winced to hear her voice quiver. She swallowed and tried again. "I hope your trip was a success." She stepped out of the stall and walked toward the stable door. Tears flowed down her cheeks, but she was determined not to let Gabriel see her distress. How could she have been so wrong about him?

Well, fine. If that's the way he wanted it, she wouldn't force herself on him. Besides, she had no time for romance. She had a bank to save, and the less she thought about Gabriel Benson, the better.

Gabriel pounded the stable wall as he watched Etta march back toward the house. He hadn't planned on seeing her until he'd grown accustomed to the idea of her marrying someone else. Although, if he were truthful, that could take decades.

Then she'd stepped into the stable, radiating the peaceful joy that was as much a part of her as her hair and skin, and anger had risen up his spine and landed on his tongue. He shouldn't have spoken to her so brusquely, but it had taken every ounce of self-control to not take her in his arms and convince her to marry him instead of William Clark.

What right did he have to speak to her of marriage? William was a professional man with a secure future, and Gabriel had little to offer. He had no job, no home of his own. He didn't even have an automobile. William Clark wasn't haunted by the war. He probably slept through the night and dreamed of spring meadows and lollipops.

Gabriel slammed the stall door but immediately regretted it when Mira squealed and bolted away from him. He sank to the ground and rested his back against the wall. He'd lost so much since that one day in France, and now it looked as though he would lose his future, too.

Cora Beck was hanging wet overalls on the line when Etta drove up to the ranch house. Cora wore a faded floral housedress and a man's battered hat.

Etta removed her Breton-styled hat and matching gloves before exiting the car. She'd considered wearing her riding clothes in order to visit the farmers and ranchers whose accounts were overdue, but since she was coming on bank business, she wore a camel-colored light wool skirt with matching jacket.

Cora raised a hand in greeting and ambled toward the dusty drive. "Morning, Miss Davis. What brings you all the way out here?"

Etta returned Cora's warm smile and removed her jacket. "Good morning. I'm calling on clients today to see how they're doing. Is Kurt or his father around?"

"Not right now, but they'll be heading in for lunch soon. Come on in, and I'll pour us some lemonade."

"That sounds wonderful. Thank you."

Etta followed Cora onto the back porch of the rambling frame house and into the kitchen.

A cardboard box of folded baby clothes sat on top of the round table.

"Sorry about the mess," Cora said as she moved the box to the floor. "I was getting some things together for our neighbor. Their baby's due any day now."

The sight of the baby clothes pricked Etta's tender heart. Cora's baby had been born too early and had died after only a few days of life, its tiny body unable to thrive. "It's generous of you to share."

Cora fingered the crocheted lace on a tiny yellow sweater. "Oh, they're just a loan. I'll get 'em back when I need 'em."

Etta wanted to comfort the young woman, but she barely knew Cora. The Beck family had been clients of the bank for many years, but Cora had married Kurt Beck while he'd been working on an uncle's ranch in Oklahoma. Etta lightly touched Cora's shoulder. "I was sorry to hear of your loss."

Cora walked to the window and gestured with her head. "We had a nice service for our little Melanie. She's right up there in the family plot, looking down on us." She glanced at Etta, smiled quickly, and returned her gaze to the window. "I know she's not really there, but it's a comfort to know she's still close. Kurt and me will have more children. I'm sure of it."

Life in rural Texas was so hard. Water was the only antidote to the summer heat, and rain could be as scarce as diamonds.

"I admire your positive outlook," Etta said. "I'm not sure I would do as well if I were in your situation."

Two men rode up to the house, their pinto horses kicking up plumes of dust.

"Here's Kurt and his pa now," Cora said. "I need to get lunch on the table."

Both men stopped outside the back door and used a wooden boot jack to pry off their dirty boots. Oscar Beck entered first, followed closely by his son. "Hey there, Miss Davis. I wondered whose car that was. What brings you out today?"

Etta offered her hand to Oscar.

Like most of the area ranchers, Oscar was deeply tanned. In keeping with the spring warmth, he wore a long-sleeved white cotton work shirt and khaki pants.

"I wanted a chance to talk to you about a few things, but don't let me interrupt your lunch. I can come back another time."

Oscar removed his broad-brimmed straw hat and hung it from a nail by the back door. "Nonsense. Just tuck in and share what we've got. As long as you don't mind plain eating."

The salt of the earth. That's how Etta's mother had described these hardworking people. They persevered through droughts and erratic cattle markets to make a living doing what they loved. "I'd love to stay for lunch. It sure smells good."

Kurt Beck removed his hat and shook Etta's hand. "Nice to see you, Miss Davis. What brings you all the way out here?"

"I'm visiting some of the bank's clients today. But don't worry. It's not bad news."

Kurt smiled broadly, his teeth whiter than normal due to his sun-darkened skin. "That's a load off my mind. We don't need any bad news." He nodded to Etta and walked to the stove where Cora dished out a fragrant meal. Kurt laid a gentle hand on Cora's shoulder and kissed her cheek.

She turned and smiled up at her husband, an everyday intimacy that stung Etta's heart. It was precisely that kind of loving touch that Etta had dreamed about sharing with Gabriel. Etta tried to picture William coming home after work, tired from a day in the office. Would he greet her with a kiss and a loving touch? She couldn't picture it.

Cora carried a large crockery bowl to the table. "Just cornbread, butter beans, and a chunk of ham," she said, setting the food on the oil-cloth covered table.

"Do we still have buttermilk?" Oscar asked.

"Sit down," Cora answered. "I'll get some."

Once they were all seated, Oscar clasped his hands and bowed his head. "Thank You, Lord for this, Your bounty, and thank You for our health. Please look over little Melanie and let her know how much we love her. Amen."

Kurt squeezed Cora's hand. Cora rested her head on his shoulder for a few seconds and then reached for the plate of cornbread. "Help yourself, Miss Davis."

Etta took a square of the golden cornbread. "I wish you'd call me Etta. I'm not that much older than you."

Cora smiled tentatively and passed the plate to her father-in-law.

Oscar slathered butter on a large slice of cornbread. "Now then, Miss Davis, what is it that brings you way out here to our place? I know I'm not behind in my loan payments."

"You're right, Mr. Beck. Your loan payments are up-to-date. But I wanted to ask if anyone from the bank has been out to collect from you."

"Just your uncle," Oscar said around a mouthful of food.

Etta's heart sank. She'd wanted to be wrong. "Carl Stanley?"

"That's the one. He first came out about, what, last September?" Oscar looked to his son for confirmation.

"That sounds right," Kurt said. "He came by and said the bank was instituting a new service. Said that since it was difficult for farmers and ranchers to get into town, someone from the bank would be coming to pick up monthly payments."

"Did anyone other than Carl receive payments?"

Oscar looked up from his plate and scowled at Etta. "Don't tell me you don't know."

Etta gazed back at the rancher, her silence implying her answer.

Oscar's fork clambered on his plate as he sat back

in his chair. "Miss Davis, are you telling me someone stole our money?"

"Did you get a receipt for the payment?"

Oscar looked at his daughter-in-law. "Cora, you handed over most of the payment envelopes. Please tell me you got a receipt."

Cora nodded vigorously. "I did just what you told me. I got the receipt and put it in the brown envelope behind the clock on your desk."

Etta wished she didn't have to burden these fine people with her problem. As bad as Carl's thievery was, the fact that he'd involved the Beck family somehow made it worse. "It's true that someone's been stealing, Mr. Beck, but it's the bank's money that's missing. That's why I need to know who's been intercepting your payments."

"Mr. Stanley usually came by himself," Cora answered. "But one time he brought a young lady with him."

Despite her years of etiquette training, Etta propped an elbow on the table and rested her head in her hand. The weeks of denying her uncle's embezzling scheme had been wasted energy. She had witnesses now. "If you saw the woman again, would you recognize her?"

Cora's eyes widened. "Oh yes. She was quite the fashion plate. Big feathers in her hat and paint all over her face. Fancy car, too."

Cora's description matched the young woman Etta had seen with Carl at Hoffman's Bakery. What was her name? "After lunch, I'd like to see the receipts so I can make a record of the collection dates. Do you know who else may have handed over payments?"

Kurt spoke up. "I saw Diego Benavidez at the feed

store a few weeks ago. He said Carl had let him drive his new automobile the last time your uncle was out at his place. Don't know why else Carl would have gone to see Diego except to collect the payment."

"This is bad business," Oscar said with an ominous scowl. "What are you going to do if Benavidez doesn't have his receipts?"

"I'm going to take his word for it and make sure the bank's ledger shows his payments are up-to-date," Etta answered. "If this comes to trial, you may be called as witnesses."

Oscar shook his head. "I stay as far away from the courthouse as possible. Only go in to pay my taxes and that's once a year. Don't be counting on me to show up."

"But, Pa, we could help put a thief in jail," Kurt argued. "You've said a hundred times how good the Davis Bank has been to you over the years. They even suspended your loan payments last year when you got hurt. I think we should do whatever we can to help."

The hard expression on Oscar's face showed little concession, but he gave one decisive nod. "Point taken. Miss Etta, if you need us, let me know."

"Thank you, Mr. Beck. I hope it won't come to a trial, but I want to be prepared. I have just one more thing to ask of all of you."

Oscar narrowed his eyes and set his mouth in a rigid line. "What more is there?"

"Will you help me keep this quiet? I'll be presenting all my evidence to the county prosecutor soon, but until then…"

"I know what you mean, Miss Etta," Kurt said. "Don't worry about us. We know how to keep a secret."

❧❧

Gabriel trudged up the gentle rise that led to his parents' barn. Was there nothing he could do to shake the dark emotions that plagued him? Ever since returning to Burnet, he'd been one degree short of bursting into rage. Visiting the families of his fallen comrades had proven futile and after learning about Etta's engagement, he was twice as irritable as he'd been before. The only relief he'd found had been in Etta's company, and now she was promised to someone else.

His mother's gentle voice sounded from the hen house. "Come on, my lovely girls. Give up the treasure."

"Chickens giving you problems, Mom?"

Sara turned, a basket of eggs clutched to her stomach. "No more than usual. Where have you been all morning?"

"Talking to the vet. One of Henry Davis's mares had a bad hoof. Dr. Scott took care of it. I'll keep an eye on her, but it shouldn't be a problem."

Sara closed the hen house door behind her. "Did you go for a ride today?"

"Not yet. Thought I'd get some lunch and then go back."

Sara gently stroked Gabriel's shoulder, as though trying to smooth his ruffled feathers. "Sometimes I wish you were still my little boy. It was easier to comfort your hurts then."

Gabriel shrugged. "No need. I'm fine."

Sara stood on tiptoe to wrap one arm around her son and hold him tightly. "I know better, but I don't know how to help. Won't you tell me what's wrong?"

Gabriel's chest expanded and contracted with a beleaguered breath.

Sara tightened her hold. "What is it, son? You know you can tell me anything, and I'll still love you."

Gabriel slid his arms around his mother's waist and rested his head on her shoulder. "I'm OK. There's nothing to worry about."

"But I do worry. I hear you go out in the wee hours of the morning. I rarely see you smile, and you walk as though you're toting a boulder on your back." His mother had always known how to comfort him, but not even she could ease this burden.

Gabriel released his hold and took the basket of eggs from her. "Have you changed your mind about riding with me? This weather won't hold much longer."

"Fine," Sara said as she headed toward the house. "Don't tell me what's bothering you. But I'm going to keep praying."

Gabriel opened the kitchen door for her. "I know you will, Mom. I'm glad you remind the Lord about me once in a while."

"He never forgets you," Sara said as she began to prepare Gabriel's lunch. "And it wouldn't hurt if you had a long talk with Him yourself."

Gabriel retrieved a pitcher of cool water from the ice box. "When are the ladies from your sewing circle coming?"

"Two o'clock. We're almost finished with Etta's quilt."

Gabriel's heart squeezed at the mention of Etta's name. Maybe he should look for work in another part of the state. Otherwise, he'd have to see William Clark living in the Davis's house. "I didn't know Etta was part of the sewing circle."

"She isn't, although she'd be welcome to join. Pour me a glass of water, too."

Gabriel filled two glasses. He placed one on the table and drank from the other, recalling how he'd done the same from the battered cup at Lorena Scott's cabin in Caldwell. She'd been proud of her water and of her son. She was content with her home and family. Maybe Gabriel should take a lesson from her.

Sara set a plate of pork roast, potatoes, and biscuits in front of Gabriel. "Leftovers from last night's supper."

"You won't hear me complaining. Is Dad coming home for lunch?"

"He usually shows up around one o'clock." His mother sat down beside him. "You need him for something?"

"I want to ask him if I can use the car tomorrow to drive into Austin. I thought I'd pay a visit to the Highway Department offices and talk to them about a job."

The smile on his mother's face meant she approved of his plan. "See there?" Sara said. "That's one prayer the Lord answered."

"You've been praying for me to get a job?"

"In a manner of speaking. I've been asking the Lord to help you find your way, and a job seems like a step in the right direction. I can't begin to understand what you went through in the Army, and you're not about to tell me, but it must have been something truly awful to trouble you the way it does."

Gabriel forced the food down his throat. Should he tell his mother of his fatal error? He'd never doubted she'd love him, but was it fair to burden her with his guilt? "Have you ever thought much about the idea of a fellow forgiving himself for a mistake he made?" he asked.

Sara was quiet for several long moments and Gabriel knew she was considering her answer. Finally, she asked, "Do you remember how Peter denied Jesus?"

"Just before the crucifixion."

"Right. I've always thought Peter must have felt tremendously guilty about that. He denied being one of Jesus's followers, and then Jesus was resurrected and came back to talk to the disciples. Can you imagine how Peter felt knowing that Jesus knew what he'd done?"

"I never thought about it before now."

"I have. Remember when you were a little boy and you'd done something wrong? Most kids are scared their parents will find out and punish them. With Peter it must have been like that but magnified a thousand times."

"I don't remember any place in the Bible where Jesus punished Peter for denying Him."

"That's true. Reverend Martin preached a sermon once about how Jesus showed tremendous grace toward Peter and that we should strive to do the same toward people who harm us. But your question has me thinking a different way. How did Peter ever forgive himself?"

Was Gabriel's mistake as grievous as Peter's? He didn't know.

"Peter was imprisoned because he wouldn't stop preaching about Jesus," his mother continued, "but that didn't stop him. I think that receiving so much grace must have changed Peter in a very profound way."

"But did Peter ever forgive himself?"

"He must have, Gabriel, because how else could he have done what he did? If he'd been going around, thinking only about what a terrible mistake he'd made, he could have never helped build the church. I mean, Jesus forgave Peter for denying Him, and once Peter received that grace, it must have been easier for Peter to forgive himself and go on with what the Lord wanted him to do."

Through the open kitchen windows, Gabriel heard his father's truck stop beside the house.

"There's your father," his mother said. "I'd better fix his plate." She got to her feet, patted Gabriel's back, and kissed him on the top of his head. "My, that certainly was a deep conversation. Maybe you should talk to Reverend Martin about it."

His mother busied herself at the stove while Gabriel finished his meal. He didn't need to talk to their preacher. His mother had given him more than enough to think about.

13

Etta had never entered the county courthouse. Her mother had once described the two-story building as "no place for a lady," and since the jail was housed within its limestone walls, Etta could understand why her mother had warned her. But Etta had business with the county prosecutor, and his office was somewhere within the imposing building.

She took a fortifying breath, straightened her hat, and marched through the front door. The tall, narrow windows allowed little light to filter into the building, and Etta stopped near the entrance to let her eyes adjust. A small placard listing the location of the various county offices had been placed nearby. No wonder this place was so busy. Everything from the tax assessor to the sheriff was housed there. At last, she found the office of county prosecutor, located on the second floor.

Halfway up the stone staircase, someone called her name. "Henrietta? What are you doing here?"

Etta placed a hand on her hat as she raised her face toward the second floor landing.

William hurried down the stairs, brows drawn and lips tight. He took her elbow and escorted her back toward the entrance. "What are you doing here, Henrietta? This is no place for you."

Etta stopped and moved her elbow out of his grasp. "Actually, I've come to see you."

William scanned the area. "You should have called. You have no idea of the type of people who frequent this building."

As if to make his point, a door opened and a uniformed deputy led three men toward the staircase. Shackled by leg chains and dressed in baggy brown jail uniforms, the prisoners shuffled up the steps, their eyes cast toward their cuffed hands.

William placed his body between Etta and the men. "See what I mean?" he asked once the men had passed. "Those men are on their way to court. I need to go so I can present their charges. Go back to the bank, and I'll come to your office as soon as I'm finished here."

"I have information about the embezzlement," Etta said quietly. "I believe it's time to turn it over to your office."

"Not now and not here," William said through gritted teeth. He placed his hand on the small of Etta's back and escorted her through the door. "I'm sorry you had to see that, Henrietta. Such distasteful concerns are best left to men. Now, you go on, and I'll see you later." William mopped his brow with a white handkerchief and left her on the sidewalk.

Etta pulled at the hem of her jacket, as though straightening her clothes could straighten her thoughts. William had acted as though she'd walked into a saloon and ordered a drink of whiskey! Surely, women weren't barred from the courthouse. After all, it was a public building.

She rubbed her temple to ease the tension that built there. No one had spoken to her in such a domineering tone since she'd been a young girl, but William seemed to think that he had the right to dictate her behavior. George Owens had made that mistake, and she'd sent him packing. Etta wondered what her cousin Nora would say if she knew how high-handed William had been.

Etta had managed to set George straight. Maybe it was time she did the same thing with William.

❧❦

Several hours later, William sauntered into Etta's office, his hat in one hand and a small bouquet of red roses in the other. "I come bearing gifts," he said with an unctuous smile. "I hope you will forgive me for not being able to meet with you earlier." He held out the flowers like a schoolboy offering an apple to his teacher.

Should she voice her resentment or swallow it?

William laid the spray of roses on Etta's desk and pulled a chair close to her. "Now then, Henrietta, what was it that was so important you felt you had to brave the dangers of the county courthouse?" He'd resumed the polite, friendly quality she'd always associated with him. Which persona was genuine? This courteous William or the one who had made it clear that she had crossed the line?

Etta thought of Nora's advice and squared her shoulders. "Surely there are women who have business in the courthouse," she said.

William crossed his legs and leaned back in the chair. "I will admit that I occasionally see a woman in the courthouse, but she is not a lady."

"A lady never has to pay her taxes?"

William removed a watch from his vest pocket and checked the time. "Her husband or another male relative takes care of that for her."

"A lady never has to appear in court?"

"Very rarely. A lady has to provide testimony in a case, but most ladies would never find themselves in a situation where they witness something unsavory."

"A few years ago, Texas admitted its first women to the bar. Are you saying that female attorneys never have reason to step into a courthouse?"

William leaned closer and took one of her hands in his. "Dear Henrietta, you should never argue with a lawyer. Arguing is what we like to do best. But to answer your question, I am sure that female attorneys have to conduct business in the courthouse. But the crux of my argument is this—female attorneys are not ladies. A lady would concede all business matters to her husband. A lady's sphere of interest revolves around her home, family, and church."

"But what about me, William? I work in this bank six days a week. By your definition, I am not a lady."

"You have been raised to be a lady, Henrietta. One only has to be acquainted with your family in order to know that. I admit I thought it peculiar that your father allowed you to work as his assistant, but out of respect for Henry, I kept my opinion to myself."

Etta's body tensed at the word. William thought it *peculiar* that she worked in a bank? She struggled not to jerk her hand away from his. "What would have happened if I hadn't been able to take his place?"

"I'm sure there's someone at the bank who would have been able to take over. If you hadn't been here, your father would have created an assistant position and trained someone. After all, once we're married, you'll be busy fulfilling your role as wife and mother. I may decide to run for a higher political office someday, and a lady such as yourself will be quite an asset."

William had everything worked out. He would marry her, tuck her at home with his mother and their children, and bring her out when he needed a demure, compliant wife at his side. He would certainly disapprove of her wish to continue working at the bank. William let go of her hand and straightened in his chair. "Now, then. What do you have to show me?"

Etta looked at the stack of folders on her desk. She needed the county prosecutor to follow through with her investigation, and that meant she needed William. Alienating him now would only facilitate the embezzler. She'd face the question of marrying William later. "I visited all of our clients who have farm and ranch loans. Every one of them reported that a representative from the bank has been collecting their payments and issuing receipts."

"Is that standard practice?"

"No. Most borrowers make payments whenever they are in town."

"Why don't they simply mail in the payments?"

"Mail service isn't available in the more rural areas. The farmers and ranchers usually pick up their mail when they come into town."

"I should have thought of that. I guess you can tell I'm a city boy. Why did the bank decide to start collecting the payments?"

"We didn't. The clients I spoke to this morning told me that Uncle Carl came to their places to make collections."

William's face crumpled in sympathy. "Oh, Henrietta. Your uncle?"

Etta nodded.

"Your uncle has been collecting payments, issuing

receipts, and keeping the money for himself?" William's tone communicated his incredulity at Carl's brash thievery.

"That's the way it looks," Etta replied. "He also recorded the payments in the ledgers. But when Arthur Lewis became head of the loan department, Arthur began keeping his own record of payments received. If he hadn't, this discrepancy might not have shown up for many, many months."

"Did Carl know about Mr. Lewis's separate record of payments?"

"Apparently not. As I told you during the last meeting of the board, Mr. Lewis was the one who called the problem to my attention. The auditor I hired confirmed that it's been happening for over a year. Also, the clients I talked with this morning described a young, pretty, fashionably dressed woman who accompanied him. Uncle Carl introduced me to a friend of his from Austin who matches that description, but I can't remember her name."

"It won't be hard to find out. Carl loves to brag and all I have to do is steer him in that direction and he'll tell me all about her. Then we may be able to convince her to testify against Carl." William propped his elbow on the edge of her desk and rested his head in his hand. "What about you, Henrietta? Are you prepared to see your uncle prosecuted for this crime and perhaps sent to prison?"

Etta rubbed her forehead, as though she could erase the headache that bloomed like a malodorous flower. "I don't know," she said on a long breath. "Do I have a choice?"

"We can always hope that he'll confess. Once we present all of our evidence, he may see he has no way out. There's also the possibility of offering him a reduced sentence if he confesses."

A pinpoint of hope lit the gloomy horizon. "You mean there's a chance he wouldn't have to go to prison?"

William dimmed that faint hope. "I don't know about that, Henrietta. Embezzlement is a serious crime. I need to look over the evidence, but if I find enough to prosecute the case, my next step would be to confront Carl at the upcoming meeting of the bank's Board of Directors."

"Perhaps the board could recommend an appropriate punishment."

"Perhaps, but the punishment phase is handled by the judge. I can make a recommendation, but the ultimate decision is his alone."

"Would Judge Thompson be involved?"

"Probably not. He should recuse himself from this case since he is acquainted with the parties involved."

Etta's head was pounding. "It's so complicated."

"Yes it is," William said. "And it can be quite unseemly. That's why ladies don't involve themselves with such distasteful matters." How artfully he'd turned the discussion back to his original point.

Etta pushed the folders toward William. "I wrote up a summary of my findings and made copies of the pertinent information for you. Will you let me know what you decide?"

"Let me take this tribulation from you, sweetheart. I'll take care of everything from this point on. Now…" William gently touched her sleeve. "…when would be a good time for me to speak to your father?"

"Oh, William, I can't…what I mean is…Can it wait until this business with Uncle Carl is finished? When I tell my father about the embezzlement, I also want to be able to tell him that the problem has been resolved."

"Poor Henrietta. So much to bear on such delicate shoulders." William patted her arm. "Very well. I'm anxious to have our engagement made public, but I understand your desire to see this matter to its finish." William stood, bent down to kiss Etta's forehead, and tucked the folders under his arm.

As he left, the pain in Etta's head traveled down her neck and established camp in her shoulders. *First things first.* She needed to settle the issue of Carl's thievery before she told William of her misgivings about marrying him.

If only Gabriel hadn't come back from his trip as cold as January frost. She'd pinned so many of her hopes on him, but he'd woken her from those foolish dreams. He obviously didn't have the same tender feelings about her that she had for him.

Her mother had always said that the Lord would guide her toward the right man, but she'd been crushingly wrong about Gabriel. Was William the right man? And if the Lord was guiding her toward William, then why did her stomach roil at the thought of life with him?

❧

Gabriel seated himself behind the steering wheel of his father's truck and offered a silent prayer of thanksgiving. The state highway department had offered him a job and a salary of twelve hundred dollars a year. Although he didn't know for sure, that was probably more than his parents had made in any year. He'd be able to buy an automobile and still put a fair amount in savings.

Gabriel drove through the crowded streets of Austin until he reached the narrow road that led home. For the first time since he'd come back, he had a future to plan for. The new job would require some travel, but Burnet was centrally located and would make a good home base. Once he'd saved enough money, he could begin building a house for himself and the family he'd always assumed he'd have.

Would memories of France continue to haunt him in the future? He'd never forget his squad. Even if he did surrender the guilt, remembering his comrades was the smallest honor he could give. But as the years passed and his life led him in a new direction, he hoped the pain would diminish. Would he be able to look at sugar and not think of Nichols? Would thunder always send him running for cover?

Just outside of the city, Gabriel crossed the recently built bridge over the Colorado River. With cement piers supporting trussed deck arches, it was the latest in bridge design. Someday, he would be on the engineering team that conceived such bridges. He could take his children to the site and explain how his team had outwitted the forces of compression, tension, torque, and shear.

But he couldn't have that family without a wife, and he couldn't have the wife he wanted.

On impulse, Gabriel swerved off the highway and followed the gravel road that lead under the bridge. He stopped the truck and turned off the engine. Quiet assaulted his ears.

What was he doing down here? He'd told his parents he'd be back by supper time, and yet something had convinced him to do some sightseeing.

Gabriel got out of the truck and walked along the banks of the wide, blue-green river, the scent of clean water filling his nostrils. Cliff swallows chattered like quarrelsome children as they darted in and out of the mud nests they'd built under the bridge. Gabriel squatted to watch tiny frogs that dared to venture away from the water in search of their afternoon meals.

He settled into a spot beneath a pecan tree and watched the ceaseless flow of the river toward the southeast. A gentle breeze cooled his brow and his eyelids grew heavy. He removed his hat and stretched out on the sun-warmed grass.

He leadeth me beside the still waters.

That was one of the many Bible passages he'd had to memorize as a boy. Maybe the writer of that Psalm had been sitting beside a river like this when the idea came to him.

He restoreth my soul.

Did Gabriel's soul need to be restored? His mother thought so. She'd say it was the Lord who had turned the truck off the highway just so Gabriel could have a quiet place to think. Although that wasn't his problem. He expended a lot of energy avoiding troublesome thoughts.

He'd been wrong the last time he thought the Lord had sent him a message. Gabriel had believed he needed to seek forgiveness from the families of his fallen comrades, but he'd apparently been wrong. Again. How in the world could Gabriel forgive himself for leading men to their deaths?

Did you shoot him?

Gabriel chuckled at the remembrance of Mrs. Patek's brash question. She hadn't been afraid to address the heart of the problem. She didn't blame him for Joe's death, and she wouldn't chastise him for his poor decision. He'd been in battle, and disasters happened in battle.

Still, it had been his indecision that kept the men in the line of fire. That was the one point he couldn't get past. He'd probably celebrate his sixtieth birthday still regretting that one day in France. Of course, if he didn't overcome the guilt, he'd be alone on his sixtieth birthday—no wife, no children, and probably no friends.

Gabriel sprang to his feet and paced along the pebbled bank. If only Etta had waited for him to figure everything out. Of course, if he could manage to forgive himself, he could also tell Etta how much he'd come to love her.

Gabriel's pacing came to an abrupt halt. Was there still a chance? She wasn't married yet. If he could forgive himself, he could move forward. Nothing would restore his comrades' lives, but forgiving himself seemed to be the only way Gabriel could have a chance to restore his future.

"I forgive myself." The whisper struggled to pass through his constricted throat. "I forgive myself," Gabriel repeated, the words coming slightly easier. "I followed my commander's orders. Even if I'd moved farther east or even headed back toward base camp, we might have still been hit." He'd said the words, but Gabriel felt no great relief. "Well," he said, heading back to his truck, "at least it was a start."

He would have to do a lot more thinking and a lot more praying before he could shrug off the guilt and grief his mistake had cost.

14

Etta looked at the sober faces of the men gathered around the conference table. By the end of this meeting, she'd know whether she would continue acting as bank president or if the Board of Directors would appoint someone else to do the job. She'd tried to steel herself for bad news, but every cell in her body seemed to tremble with nerves.

Judge Thompson called the meeting to order. "We convene today in special session to discuss the matter of a shortfall in the bank's accounts. Are you ready, Mrs. Swanson?"

Carolina nodded. "I typed up the minutes from the last meeting. Would you like me to read them now?"

"Can we dispense with the regular procedure?" asked James Moore. "I need to get back to the store."

"Always in a hurry," teased Mayor Robinson. "Can't your employees get by without you for a few hours?"

Judge Thompson rapped his knuckles on the table. "All right, gentlemen. If time is a concern, let's skip the minutes and turn this meeting over to our county prosecutor. William, you said you had some information to share with us."

A week had passed since Etta had given her information to William.

Uncle Carl had come into the bank every day with

his usual genial smile and flirtatious manner. Did he have no conscience at all? Her mother had been honest, respectable, and upright in every way, but her mother's brother had betrayed people's trust and deceived his family.

William stood, removed his watch from his vest pocket, and opened it. After placing it on the table next to a stack of documents, he cleared his throat and addressed the group. "Thank you, Judge. As I'm sure you all remember, Miss Davis disclosed a problem in the loan department during our last meeting. It was decided she would investigate the matter further and report back to us. She met with clients whose accounts were past due and discovered that an employee of the bank had collected the payments and issued receipts. However, he pocketed the payments. In an attempt to hide his theft, he entered the payments in the bank's ledgers. However, when Arthur Lewis became manager of the loan department, he kept a separate ledger that reflected the true payments. That's how the embezzlement was discovered." William paused for a drink of water.

"Well, don't keep us in suspense," James Moore said. "Who was it?"

"Carl Stanley," William answered in a calm, confident voice.

The men's surprise was evident in the silence that met William's announcement.

Carolina caught Etta's gaze and nodded. Apparently, Carolina had had her own suspicions about Uncle Carl.

"That snake in the grass," Mayor Robinson said in a quiet voice. "I would've never thought…"

"Are you sure about this?" Judge Thompson

asked.

"Quite sure," William answered. "I followed up on Miss Davis's discovery. All the borrowers confirmed that Carl had made personal visits in order to collect their payments. Furthermore, Carl has a lady friend, a Miss..." William referred to his notes. "Miss Florence Edwards of Austin. I spoke with Miss Edwards myself, and she readily verified that she had accompanied Carl while he conducted bank business. Once I explained that she was in danger of being charged as an accomplice, she quickly disclosed that Carl had opened a bank account in her name, but she avows that she's never accessed the funds. "

James Moore shook his head. "Of all the underhanded, devious tricks. What happens next, William? Will you arrest Carl?"

William ignored Mr. Moore's question and directed his attention to the entire group. "If you recall, Carl suggested that he would be the best person to fill in as bank president during Henry Davis's absence."

"Fat chance of that happening," Mayor Robinson said.

"Nevertheless, we agreed to meet with Carl to discuss the matter at a later date. I took the liberty of informing him about today's meeting. He should be here in..." William looked at his watch. "...in approximately ten minutes."

"You're going to confront him with the evidence?" Judge Thompson asked.

"That is correct. The sheriff and a deputy are standing by, ready to arrest Carl once this meeting is over. But I didn't want to waste the opportunity to question him with all of the members of the board present."

James Moore spoke. "What are the chances of recovering the missing funds?"

"That's one of the issues I intend to speak to Carl about. With any luck, Miss Edwards's bank account will contain most of the stolen funds. I am in the process of requesting a warrant to access that information. Since the account is in a bank in Austin, I had to go through the court in Travis County."

"You're going to corner that rat and hope he confesses?" asked Mayor Robinson.

A small smile crossed William's lips. "That is my plan."

Judge Thompson rubbed his chin. "It might work. Carl Stanley has always been interested in what people think of him. The threat of being disgraced may just be enough to push him over the edge." A long minute of silence followed Judge Thompson's statement.

William resumed his seat, took another drink of water, and gazed out the nearby window.

Mayor Robinson was the first to break the quiet. "While we're waiting for Carl, I'd like to discuss whether Miss Davis should be allowed to continue acting as bank president. I called on Henry today."

Etta sat up in her chair. No one had told her the mayor had been out to the house. Had her father been ready to receive visitors?

"I know," Mayor Robinson said, glancing at Etta, "I probably should have checked with you first. But I wanted to see for myself how long it will be until your father returns to the bank. I have to tell you, gentlemen, I don't foresee Henry resuming his position for many months."

James Moore interrupted the mayor. "Where are you going with this, Edgar?"

"I'd like to throw my full support behind Miss Davis," the mayor answered. "There's no one better suited for the job, and she's handled this embezzlement mess with admirable efficiency."

"I agree," James Moore said. "I have no qualms about leaving Miss Davis in charge until her father feels up to returning. What about you, Judge?"

Judge Thompson's bushy white eyebrows rose as he looked at Etta. "Do you want to continue, Miss Davis?"

Etta cleared her throat before answering. She wanted to make sure her voice didn't reveal how nervous she was. "Yes, Judge Thompson."

"There's one thing we haven't considered," William said. "Henrietta acted as her father's assistant and was able to step in when he became incapable of continuing. If she chooses to step down, there is no one to take her place."

"Why would she choose to step down?" Mayor Robinson asked. "She just said she wanted to remain."

William glanced at Etta and smiled. "Miss Davis is a young woman, gentlemen. She may want to get married someday."

The other men all looked away or squirmed in their chairs, apparently embarrassed that they'd never considered Etta's marriage prospects.

"I see your point," the mayor said. "Miss Davis needs an assistant."

"Precisely," William replied. "The bank has never had a vice-president, but this experience shows us that one is needed."

"Who would you recommend for such a position, Etta?" asked Judge Thompson.

Etta only needed a few seconds to come up with

an answer. "The most suitable candidates would be Mrs. Swanson or Arthur Lewis. Mrs. Swanson has worked here for many years and knows all of the bank's procedures. Mr. Lewis has taken great initiative since taking charge of the loan department."

"Two women in administrative positions?" James Moore asked, his incredulity evident in the tone of his voice. "That's really pushing things."

"Don't worry," Carolina said with a soft laugh. "I'm not interested in taking on more work. Mr. Davis gave me a job when no one else would, and I've tried to repay his consideration with loyal service. But I've reached the age where I'd like fewer responsibilities rather than more."

Etta smiled at Carolina. When this matter was resolved, she'd speak to Carolina about changing her job requirements. After all, Uncle Carl's position would soon be vacant.

"Very well," Judge Thompson said. "If Etta will speak to Mr. Lewis and ask him if he's interested in the position, we'll put it on the agenda for our regularly scheduled board meeting."

A knock postponed Etta's response.

Carolina rose and opened the door.

Carl stood at the threshold, his straw boater in his hand and a broad smile on his face. "Good afternoon, everyone," Carl said as he entered the room. "I hope you're all enjoying this beautiful spring weather. There's no better time to be in Texas, that's what I always say." Carl pulled out the only empty chair and settled into it. "I was delighted to receive a note asking me to attend today's meeting. May I assume you've reached a decision about Etta's place at the bank?"

William stood. "Carl, would you please tell us

how long you've been an employee of the Davis Bank and Trust?"

"It will be two years in November. If Henry could talk, I'm sure he'd tell you what a great job I've done."

"What areas of the bank are your responsibility?"

"Personnel. I interview and hire tellers, bookkeepers, and secretaries. I also make sure they're doing their jobs and handle any problems that arise. Henry's in charge of the management level, and I do everything else."

"Do you have any day-to-day responsibilities that involve cash?"

"Not usually, but I've always been willing to fulfill any duty assigned to me."

"Is that why you collected payments from farmers and ranchers who have loans with the bank?"

Carl's Adam's apple bobbed as he swallowed. "Why, yes it is. I know it's difficult for those clients to get into town, so I took it on myself to collect the payments and to issue receipts."

"Were these payments made in cash?"

Carl adjusted his purple-striped tie as though he felt the noose tightening around his neck. "Why, yes they were. Clients with checking accounts are mostly our business owners. Almost everyone else operates on a cash basis."

"What did you do with the cash once you'd collected it?"

Carl crossed his legs, uncrossed them, and shifted in his chair. "Well, I entered the payments in the general ledger and added the cash to a teller's drawer. That's the way we always do it."

"I'd like you to examine this ledger." William placed Arthur Lewis's record of payments in front of

Carl. "Do you recognize it?"

Carl turned the pages as he frowned over the small, black book. "No, can't say I do. It's too small to be one of the ledgers we keep at the bank."

"This is a separate ledger kept by Arthur Lewis. You know Mr. Lewis, correct?"

"Of course. Arthur's office is only a few feet away from mine."

"Were you aware that Mr. Lewis kept a separate ledger of loan payments?"

Carl pulled his collar away from his neck. "No, can't say I did. If I had, I would have reported the collections I made. If my minor oversight has caused a problem, it can easily be rectified by checking the general ledger."

"Are you acquainted with Miss Florence Edwards of Austin?"

Carl removed a white handkerchief from the inside pocket of his jacket and wiped his upper lip. "Yes, I know Miss Edwards. In fact, I introduced her to Etta a few weeks ago. Do you remember, Etta?"

Despite his duplicity, a twinge of sympathy touched Etta's heart. Carl was walking farther and farther into the trap. "Yes," she answered. "I remember meeting her."

William continued drilling Carl with questions. "Miss Edwards told me that she sometimes accompanied you when you made your collections."

"Only once. Flo loves fast automobiles, and my car was built for speed."

"Miss Edwards also told me that you opened a bank account in Austin under her name."

Carl's gaze dropped. "Oh, well, gentlemen…this is rather a delicate matter and definitely not one to be discussed in front of the ladies."

William pursued the question. "I believe Miss Davis and Mrs. Swanson will survive any shocking revelation. Would you like to explain why you are making deposits under Miss Edward's name?"

"Well..." Carl cleared his throat. "Flo is a special friend. I...uh...help her financially in exchange for her...uh...friendship."

"Miss Edwards is a kept woman?" William asked.

"That's a harsh way to describe my friendship with Flo. She has a job at a dry goods store on Congress Avenue, but as I'm sure you can imagine, her salary provides only for the most basic necessities of life. It is my pleasure to provide her with the occasional treat such as a new hat or a small item of jewelry. She is most grateful for whatever favor I show her."

William placed three sheets of paper in front of Carl. "The paper on the left is a list of shortfalls the bank has experienced during the last fourteen months. There is a regularly occurring discrepancy between the cash in the tellers' drawers and the amounts recorded in the general ledger."

Carl shook his head and pointed to the sheet of paper. "This is what I was talking about, gentlemen. I know little Etta tried her hardest, but an error like this could end up costing the bank a lot of money."

"Indeed," William said. "The second paper is a record of the payments you collected. Most of the clients had receipts signed by you."

Carl rubbed his chin. "I'd have to look at the general ledger to make sure this is correct. There have been too many for me to remember."

"Miss Edwards turned over her bank book to my office. The deposits equal the amounts you collected minus approximately two thousand dollars."

Carl squirmed in his chair. "Hmm…that is a coincidence."

"According to Miss Davis, your salary is seven hundred fifty dollars a year. How is it possible you deposited close to five thousand dollars in Miss Edwards's account?"

"Me? Oh, no. Flo must have made these deposits." Carl scooted his chair away from the table and glanced at the door.

"Miss Edwards and the tellers at Texas Trust disagree. Miss Edwards says you made the deposits and the tellers describe a well-dressed, sandy-haired man in his forties. They also report that he drives a yellow Hudson."

Carl's chair screeched on the wooden floor as he stood. "What is this? Are you accusing me of stealing payments and falsifying ledgers?"

"In my role as county prosecutor, I am prepared to file charges of embezzlement against you."

Carl's face turned crimson. "That's ridiculous! I tried to help out the bank's customers and I get accused of a crime? If Etta's lost the bank's money, you need to lay the blame on her. I refuse to stay here and let you besmirch my good name." Carl grabbed his hat and strode toward the door. But when he opened it, the sheriff and a deputy blocked his exit.

William nodded to the sheriff and the two officers grasped Carl's arms. "You're going to spend the night in jail, Carl. I'll be by to file charges."

"This is madness!" Carl yelled. "I haven't done anything wrong. I can produce every dollar I collected."

William signaled with his hand for the sheriff to

take Carl away. Through the open doorway, Etta could hear Carl angrily protesting his arrest.

As the sound of Carl's furious voice subsided, everyone around the conference table sat back in their chairs and sighed heavily.

"I never would have thought..." James Moore muttered.

Judge Thompson placed his palms on the table. "Mrs. Swanson, please note that the board will meet again in two weeks. That should be enough time for Mr. Clark to bring us up-to-date on the case against Carl and the prospect of recovering the stolen funds."

"Do you need more time, William?" asked the mayor.

William stacked his papers and returned his watch to his vest pocket. "No, two weeks should be plenty."

"Very well, then," Judge Thompson said. "As chairman of the Board of Directors, I hereby call this meeting closed."

After the men had shaken hands with each other and filed out of the room, Etta folded her arms on the table and rested her head on top of them. Her neck and shoulders ached as though she'd been carrying the weight of the world.

Carolina touched Etta's shoulder. "Your father would be so proud."

Carolina's kindness moved Etta to tears. She'd successfully controlled her emotions during the meeting, but now that it was over, everything she'd held back rushed to escape her self-imposed blockade.

"Do you want a few moments alone?" Carolina asked.

Etta retrieved a handkerchief from her jacket pocket and nodded.

Carolina patted Etta's shoulder, refilled her water glass, and left without saying another word.

Etta's breaths came in ragged sobs. Her father wouldn't be proud if he saw her now. Women weren't considered suitable for business because of their emotional natures, and wasn't she fulfilling that opinion? Gabriel had told her she needed to be more of a man, but how in the world could she be something she wasn't? Etta sipped her water and took several deep breaths. She had to tell her father about Carl and the impending trial, but at least she could tell him the problem had almost been resolved.

∂∙∕

The sun was setting by the time Etta turned onto the drive that led to her house. Wisps of pale yellow and pink clouds stretched along the sky, and the first stars blinked to life. She hesitated outside the kitchen door to gather her thoughts and to put on her best face.

If Rosa got a hint that Etta was troubled, Rosa would also be upset.

After several deep breaths and a few practice smiles, Etta climbed the steps and walked through the back door. "Evening, Rosa. How was everything today?"

Rosa was at the counter, chopping onions. "Good day today. Your papa walked to the stable and back without Charlie's help. Charlie said the horses were so happy to see him, they sang and danced."

"I wish I'd seen that," Etta said with a laugh. "I'll go up and see Papa now."

"No, mija. He's sleeping right now. I just checked on him."

"Where's Mr. Simpson?"

"He went into town with my brother."

"Oh? Is Mr. Simpson making friends with your family?"

A shy smile lit Rosa's face. "You could say that."

Etta nudged Rosa with her shoulder. "Is there something I need to know?"

Rosa's cheeks grew a charming shade of pink. "Well...maybe..."

This time, Etta's smile was genuine. "Is Mr. Simpson going to be asking for long-term employment soon?"

Rosa ducked her head. "Well, mija, you know, your papa is going to need help for a very long time. Somebody to take care of the little things he needs. Plus, Charlie could help around the place with the horses and the garden after Benito goes to college."

"I see. I think that's a very good idea."

Rosa's dark eyes glistened with excitement. "Really, mija? You don't mind if me and Charlie...well...he asked me if I would marry him and..."

"And?"

"I said maybe."

"Maybe? What are your reservations?"

Rosa wiped her hands on her apron. "I can't leave you and your papa all alone. You need me now more than ever. But Charlie, he said that as long as he could find work, we would stay in Burnet."

Etta would gladly find work for Mr. Simpson if it made Rosa happy. "Do you think your brother will give his permission?"

Rosa's voice took on a serious tone. "He will if he knows what's good for him."

Etta laughed with Rosa. It had been a long time since Etta had something to celebrate. "Are you happy, Rosa?"

Rosa scooped the chopped vegetables into a black skillet. "I think so. My husband, he died a long time ago and…well it might be nice to have somebody special again."

Etta put her arm around Rosa's shoulders. "If you're happy, I'm happy. Mr. Simpson will have a job in Burnet for as long as he wants it. If not here at the house, then I'll find something for him to do at the bank."

Rosa embraced Etta. "*Gracias, mija.* I'll tell Charlie when I see him."

"Now, what can I do to help with dinner?"

Rosa touched her forehead with her palm. "Oh, I almost forgot. Miss Sara called a few minutes before you got home. She wants you to come see her."

"Now?"

"That's what she said. You go on, and I'll finish the dinner. When Charlie comes home, he'll wake up Mr. Davis, and we'll eat."

Etta headed toward the kitchen door. "Just think, Rosa. You're going to be a bride. We'll have to find you a new dress."

"Nothing too fancy. I'm too old for those dresses that look like clouds of lace. Besides, I already had a big wedding when I was nineteen."

"As soon as you have the date, we'll go shopping. I haven't shopped for new clothes in a long time."

The image of Rosa's shining eyes and smiling face stayed with Etta as she walked the short distance to the Bensons' house.

Charlie would have never come into their lives if

her father hadn't needed him, and now Charlie would change Rosa's life as well. One person's life touched many others, sometimes by accident, sometimes by fate.

Like Gabriel. Even though Etta had been acquainted with Gabriel all her life, she hadn't known him until recently. The time she'd spent with him had been powerful and life-changing. He'd encouraged her to prove herself, and he'd trusted her with his secret. Unlike George Owens, Gabriel hadn't befriended her as a way to gain control over the bank, and unlike William Clark, Gabriel didn't expect her to resign from the bank in order to stand by his side while he climbed the ladder of success.

However, Gabriel had returned from his travels a different person. Where he'd once been good-humored and friendly, he was now cold and surly. She'd stayed away from Gabriel since he'd tended Mira's hoof and she'd told herself that dreams of loving him were foolish.

How peculiar life was. She'd rebuffed George's interest; she'd probably decline William's offer, and the one man she cared for didn't return her feelings. How did other women maneuver the complicated world of love?

As she neared Sara's house, Etta saw that Mr. Benson's truck was not parked in its usual spot. Hopefully, that meant Gabriel wasn't at home. As much as Etta wanted to see him, dealing with his churlish disposition would be too much after everything that had happened at the board meeting.

In keeping with the warm spring weather, Sara's front door and windows were open. Etta knocked on the doorframe and called, "Sara? You wanted to see me?"

Sara's voice sounded from within the house. "Come on in, Etta."

Etta walked through the doorway. "Where are you?"

"In the kitchen. Come on back."

Etta checked the house as she passed through the parlor and hallway. Gabriel was not in sight. "Rosa told me you wanted to see me."

Sara placed a lid on a blue metal roasting pan and slid it into the oven. "You've been so busy lately we haven't had a chance to talk."

"Where's your family?"

"Gabriel went with his dad to unload some lumber. I'm not sure how long they'll be."

Etta breathed a sigh of relief. She wanted to see Gabriel. Really, she did, but another round of poorly-veiled insults might reduce her to tears.

Sara closed the oven door and washed her hands. "Come sit down. I want you to taste the rice pudding I made this morning. I got a new recipe from a magazine." Sara spooned the pudding into a bowl.

Etta had always loved coming to Sara's house. From the outside it was a simple white-frame house with tall windows to catch every available breeze, but inside the warmth of love suffused every room. Faded forget-me-nots embellished the kitchen wallpaper and the shelves held mismatched plates, but Etta thought it was the nicest room in the house.

The kitchen was where Sara cared for her family. She concocted home remedies to treat everything from the sniffles to skinned knees, and although company was shown into the parlor, those close to her were entertained at the well-used kitchen table.

"Now then," said Sara, setting a bowl of pudding and a spoon in front of Etta, "catch me up on everything that's been going on."

Etta tasted a spoonful of the sweet, creamy pudding. Sara had always been a good and loyal friend, but Etta couldn't talk to her about Gabriel. "The pudding's delicious. Very smooth."

"Good. First, tell me what happened when you went to Austin. Did Nora chaperone you?"

It seemed as though years had passed since her weekend with Nora. "Oh, yes. And she gave me quite a talking to about my inability to refuse George Owens's attentions."

"That's an important skill for every woman to know. Did you set him straight?"

"I tried. Turns out he was more interested in taking control of the bank than he was in romancing me."

"He said that?"

"He sure did. Nora couldn't believe it either."

"Good riddance, I say. What's this I hear about you and William Clark? His mother has been spouting off about her son proposing to you. Does she know what she's talking about?"

Etta tilted her head from one side to the other. "Sort of. William did ask permission to talk to Papa about marrying me, and at first, I thought it might work. I mean, William's always been very kind. He always compliments me in one way or another, and the Clarks have been friends of the family for years and years."

"But?"

"But it's become clear that marriage to William would be like voluntarily entering a cage. He wants someone who'll care for his mother and be content to raise his children and stand in his shadow. He'd never sit still for a wife who wants to work outside the home."

"There are plenty of girls who would be satisfied with that kind of life, but you're not one of them, Etta. The Lord gave you a kind heart and a sharp mind. It would be a shame to waste them on Ida Clark's many imagined aches and pains."

"What I can't understand is why I've suddenly received the attention of two men. I went years without attracting more than polite greetings."

"But that's when you were still hiding from life. Remember how Catherine used to encourage you to attend the young people's group at church?"

Etta frowned and pressed her lips together. "I'm too old for that group."

"No, you're not. That was just an excuse to hide. And whenever you went to horse shows, your mother practically had to make you attend the dances."

Etta shifted in the hard wooden chair. Sara's depiction of her was right on the money, and Etta didn't like it one bit. "I was afraid no one would ask me to dance."

"Did that ever happen?"

"Not really. I never was the belle of the ball, but I was never a wallflower, either."

"That's what I'm saying. You never gave any of the young gentlemen a chance to know you."

Etta propped her elbow on the table and rested her chin in her hand. "I never thought of it that way before, but you're right. I was hiding."

"Now that you've been forced to step into the spotlight, people are seeing you for who you really are."

"And who would that be?"

"A lovely, intelligent, brave woman who refuses to let the world beat her down."

Etta thought about her earlier tears in the conference room. "I don't know about that. You should have seen me at today's board meeting."

"What happened?"

"Remember when I told you about someone stealing from the bank?"

"Of course. Did you find out who it was?"

"It was Uncle Carl."

Sara fell back in her chair and slowly shook her head. "I wish I could say I was surprised."

"Do you know something I don't?"

"Your mother and father quarreled about Carl working at the bank."

"Papa didn't want to hire Carl?"

"No, your *mother* didn't want him to hire Carl. Your uncle lost his job in San Antonio because he was suspected of overcharging the customers and pocketing the extra money. He was given a choice—either leave town or face an investigation."

Why hadn't her parents told her? She would have seen Carl in a different light if she'd known about his past. "I never knew he was in trouble with the law."

"Carl was a few years ahead of Catherine and me in school. He was always a troublemaker, always looked for the easy way out. Catherine knew what kind of person her brother was, and she didn't want Henry to give him a position that had anything to do with money."

"But Papa hired him anyway. I kept hoping I was wrong about Uncle Carl, but when I'd gathered enough evidence, I gave it to William."

"And what did our county prosecutor do?"

"He confronted Carl at today's board meeting."

Sara rolled her eyes. "That must have been quite a show."

A painful tightness constricted Etta's throat, as if the words were too distressing to say. "It was awful, Sara. The sheriff took Carl to jail."

"Oh, Etta." Sara wrapped her hands around Etta's forearm. "I'm so sorry you had to go through all that. Does your papa know?"

"Not yet. I was going to tell him, but he was napping when I got home. To tell you the truth, I'm afraid of what the news will do to him. He'll want to know how I let this happen."

Sara lowered her chin and looked at Etta. "I think you've got your calendar a little mixed up."

"What do you mean?"

"Didn't you tell me the records showed the funds had been stolen over a long period of time?"

"That's right."

"Then Carl started stealing while your father was still in charge. You stopped the thief, Etta. If it weren't for you…"

Sara was right again. Why hadn't Etta realized Carl had started stealing while her father was overseeing the bank's daily operations? "Do you think Papa will see it that way?"

Sara fisted her hands on her hips. "If he doesn't, I'll march right over there and give him a piece of my mind."

Etta chuckled in spite of herself. "Papa wouldn't like that."

"I'm sure he wouldn't. But…" Sara stood. "I have

something he will like." Sara left the kitchen but returned a few seconds later with a blue-and-white quilt draped across one shoulder.

Warmth spread through Etta's chest. "Oh, Sara. It's so beautiful. I never imagined. How can I ever thank you?"

Sara smiled and folded the quilt into a neat rectangle. "No thanks necessary. We were happy to finish it for Catherine."

"Will you give me a list of the ladies who worked on it? I'd like to write them a note."

"That would tickle them pink."

Etta took the quilt from Sara and lightly touched the patchwork. Her mother's stitches, her stitches, and the stitches of her mother's friends. Each stitch a prayer. Each stitch an act of love. Etta laid her head on the quilt and let the love seep into her. "I miss Momma so much. She used to say that the world was filled with a thousand little blessings, and it was up to us to find them. I wonder what blessing she'd see in everything that's happened during the last few months."

Sara sat next to Etta and stroked her hair. "Oh, I don't know. A husband who's getting better every day and a daughter who's grown into a strong, capable woman?"

Tears filled Etta's eyes again, but this time they were not tears of anger or sadness.

Sara caught a tear with her fingertip and smiled warmly at Etta. "You're one of those thousand little blessings, Etta. You're a blessing to your family, to the people who work at the bank, and to everyone who knows you."

Etta buried her face in the quilt and gave thanks for Sara's friendship. Later, she'd make sure to find time to thank the Lord for every blessing He'd given her through this difficult time.

15

"Your papa is waiting for you in the dining room," Rosa said as soon as Etta returned home. "Oh, is that your momma's quilt?"

"Isn't it beautiful?" Etta passed the quilt to Rosa and stepped to the sink to wash her hands. "I'm going to give it to Papa tonight."

Rosa examined the top-most quilt square. "You did a good thing, *mija*. It's not as good as having your momma here, but now your papa can wrap himself on cold nights and remember her love. Later, you can put it on your children's beds and your grandchildren's beds. Your momma's love going from generation to generation."

Etta's heart swelled with emotion. Her mother's quilt would be as warm as a good-night kiss. Like the sun's rays, the pure, sweet love would go on and on.

"Now," Rosa said, handing Etta a towel, "dry your hands and join your father in the dining room. I'll bring the food."

Etta held out her arms and Rosa passed the quilt back to her. Eating in the formal dining room had been one of her mother's traditions. Breakfast and lunch were usually eaten in the kitchen, but dinner was always served with candlelight on the polished mahogany table. Since her father's stroke, Etta had shared the evening meal with him in his bedroom. Reinstating her mother's tradition was yet another sign of his recovery.

"Evening, Papa," Etta said as she kissed his cheek. "You're looking well."

He smiled crookedly, the right side of his face still unable to move as well as the left.

"I have a gift for you." Etta sat in the cushioned chair on her father's right. "Do you remember the quilt I was working on? The one Momma started?"

Henry nodded.

"Sara Benson and the ladies from the sewing circle finished it for me." Etta spread the quilt on her lap. "It's for you, Papa. I prayed every night as I sewed the squares together. I asked the Lord to help you recuperate. Your recovery shows me those prayers were answered."

Henry reached across the table with his left arm and gently touched the quilt. His eyes shone with unshed tears and his mouth opened and closed as though he struggled to form words.

"Lov…" He paused, closed his eyes, and tried again. "Love…ly."

The invisible weight that Etta had borne for such a long time lifted from her shoulders. She knelt next to her father's chair and laid her head on his knee. "I miss Momma so much, Papa. I'd bring her back if I could." Etta swallowed the sob that threatened to escape her aching throat.

Her father's dry palm caressed the crown of Etta's head. "Thank…you…Etta."

Etta turned her face toward his. Through the prism of her unshed tears, her father's face seemed younger and healthier.

Rosa entered the dining room, a tray with two bowls in her hands. "What's this? Nobody wants to eat tonight?"

Etta stood and refolded the quilt. "I do. What's for dinner?"

Rosa set the bowls on the table. "We start with corn chowder. You still like that, don't you?"

"Of course," Etta answered.

Rosa tucked the tray under her arm and reached for the quilt. "Give me that beautiful coverlet. I'll put it on Mr. Henry's bed."

"Thank you," Etta answered.

"Now eat, *mija*. You're too skinny!"

Etta grinned at her father as Rosa bustled out of the dining room. "Does she boss you around as much as she does me?"

Henry shook his head. "Rosa...no. Charlie...yes."

Etta laughed softly. It was such a relief to have a conversation with her father again. "Did Mr. Simpson tell you he'd asked Rosa to marry him?"

"Yes."

"I assured Rosa I'd find a job for Charlie for as long as he wanted one. I hope that's all right with you."

Her father's face was expressionless, but after several seconds he said, "Good...idea."

While they ate in silence, Etta tried to disregard her father's sometimes clumsy attempts to get the soup from the bowl to his mouth. If their situations were reversed, she'd cringe if he tried to feed her or criticized her efforts to feed herself. Surely, the Golden Rule fit this situation as well as it fit every other aspect of her life.

Rosa cleared away the empty bowls and served them pork chops with macaroni salad. She had cut the meat into bite-sized pieces for Henry. He grasped the fork with his left hand and scooped up a bite of salad.

As much as she hated to ruin the contented feeling that flowed between them, she needed to tell her father about the embezzlement. "There's something else I have to tell you, Papa. About the bank."

Henry rested his fork beside his plate and looked at her expectantly.

Etta's mouth was suddenly dry. She sipped from her glass of ice water and took a deep breath. "Several weeks ago, Arthur Lewis brought a problem to my attention."

Her father nodded but did not try to utter a word.

"Since becoming loan manager, Mr. Lewis has been recording payments in his own ledger. He noticed that several clients were in arrears and sent them reminder notices."

Henry nodded again. He was following her story with no trouble.

"But the clients came in with receipts, showing the payments had been made. Then some money went missing from the tellers' drawers."

Henry frowned for the first time, and Etta hastened to explain. "I looked into the books and realized that either there was a mistake or someone was stealing. Right away, I called the Worthington accounting firm in Austin to have the books audited. They sent George Owens."

"Good," Henry said slowly. "Good."

"George found that the farm and ranch loans were missing several thousand dollars. That information, plus the discrepancy in Mr. Lewis's ledger, led me to believe that someone was intercepting loan payments. I drove out to visit our clients, and I discovered that Uncle Carl had been collecting their payments."

The tips of her father's ears turned red, and his hand fisted on the table. "Carl...took...?"

"I'm afraid so, Papa. I turned the information over to William Clark, and he completed the investigation. He found a young woman in Austin who is Carl's friend. Carl opened a bank account in her name. William thinks that almost all of the missing funds are in that account."

The dishes rattled as her father pounded the table with his fist. "Carl? Carl?"

"I'll ask William Clark to come out and talk to you. He can explain the legal side better than I."

Henry rubbed his head with his left hand and moaned.

Alarm darted through Etta's body. Was it too much for him? Should she have waited?

Henry lowered his arm and clenched his jaw. "I...I should have..."

Etta wrapped her hand around his forearm. "It's all right now, Papa. The problem has been resolved, and Carl is in jail. It won't take long for our investments to bring in enough to cover any losses."

Henry shook his head. "Wait." He obviously needed time. Time to process what she'd told him and time to recover from the shock.

She sat quietly, moving the food around her plate and watching her father from the corner of her eye.

Henry drank his water, dabbed at his chin with the linen napkin to dry the portion he'd spilled, and sat back in his chair. After several long breaths, he said, "Etta?"

"Yes, Papa?"

"Good...very good."

Etta's heartbeat raced with joy. Her father

approved of how she'd handled the problem. If his speech were restored, he might even have more praise. "Oh, Papa. I didn't know what to do. I felt so betrayed and angry, and all I could think about was what would Papa do if he were here?"

Henry reached across the table and covered her hand with his. "You did right...Etta."

Etta squeezed her father's hand. "Thank you, Papa."

"Now eat," he said with another crooked smile. "Too...skinny."

Their shared laughter rang through the silent dining room.

Everything was going to be all right just like her mother always told her.

❧

At dawn the next day, Etta retrieved the flat basket and small pruning shears her mother used for collecting flowers and walked to the garden. Her mother's yellow roses bloomed abundantly along the perimeter of the flower beds and purple larkspur and irises pushed their way toward the sun. Every season produced a different palette of blooms, but spring was definitely when the garden strove to be its most flamboyant.

Etta clipped several blossoms and placed them in the basket. Her mother's garden was yet another way her love outlasted her earthly life. Like the quilt, the garden could bestow love for many generations.

Once satisfied that she had enough, Etta headed to the hill where the Davis family cemetery was located. The pink evening primrose still adorned the land, but the other wildflowers were beginning to fade. *They'll be back next spring.* Like every other cycle of life, there was no way to hurry it and no way to stop it.

The wrought-iron gate at the top of the hill squeaked as Etta opened it. She knelt beside her mother's grave and placed some flowers beside her headstone. The inscription was perfect. *Beloved wife, mother, and friend.* Life was all about love. Love of family, friends, even enemies.

"I miss you, Momma," Etta said in a soft voice. "I know you're not really here, but I miss talking with you."

A curious mockingbird landed on a nearby fencepost and tilted its head to get a good look at Etta. "Shouldn't you be hunting a juicy bug for breakfast?" she asked with a smile.

In response, the bird flew to a low-hanging branch of an oak tree and began to sing its own joyful greeting to the dawn. At times like these, when all seemed right with the world, Etta's heart filled with gratitude. Life really was full of blessings. If only she could remember to look for them every day.

Etta closed her eyes and raised her face to the sky. "Thank You, Lord," she began. "Thank You for giving me such a wonderful mother. Thank You for Papa's health. Thank You for Sara and Nora and everyone else who has helped me during the last few months." She took a few deep breaths and let the scent of clean earth and morning air fill her body.

"I don't know what to say about Uncle Carl," Etta continued, "but I know he'll need You to comfort and guide him. If he did wrong, he will suffer the consequences, but I don't want him to suffer more than is necessary." She'd be happy if Carl returned the money and disappeared from their lives, but would he learn his lesson?

"Please remember Gabriel, Lord. I hope he will be healed of the grief and guilt he carries with him. If he's the man meant for me, let me know, and if he's not the right one...then help me accept it." Invisible bands of longing wrapped around Etta's chest. She couldn't forget the gentleness of Gabriel's touch and the strength of his arms. Had she misunderstood her own feelings? Was it merely her inexperience that led her to believe her future was linked with his?

She touched her mother's headstone and got to her feet, the mockingbird continuing its serenade as she made her way down the hill.

అంత

Gabriel gathered pink wildflowers on his way to Etta's house. It was too early to call on her, but he was afraid he'd already waited too long. As he crossed the footbridge over Hamilton Creek, he saw her.

As it always did, his heart fluttered at the sight of her. The morning sun silhouetted her body as she ambled down the hill, a basket hanging from the crook of her elbow. She was surrounded by a halo, as though her goodness could not be contained within her body. Before he could decide whether to call out to her, Etta noticed him. She stopped, apparently trying to decide if she should speak to him or go to her house.

Gabriel strode toward her, his Bible tucked under one arm and a hastily-gathered bouquet of wildflowers in the other. "Good morning, Etta."

She smiled her usual warm smile. "Good morning. It's going to be a beautiful day."

The fact that she was smiling and talking to him bode well. "I hope so," he said. Then he held out the pink blooms. "These are for you."

"You picked flowers for me?"

"I suppose I should've gone into town and visited the florist, but…I don't know…if the earth offers flowers, why not take them?"

Etta took the bouquet from his outstretched hand. "These are nicer. You went to the trouble to pick them."

They stood in the dew-dampened grass, their shadows long in the morning sun, and looked at each other.

Gabriel's heart beat rapidly and his breath caught in his throat. He had so much he needed to say and no idea how to say it.

"How's your family?" Etta asked.

"They're fine. How's your father?"

"He can walk short distances now, but he has to use a cane, and his speech is much better."

Gabriel mentally kicked himself. Was he really wasting time with small talk? "I want to apologize for how I behaved the last time we met. I shouldn't have spoken to you in such a rude manner."

Etta lifted her chin. "It's all right. I imagine you were tired after your trip."

He didn't deserve her pardon, but she'd given it nonetheless. Etta's heart was as kind as the Good Samaritan. "The thing is, I'd heard about you marrying William Clark and…well, I was jealous."

Etta stepped closer to him. "Jealous?"

"And angry. I'll admit to that, too. I thought…well, I thought you and I had a kind of understanding before I left, but, thinking back on it, I realized that I'd never said the words I needed to say."

"What words?"

Gabriel fought to take a breath. Why did his chest feel so constricted and his stomach so tense?

Etta must have seen his distress because she didn't force him to answer her question. "I'm not going to marry William."

A gush of fresh air filled Gabriel's lungs, and the invisible weight he'd been carrying around his neck receded into nothingness. "You're not?"

Etta looked toward the horizon. "I wouldn't be a good match for what William wants in a wife."

"How could you not be?"

She didn't look at him, but her smile indicated that she appreciated the compliment. "William wants someone who'll look after his mother, care for his children, and support him when he runs for political office. As much as I'd like to have a husband and children, I'm not willing to mold myself into someone William wants me to be. If I ever marry and have children, I'd like to keep working at the bank."

Poor William. Poor, brainless William. William didn't realize Etta was perfect just the way she was.

Gabriel's spirit lifted for the first time in weeks. He reached for Etta's hand. "Would you like to walk over to our spot?"

Etta shifted her gaze to the shady spot where they had shared a picnic. Then she placed the pink flowers in her basket and slid her hand into his.

His spirit celebrated the small intimacy. He intended to ask her to put her trust in him for the rest of her life, and the ease with which she'd taken his hand nurtured his hope. "I'll never forget the first night I saw you here," Gabriel said as they reached the shady spot by the creek.

Etta placed the basket on the ground and settled onto one of the large rocks. "Papa's come a long way since then. It wouldn't surprise me if he returned to the bank in a few months."

"You did right by him."

She smiled again. "Charlie Simpson turned out to be an angel in disguise. Not only did he help Papa, he also made Rosa very happy."

"How's that?"

"He proposed to her! I was so surprised when she told me."

"Are you worried about losing a housekeeper?"

"Oh no. Rosa's a member of the family, and it appears that Charlie will become the same."

Gabriel sat next to her. "So one problem is on its way to being resolved. That leaves the missing funds from the bank. Did you ever find out who was stealing?"

Etta propped her elbows on her knees and covered her eyes with her hands. "I'm sorry to have to tell you this, but my suspicions were correct. It was Uncle Carl."

Gabriel felt her anguish in his own heart. "That's really tough, Etta. We rely on our family when times are hard, but your uncle deceived everyone. You'll never be able to trust him again."

"Papa was so angry."

"I can imagine. But I bet he was proud of the way you handled it."

Etta uncovered her eyes and looked at Gabriel. "I hope so."

Should he ask her now? Maybe he should wait until they were in a romantic setting. But when would that be? "By the way," he said, "I landed a job."

"Good for you! I didn't know you were looking."

"Well, I can't spend my life helping my father make deliveries and exercising your horses."

"You strike me as the kind of man who needs to be active."

"That's true, plus I want to make a mark on the world. I got a position with the State Department of Highways. They've only been in existence for two years, and in many ways, they're still trying to figure out what needs to be done. I don't know if you've heard this, but Texas is a big state. Lots of highways, bridges, and dams need to be built."

Etta rolled her eyes at his comment about the size of Texas. Everybody knew it was the largest of the forty-eight states. "You'll be putting your degree in civil engineering to good use."

"That's the plan."

Etta bit her bottom lip and an expression of concern crossed her face. "Will you have to leave Burnet?"

Was it too much to hope that she wanted him to stay? "I'll motor into Austin most days and work in the office there. But I'm sure there will be some travel once construction starts."

Etta's shoulders dropped and she placed a hand over her heart. "I'm glad you're not going too far. You've only been back for a short time."

It wasn't a declaration of undying love, but at least she liked having him around.

"Why do you have your Bible?" Etta asked.

Gabriel reached beneath his arm and retrieved the book. "My plan was to catch you before you went to work so I could apologize for my bad manners. Then I was going to take one of your fine horses for a ride and spend some time reading the Good Book."

"Anything in particular?"

"The story of Peter denying Jesus just before the crucifixion. Do you remember that Scripture?"

"Sure. Peter was so human. Remember how he could walk on water as long as he kept his eyes on Jesus, but his fear made it hard for him to believe? It was also fear that caused him to deny Jesus."

Gabriel rubbed the Bible's black leather cover. "Mom and I were talking about the story a few days ago. Do you think Peter ever forgave himself for denying Jesus?"

"That's an interesting question. Why do you ask?"

"The last time you and I sat here, you prayed for me. I thought I was supposed to accept the blame for my mistake and ask for forgiveness. But I was wrong. Turns out I was supposed to forgive myself."

"I never thought you did anything wrong."

Gabriel shook his head, negating her effort to comfort him. "Etta, when I regained consciousness that day, the earth smelled of gunpowder and blood. There were bodies and parts of bodies scattered like garbage. The world was silent--no voices, no wind in the trees, not even birdsong. It took a minute to realize what had happened, and when I did, it felt as though someone had yanked my heart out of my chest and ground it under his boot heel. I began to shake so badly I couldn't see straight." He fell silent, struggling to contain his emotions.

Etta laid her hand atop his clenched fist, and, despite his distress, he smiled at the simple act of tenderness.

"Finally," Gabriel continued, "some French

soldiers helped me back to the aid station. I didn't have a scratch on me. Ten men dead, blown apart in some cases, and I hadn't lost one drop of blood. I'm the one who led them to their deaths. How can you say I didn't do anything wrong?"

Etta bowed her head. She was praying.

What a wonderful mother she would make. She'd teach their children about the Lord and keep Christ at the center of their family.

Although he already cherished her, his love strengthened at the thought of the family they'd build together.

After several minutes, Etta raised her head. "What if our circumstances were reversed?"

Gabriel frowned in confusion. "What if you'd gone to the Army and I'd stayed in Burnet?"

Etta grinned in response. "The only way you'll ever find me in the Army is if I'm drafted."

"Let's hope that day never comes."

"Amen to that. But seriously, Gabriel. What if I'd done something that led to the deaths of many people? Let's say I was driving my father's car and another automobile hit us, killing all the passengers but me. Would it be my fault?"

"Of course not."

"But I could apply the same rationale to that situation that you've applied to yours. Those passengers were there because of me. Even though I couldn't have known the other automobile was going to hit us, I was the one who'd brought them to that spot at that time."

Gabriel narrowed his eyes. Her line of reasoning was sound, but she was letting him off easy again.

"Do you remember when Jesus told the disciples

the two greatest commandments?" Etta asked.

"Love the Lord with all your soul and love your neighbor as yourself?"

"That's right. I was thinking about the last part of that Scripture. You wouldn't hold me responsible for the passengers' deaths. That grace would be a way of loving your neighbor. So, if you love yourself the same way you love your neighbor, you'd have to forgive yourself as well."

Gabriel could almost see the mathematical logic problem written on his professor's chalkboard. His engineer's mind knew the syllogism was sound, so why was it so difficult to release his guilt? "Were you praying for the right words to say a few minutes ago?"

Etta nodded.

"That's what I thought, because you sure found them." Gabriel stretched his long legs in front of him and considered Etta's words. "In my heart, I know you're right. But I can't get those men out of my head. They slip in and out of my memories like minnows in shallow water."

Etta looked toward the hill where the Davis family cemetery was located. "My mother used to sing hymns when she worked around the house. Does your mother ever do that?"

"All the time."

"One of my mother's favorites was 'What a Friend We Have in Jesus.' Do you know that one?"

"Sure." He sang a few bars.

"I didn't know you could sing."

"Most people would say I can't."

Etta laughed softly. "I was thinking about the line at the end of each verse. 'Take it to the Lord in prayer.'"

"You think I should pray about forgiving myself?"

"Wouldn't hurt."

"I know it wouldn't hurt, but…" Gabriel searched for the words. What did he need? Why wasn't prayer enough? "I wish I could do something real and concrete. I'm not saying prayer isn't effective, but I need…oh, I don't know."

"Let me have your Bible."

Gabriel looked askance but passed the book to her. She reached into the basket and retrieved one delicate pink flower. "I remember the story about the soldier who craved sugar. What was his name?"

"Private Nichols."

Etta opened the Bible to a random spot and placed the flower between the pages. "May the Lord keep Private Nichols in the hollow of His hand and bless Private Nichols's family." She selected another flower and turned to another page. "Give me another name."

"Anthony Blake."

"May the Lord keep Anthony in the hollow of His hand and bless Anthony's family." She gently positioned the flower between the pages and looked at Gabriel expectantly.

Etta was showing him how to give the problem to God. It was a tangible way to remember his men and leave his burden on the altar. The flowers would dry between the thin pages of the Bible and someday fall into nothingness. Perhaps his guilt would fade in the same way. Gabriel took the Bible from her and flipped the pages until he reached the Psalms. "May I have a flower?"

Etta positioned the basket on her lap and offered him a pink blossom.

"This is for Corporal Sam Hutchins," Gabriel said,

laying the flower over the printed words. "Sam was a good man, even-tempered and dependable. I pray that the Lord will keep Sam close to His heart." Gabriel looked at Etta.

"Does it feel right?" she asked. "Does it feel like a valid way to pray for the men in your squad?"

Gabriel took a few moments to examine his feelings. He'd never really thought about his men being in God's care, but surely, they were. There was no more war for them, no more hunger, thirst, loneliness, or fear. "Thank you, Etta." Gabriel's voice was thick with emotion. Etta had understood his pain, listened to his grief, and eased his heartache. She had helped him heal like no one else.

The sound of neighing horses caused Etta to look toward the stable. "Benito must be starting work. I hear Mira saying good morning."

In the distance, Gabriel saw the teenaged boy lead Antares out to the pasture. The stallion sniffed the air, pranced among the wildflowers, and headed toward them.

Etta stood and the horse trotted straight toward her outstretched hand. "Good morning," she said to the animal. "Are you ready to start your day?"

Antares used his muzzle to nudge Gabriel's shoulder.

"All right," Gabriel said. "I know you're there. Sometimes I think this horse is as spoiled as a rich lady's lap dog."

"Oh, he is," Etta concurred. "I don't know who spoils him more, you or Papa."

The horse placed his nose on Gabriel's head and blew hard enough to ruffle Gabriel's hair.

Etta laughed at the stallion's antics. "You'd better

pay attention to this horse before teeth are involved."

Gabriel tucked the Bible under his arm. Stroking the horse's forehead and neck, Gabriel spoke softly to the animal. "Where do you want to go today? Shall we ride west until we get to the Rockies or south to the Rio Grande?"

Antares flicked his head, as though agreeing with the idea and then wandered toward the gate where the mares were congregating.

Gabriel glanced at Etta. "Would you like to walk to my house? I'm sure Mom's got breakfast on the stove."

Etta touched his Bible. "Don't you want to finish praying?"

"I will, but not right now. I need some time. Besides, there's something I'm determined to ask--"

"Oh!" Etta's eyes widened and one hand covered her mouth. "Papa's walking to the stable! Look, Gabriel."

Gabriel fixed his gaze on Henry Davis. The older man walked haltingly with the use of a cane but made steady progress.

The mares trotted along the fence line, neighing loudly and swishing their tails in excitement.

The happy gleam in Etta's blue-gray eyes matched her wide smile, and Gabriel silently rejoiced with her. First she'd lost her mother, and then her father's health had been jeopardized. The past few months had been physically and spiritually arduous. Thank goodness Etta could set aside at least one worry.

"Do you think your father's able to talk to me this morning?" Gabriel asked.

"Probably. Would you like to have breakfast at our house instead?"

Gabriel had expected to be anxious when he finally got around to proposing, but rather than nerves, a feeling of quiet assurance filled his heart. He touched Etta's elbows and softly turned her to face him. "Etta…"

She lifted her face and looked at him, her sweet lips parted as though on the verge of a question.

Gabriel touched her cheek with his fingertips. "Etta, since I came back, you've been my best friend. When I took that trip to visit the families of my men, all I thought about was how much I wanted to talk to you. Whenever I was disappointed or angry or frustrated, I wished I could sit with you in a quiet place and simply be with you." Gabriel moved closer until the toes of his boots touched her feet. "I don't know when it happened, but I've fallen in love with you, Etta."

Her eyes widened and a tentative smile teased the corner of her lips.

He cradled her face in his hands and gazed into her lovely, kind eyes. "I love your gentleness and your sweetness. I want to build a home with you, a home bursting with laughter and love where friends and family are always welcome." Gabriel kissed her forehead. "I want you to be the mother of my children, Etta. When we stand before the congregation to have our children baptized, I want everyone to know how blessed I am to have you for a wife." He slid one arm around Etta's shoulders and held her against his chest. "And when I'm an old man, I want to sit by you in the evenings as we watch the fire dwindle. Then we'll climb into bed and hold each other while we sleep. I will cherish your love for as long as I live." He bowed his head and brushed his lips against hers.

Etta took a sharp breath as though surprised by his

loving touch but then rose to her toes, wrapped her arms around his neck, and gave herself to his kiss.

Gabriel pulled her body closer, rejoicing in her willingness. Her kisses were as sweet and honest as the rest of her. If he kissed her every day for the next fifty years, he still wouldn't have enough. "Oh, Etta," he whispered. "Please marry me. Be my wife. Be my friend. Be my love."

Etta nestled her head on his shoulder and relaxed in his arms.

The tenderness of the moment warmed Gabriel's heart. Once they were man and wife, he'd hold her like this every chance he got. "What do you say, Etta?"

Her eyes shone with love and joy. "You've made my dreams come true, Gabriel."

"So you'll marry me?"

"Of course."

Gabriel encircled her waist and lifted her off the ground. "I love you, Henrietta Davis. I'll do everything I can to make you happy and keep you safe."

Etta flung her head back as peals of laughter rang toward the sky. When at last Gabriel set her on her feet, she lifted her mouth to his. "I love you, too, Gabriel." Her whispered words tickled his lips.

Gabriel kissed her again, all of his love, joy, and hope bound up in that act of love. "It's time to visit your father. There's a question I need to ask him."

Etta's smile erased any lingering doubt from Gabriel's soul. He closed his eyes, sent a prayer of gratitude to his Creator, and took his beloved's hand.

Side-by-side, Gabriel and Etta walked into their future.

Thank you for purchasing this White Rose Publishing title. For other inspirational stories, please visit our on-line bookstore at www.pelicanbookgroup.com.

For questions or more information, contact us at customer@pelicanbookgroup.com.

White Rose Publishing
Where Faith is the Cornerstone of Love™
an imprint of Pelican Ventures Book Group
www.PelicanBookGroup.com

Connect with Us
www.facebook.com/Pelicanbookgroup
www.twitter.com/pelicanbookgrp

To receive news and specials, subscribe to our bulletin
http://pelink.us/bulletin_

May God's glory shine through
this inspirational work of fiction.

AMDG

www.ingramcontent.com/pod-product-compliance
Lightning Source LLC
Chambersburg PA
CBHW020414260626
47156CB00007B/2389